LATE HARVEST

LATE HARVEST

Kay Stephens

severn
House

This first world edition published in Great Britain 2000 by
SEVERN HOUSE PUBLISHERS LTD of
9–15 High Street, Sutton, Surrey SM1 1DF.
This first world edition published in the USA 2000 by
SEVERN HOUSE PUBLISHERS INC of
595 Madison Avenue, New York, N.Y. 10022.

British Library Cataloguing in Publication Data

Stephens, Kay
   Late harvest
   1.   Remarriage - Fiction
   2.   Domestic fiction
   I.   Title
   823.9'14 [F]

   ISBN 0-7278-5583-2

Typeset by Hewer Text Ltd.,
Edinburgh, Scotland.
Printed and bound in Great Britain by
MPG Books Ltd, Bodmin, Cornwall.

The greatest gains and values are farthest from being appreciated. We easily come to doubt if they exist. We soon forget them. They are the highest reality.

Henry David Thoreau, 1817–1862

One

How had this longing to get away become so insistent? Caroline unlocked the door of The Sylvan Barn and gazed across the spacious entrance hall where antique furniture, white walls and the gleaming wooden floor combined to create precisely the degree of elegance that she'd planned. She could never leave all this. Could she?

Today had been bad – not spectacularly bad – just grimly so. The fact that Malcolm had overlooked their anniversary was only partially responsible for her distress. She was a realist, knew that the sparkle didn't last for ever.

Those early days, when she had wanted Malcolm to rely on her, had turned into this morass where she endured being taken for granted. She seemed to have changed so utterly that she felt diminished. And Malcolm . . . ? She knew him too well. If he surprised her now it was because he was *not* being shaken into seeing what was happening to her.

Caroline found it increasingly difficult to recognise the person she was becoming. It wasn't at all like her to feel so often that somewhere deep inside, concealed from everyone, she was weeping. There had to be a solution – one which she would find.

She hadn't created this lovely home to be scarcely noticed while their married life grew intolerable. But if she managed to suppress tears, she was coping less well with problems accompanying them here from Malcolm's office.

She loved him so deeply that she couldn't bear to see him worn down by uncertainty. Over the last six years, since 1987, they had waited to learn the route this planned rail link would take. And she had exhausted every possible means of reassuring Malcolm that its impact on their business might not be too grave.

Caroline yearned for the time which now seemed long ago, when career and love had flourished within their own boundaries. And when stepsons were small enough to reprove for a television left blaring out that unmelodic tune heralding *Meridian Tonight!*

The word "Folkestone" jolted her into hurrying through to the drawing-room to stare at the screen.

"Mother . . ." she gasped, her surprise total. "That is my mother!" Smiling, Caroline paused beside the sofa to watch. People were marching through the streets, protesting against the removal of the town's name from road signs. Good for them! She had wondered what sane government body could justify replacing "Folkestone" with "Eurotunnel". There she was again – Lucy Forbes, tall and erect, her glorious white hair contrasting with the red placard she carried.

Eager for a closer look, Caroline rushed towards the set, but the camera angle shifted to the uniformed band leading the demonstration. The shot switched again to the town's mayor, straightening his tie along with his thoughts ready for the interview.

Behind her the telephone rang just as the man began speaking. "Get that, would you, Chris?" Caroline called.

Her stepson did not respond. Being ignored fuelled her exasperation. She turned off the television sound and hurried to lift the receiver.

"Hello, dear," Lucy Forbes began. "Sorry to bother you, but—"

"Mother, I've just seen it. On television. It was great!" And it was also a reminder about taking positive action.

"Yes, well . . . Wanted to do my bit. Thing is, though, I've had a slight accident."

"Oh, no . . . What, at the demonstration? How bad . . .?"

"When we were dispersing, actually. Nothing serious, darling. Somehow tripped—"

"Not over your placard?"

"Don't think so. The pavement edge, I'm sure. Twisted my ankle."

"How bad is it? Where are you?"

"At Vinnie's, it happened just round the corner from her place. The St John's people were very helpful, brought me straight here."

2

Pity you didn't get them to take you home, Caroline reflected, recalling her mother's aversion to operating the lift alone. "Want me to come over?"

"Oh – I've just remembered the date. Forget about me. Malcolm will be taking you somewhere nice."

"No."

God, Caroline thought, *do I sound this forlorn, pathetic?*

"You're leaving celebrating until the weekend, are you?"

"Yes, that's it," she agreed swiftly, and willed her mother not to go on about anniversaries. "I can come over this evening."

"If it's no trouble. I'll be all right if only somebody can get me back to the flat."

"Be with you in forty minutes – less if there's not much traffic."

The front door slammed. Caroline turned, glancing over her shoulder as Malcolm reached the drawing room doorway.

"That for me?" he enquired, after she had replaced the receiver.

"No, it's all right. Mother." She noticed how worn her husband looked, how his large frame sagged, and remembered the appointment he had kept. "What did the optician say? How are the eyes?"

"Sight's no worse than last time, don't need the lenses changing. But—"

"Oh, that is good news. So we can stop worrying."

"About that, yes."

"Mother's problem doesn't sound very bad. Just a slight sprain, her ankle. And for a good cause too. Hardly seems fair, does it?"

Malcolm was looking blank. She explained about the demonstration against the word Folkestone being taken off the road signs.

"Don't tell me Lucy took part."

"Indeed, she did. Carrying a splendid banner."

"Ought to have more sense at her age. What time's dinner?"

Caroline reminded herself she'd shown him he could expect punctual meals. That had always been a part of proving how much she cared.

"I've only just come across from the farm office. Took a couple of calls there. East Malling research station – with answers about new root stock for the far orchard. And a regular strawberry picker. They'll both ring again."

"The way things are, we shan't be restocking any orchards."

Caroline smiled, hoping to counteract Malcolm's gloom about their decline as the foremost fruit growers in Kent. "You're ready for a break. You'll find the meal's no problem, there's plenty in the freezer. If you give Chris a shout he'll see to it. He's somewhere around."

"So you have remembered Mrs Dacre's still away. I can stick something in the microwave myself, less trouble in the end. You're evidently going out then?"

"Got to, sorry. Can't leave Mother at Vinnie's all night, she's only got the one bedroom." And Caroline herself was in need of some respite. Getting away would provide space in which to find solutions. Malcolm had enough on. She was the one who had to prevent the security they felt it their love for each other from eroding all vitality.

Malcolm remained rooted in the doorway even while Caroline was hurrying past him to the airy entrance hall. She wished his grey eyes didn't look so anxious, there was no reason that they should. She would only be out for a couple of hours. And she had stocked the freezer yesterday, from Marks & Spencer's as well as Sainsbury's.

"All right if I take the Jag?" she enquired. "Mine's not starting very well."

He nodded. "Fine. Take care." He tossed her the keys, ran a hand through his brown hair. "About the optician—"

"You said, Malcolm. Your eyes are OK." Yet again Caroline smiled reassuringly – she would need to tackle his habit of worrying about everything. She turned and strode briskly across the expanse of polished boards towards the outer door.

He watched her, noting the familiar purposeful step, the set of her head with its mane of glossy hair – not unlike a lion's in shade, nor in the way it framed her fine-boned face.

As always, Caroline relished driving the Jaguar. Her soul also rose with each mile of the M20 as she headed towards her old territory. Beautiful though their own village was, she loved the area around Folkestone. Occasionally she ached with nostalgia for the home where she had grown up, overlooking the sea at Hythe from its terrace above steep gardens. It had provided a blissful childhood.

Nearing the end of the motorway, Caroline felt sickened. Throughout the development of the massed railway lines, the additional roads and these tunnel workings she'd been horrified. Today, distress about this impairment around Cheriton was extended as she contemplated the damage its rail link would cause the downland where her husband's people had grown fruit for generations.

Sighing, she consigned regrets to the back of her mind until she might resist the planners. She was determined to fight back. Maybe she should accompany Malcolm to a few of those protest meetings. If only there didn't always seem to be so much that only she herself could tackle! But first, she would at least nourish her flagging spirits with Lucy's participation in today's protest.

Lucy's exhilaration was overriding any pain from the ankle when Caroline was welcomed into Vinnie Hammond's cramped living-room.

"Vinnie recorded the report," she exclaimed as soon as Caroline straightened her back after kissing her mother. "Do you want to see it?"

"Later perhaps, I saw most of it, you know. Got to get you back to the flat, haven't we?"

"There's no rush," Vinnie began from her wheelchair, then frowned. "Or is there, my dear? I suppose you left Malcolm to fend for himself?"

"With Christopher's help, he was in the house somewhere."

"So, Malcolm isn't on his own," said Lucy. "That's all right then, dear."

Caroline nodded, yet why was she feeling, disturbingly, that Malcolm was troubled by more than his perpetual business problems?

"I've a favour to ask you," Lucy began, smiling towards her daughter. "When you've installed me in the flat, could you possibly pop back here?"

Vinnie was gazing awkwardly at them both. "Oh, Lucy, you

shouldn't have. Caroline, take no notice. I'll let Scamp out into the garden."

"He hasn't had a walk all day," Lucy persisted.

Since Vinnie's arthritis had confined her to that chair Lucy had walked the Yorkshire Terrier, savouring the contact with a pet forbidden in the flats.

"Sure, I'll see he has a walk. Just so long as we do get you back home now, Mother." Her unease concerning Malcolm might seem to her unwarranted, but it was slow to shift.

Lucy fussed, as normal, in the lift while Caroline prayed it would not stick and prove this ridiculous dread well-founded. Taking her arm, she encouraged her the few yards along to the flat.

"There now, you should be fine so long as you don't overdo things. Haven't you a footstool somewhere? I'll just see about a meal for you."

"There's no need, darling. All under control. Take a look. The oven was timed to come on at six. When I've washed my hands it'll be cooked."

"I'll set the table for you."

Shaking her head, Lucy beamed. "That's ready as well. In my little sun room. Now the better weather's coming, I eat there every evening."

"Good idea."

The flats had sold so well because of their view over the sea. On a clear day France was visible. At the moment a faint haze disguised the horizon, but the sky was glorious with the few clouds exhibiting a spectacular spectrum of colours.

Before leaving, Caroline checked again that her mother could cope, and didn't need a visit from the doctor.

"I'll ring him if the ankle feels any worse, dear. But the ambulance man said this strapping should be sufficient."

"Well, I'll give you a call, anyway, in the morning, just to be sure."

Ten minutes later, walking Vinnie's dog across The Leas, Caroline was reassured by looking upwards to see her mother busy with knife and fork, sitting framed by flowering plants near her sun room window. They exchanged a wave before the Yorkie tugged on his leash, dragging her with him as he scampered towards a massive German Shepherd.

The dog's owner laughed, calling "Heel, Captain," then nodding his satisfaction as the command was obeyed unfalteringly.

Caroline smiled. "You've got him trained!"

"He's not so impulsive as yours, perhaps. Though maybe not quite so much fun either . . ."

"You like Yorkies, do you? Scamp isn't mine, anyway. Exercising him for a friend."

"Thought I hadn't seen you before." He was appraising Caroline's streamlined figure, his glance courteous yet knowledgeable.

"You live round here, then?" she asked.

He was tall, tanned and appeared very fit. His eyes, a penetrating blue, expressed youthful energy strangely at odds with his white hair and moustache. And those eyes regarding her so intently registered his approval of what he saw. Caroline couldn't have ignored her urge to learn more about him.

The stranger smiled. "Until this job's completed."

"And your work is . . .?"

"Civil engineering. In connection with the Tunnel."

Caroline did not speak. She contained disappointment and increasing disapproval, and wondered why she should care what his work might be.

She turned her mind to their surroundings: the wind coming in from the sea that glinted below the cliffs here, elegant houses and hotels, their pleasing gardens. Her expression must have spoken for her because the man grinned, ruefully.

"In the main, that does seem to be a stopper of conversation."

She almost admitted to the regret that was rising instinctively. Something about him convinced her he'd have plenty to say that would interest her. Instead, she shrugged, murmured that it was time to be getting back, and hustled Scamp home to his mistress.

Steak pie and chips heavy on his stomach, Malcolm glanced at the clock. If he hurried, he should catch Anne before evening surgery finished. He was desperate to hand over the letter from the optician, to be reassured that the man's alarming words had been an exaggeration.

He took Caroline's keys from the hook near the door and rushed out to her Renault Clio. He adjusted the seat to his six foot two inches and turned the key several times, abortively. Her reason for taking his car finally penetrated the dread weighing him down.

Malcolm dashed back into the house, and called to his son who had darted upstairs to change as soon as they had eaten.

Carrying squash gear, Christopher came charging down to the hall, brown hair flopping on to his deep forehead.

"What is it, Dad? I'm late already."

"Any chance of a lift as far as Anne Newbold's?"

"Not really on my way. Suppose I could drop you by the village hall, if you like."

Blue eyes dared him to expect more than that.

Malcolm nodded. "You're on. Thanks." He tried to discard memories of ferrying his sons all over Kent in the days before they could drive.

The open MG racing around bends between high hedges rather precluded conversation. Malcolm was not sorry. He was too pre-occupied to feel perturbed by Christopher's reckless driving, much less to be in the mood for making small talk.

The car plunged the last few yards to the junction with the High Street, swung left and stopped, engine still revving, before the village hall.

"Thanks, Chris."

His son shouted back "OK. See you." And was away before Malcolm had turned towards the steep lane confronting him.

He cursed the planner generations ago whose network of roads criss-crossed this hillside, yet neglected to provide access between his farm and the doctor's surgery.

Malcolm glanced at his watch as he began plodding upwards. If Anne kept strictly to surgery hours tonight, his journey would be wasted. Willing himself to speed up, he fixed his gaze on the distant corner of Birch Tree House and trudged forward.

He saw her as soon as he started up the path. Inserting in the window a card detailing out-of-surgery hours instructions, Anne

"Certainly, we've published nothing yet on the repercussions of the Eurotunnel scheme. We'll have to consider your options. You could either come up with an item yourselves, or I suppose I might arrange for a journalist to do an interview."

They discussed further details while Amanda's violin scraped plaintively beyond the dividing wall. By the time Caroline was leaving her head had begun to throb.

"What's really worrying you, Caroline?" Julian asked, taking her empty glass.

Startled, she faced him. "Nothing really." But she faltered, feeling defenceless.

"Oh, come on," he said. "I know you. You always have dressed with infinite care when you're putting on a front. Is it your stepsons perhaps? Can't have been easy taking on a ready-made family."

"No, they're fine. At least . . . It's not so good about Christopher . . ."

"Oh?" Julian sounded amazed. He sat down facing her, leaned forward, his eyes puzzled as well as concerned. "But I thought . . . Malcolm said he was doing so well last time we met. That agricultural college had given the lad a good grounding."

"So it has." Caroline swallowed, choked by the distress mounting for weeks. She sighed. "You may as well know, it isn't as if we moved in the same circles. The farm's not doing as well as it was. We lost some ground to the M20 extension, it split our land in two, now it's less easy to manage. Then there's the way imported fruit floods the market, lots of growers are grubbing out their trees."

"I'm sorry. Poor Malcolm."

And me? thought Caroline. *I'm suffering too, more so perhaps because of loving him so much yet being unable to help. Hardly bearing to watch his destruction.*

She swallowed yet again. "The worst is that he's had to tell Chris that he can only keep him on another few weeks."

"Malcolm will change his mind over that, I'm sure. He'll not let somebody of Christopher's calibre go to anyone else. More's the pity – I could use him here."

On the way out, she interrupted Amanda's practising to say goodbye. Saddened beyond words – she ought to have known what

39

to say to her daughter, but was too upset to think of a single thing –
Caroline stood in the doorway, trying to create a smile.

"You look dismal, Mother. Is it something Daddy's said?"

She shook her head. "No, darling. Just – things." *And leaving you
here like this.* "Keep in touch, won't you?" she said, her brightness
forced. "Don't forget there's an open invitation to come and stay."
They were both well aware, though, that Amanda had never shown
any inclination to take that up.

Her daughter nodded, then looked down at her violin.

"What are you playing?" Caroline asked.

"Couldn't you tell? Was it that bad?" Amanda demanded, her
pallor increasing.

"We were talking, darling, not really listening."

"That figures."

"Play me something now, I've got time to sit and—"

Amanda interrupted. "I'd rather not. Sorry. I'd feel idiotic."

Her abortive attempt at improving their relationship left Caroline
even closer to uncharacteristic tears. Heading towards her car, she
longed to be back when Amanda was in her school years and
discussing her progress had provided some basis for contact.

*I might have succeeded in getting Julian to promise us space for a
feature,* she thought, driving through the Sussex lanes. *I just wish the
encounter hadn't reaffirmed how inadequate a mother I am. I've got to
work to put that right.*

She wasn't feeling up to that, any more than she really felt capable
of facing anything at home. Instinctively, she took the next turning
for Appledore, then headed towards the coast. Her mother would be
surprised to see her, but Lucy Forbes wasn't easily dismayed. And
after all, Caroline needed no more than a bit of understanding –
someone to hear out this need to improve things with Amanda.

She had reached a straight stretch of the road over Romney
Marsh when she realised that she wouldn't confide in her mother.
She knew Lucy, who mightn't be perturbed by a sudden arrival, but
would worry afterwards.

Her head ached appallingly, obliterating concentration. She drew
off the road, stopped the engine, and rested her head on the steering
wheel.

seemed about to lock up. Hoping to trade on their long-standing friendship, Malcolm waved to attract her attention.

The door opened and he staggered, breathing heavily, over the threshold.

"You're in bad shape!" Anne remarked, but her smile assured him that he was more than merely another patient.

"I hope you'll forgive my arriving just as you've so evidently finished for the day."

"You'd better come through, Malcolm. You look in need of a chair."

"That bad, eh?" he said, but failed to convey his normal humour.

"Is it the breathlessness that's brought you to me?" Anne enquired, removing her stethoscope from a desk drawer.

"Not really. At least – could be a symptom." He took out a pigskin wallet from which he removed an envelope. "Saw the optician today. He gave me this for you. Probably fussing unnecessarily . . ."

Anne slit the envelope, studied the contents. Her hazel eyes professionally veiled, she turned back to him. "He told you, I imagine, what this says. About the arteries?"

"That they show signs of becoming fouled-up, or some such."

"We'll do tests, of course. Beginning with blood pressure."

Asking him to remove his jacket and roll up a sleeve, she moved the apparatus to his side of the desk.

"You're what age now, Malcolm?"

"Forty-one last birthday."

The doctor glanced towards his waistline as she clamped tight the velcro fastening and began pumping. She was frowning while she repeated the procedure and noted the readings on her pad. As she returned to her chair she faced him.

"Your blood pressure's way up, I'm afraid. We need to treat this seriously. I'm going to take blood samples, have cholesterol levels tested. We must consider everything. Weight?"

"I am waiting," Malcolm quipped. High blood pressure was quite a relief, his mother had taken tablets for as long as he remembered.

Anne gave him a look. They'd always enjoyed a joke together during the years they both served on the local parish council. She felt shaken and saddened that Malcolm had let his health deteriorate so radically during that relatively short period since his resignation. But she must contain her own reaction for now, concentrate on what was best for him.

"I mean it about your weight," she said, checking him before he replaced his jacket. "Just slip off your shoes and step on that scale. how tall are you? Six-one, -two?"

Anne had a chart open on her desk, and frowned again when she compared his weight with some expert's concept of the ideal.

"You could begin by losing a couple of stones, Malcolm. I suspect we shall find the cholesterol's pretty high, and it won't hurt you if the diet to reduce that is the one you start on today."

"Come off it, Anne. You know me. Far too busy to be picky about food."

"All this entails is sensible eating," she persisted firmly, pushing photocopied diet pages towards him. "Caroline's responsibility really. She's kept her own figure trim enough, I'm sure she'll only be too eager to cooperate."

Malcolm stilled a shrug and contained a wayward urge to reveal that this was not the first evening that his wife had found other people's needs more imperative than his own.

"What did you eat today? Breakfast . . .?"

"Toast, marmalade."

Her glance was shrewd. "Nothing else?"

"Er – well, that was after bacon and sausage. I'm a farmer, for heaven's sake, Anne. Not some pen-pusher."

She smiled, knowingly, hazel eyes lighting. "Is it lifting all those bushel boxes that you call heavy? Or spraying apple trees?"

"It's still outdoor work, a man's job."

"I'm not disputing that, love. Come down off the high horse. It's not necessary with me, remember. Are you going to tell me what you ate during the rest of the day? Or daren't you let on?"

"Had to meet someone at lunchtime. Pie and a pint, that sort of a thing."

"I hope Caroline gave you a salad tonight to compensate?"

He shook his head. There was no way that he would admit to the steak pie and chips. Even though he'd been driven to making that choice. Caroline knew he hated all those supposedly healthy ready meals with which she stocked the freezer.

"Give the diet a go, please," said Anne solemnly. "And we'll discuss this again when I have the blood test results. Meanwhile – what's really troubling you, Malcolm?"

"What do you think? You know why I came off the council. Whatever we do at local level, it's County Hall who should be doing more. And the government are driving us into the ground. From being the biggest grower in Kent, I've dropped to having a farm that's barely paying its way. Now this bloody rail link is destined to cut right through my land. Even disregarding the ground that will be sacrificed, there's no hope of managing the rest effectively. It was bad enough when the motorway sliced through it. When the rail route was announced in March I could have topped myself."

They would have to check this encroachment on their lives or have the whole county ruined.

Anne was nodding sympathetically. Hardly anyone in the area was unaffected. Some of her patients would lose their homes. Others, like Malcolm, could face bankruptcy after the curtailing of their land.

"You'll be compensated, though, surely? As a community, we're to ensure that no one misses out on that."

"If I get anything, you can guarantee it'll be minimal. Might have been better off if they were taking every last acre."

"What about Graham? How will he be affected?"

Malcolm snorted. "Scarcely at all. You know my brother. Has his finger in so many pies that losing a bit of land won't matter."

"And you couldn't take a leaf out of his book?"

"What – start distributing fruit? Importing? That's what he's doing now. Never! If I go bankrupt tomorrow, I'll not resort to that. Cutting our own throats, that's what importers are doing."

"I see. Well . . ." She sighed. "Let's hope things don't turn out so badly as you fear. What does Caroline think? She's always seemed very go ahead."

"Oh, she thinks like Graham. Keeps urging me to either go in with him, or set up a similar business. She even had the nerve to suggest that this wretched Channel Tunnel should accelerate import procedures."

Anne refrained from commenting that, from her estimation, it should.

"But exports as well, perhaps?" she suggested.

When he didn't respond she accepted that he was refusing to contemplate any potential benefits from that tunnel scheme.

"Tell me how your sons are getting on – Nicholas is in his second year at Cambridge, isn't he?"

"Yes. Doing well, from his account."

"Reading English, isn't he?"

Malcolm nodded.

"And Christopher – is he taking to fruit farming?"

"Seems keen enough, on the whole. So long as it doesn't interfere with his other interests."

"Ah – yes. He plays squash with my nephew quite often."

"That's where he is tonight. Then there's the clay shooting. Wish sometimes that he'd take to potting the birds ravaging my orchards. Still, he's a likeable lad and some of his 'green' notions are quite worthy. Caroline's influence, of course."

"She's turned out a marvellous stepmother, I think."

"Oh, yes." If only Caro hadn't seemed to win over his sons *too* completely, drawing their allegiance to her. Away from himself.

"You have a great deal to look forward to, you know, Malcolm. A good family, one son already following in the proverbial footsteps."

He sighed awkwardly. "Except that I don't know how I can keep him on. Can't continue paying him beyond next month."

"As bad as that, is it?"

"Don't breathe a whisper, not where it could get back to him. I shall tell Chris myself. When I can find the words. There's no easy way."

"I'm sorry, Malcolm, that things are as grim as this. I'd no idea. And, without wishing to hammer home the point, this really is the time for taking more care over your own well-being. You're aware what stress can do, I'm sure."

She rose with him, walked at his side as far as the outer door.

"Make certain that you come back for those results," she said, and placed a hand on his arm. "And don't forget you don't have to battle alone. I'm always here."

Thankful that surgery was finished and she needn't face anyone else, Anne closed the door after him. She leaned against its panels, perturbed. Had she done anything like enough? Could she have said more – to make Malcolm feel better? To make *her* feel that she'd come somewhere near to conveying her determination to see him through this crisis?

She had been so shocked, utterly taken aback to recognise how ill Malcolm looked. And when his B.P. had confirmed the evidence of her initial glance, she'd sensed instinctively that those blood tests eventually would only bear witness to the seriousness of his condition. Even if he'd been a near relative, she wouldn't have felt more distressed. But then, she and Malcolm Parker always had seemed close. His keen mind and ready wit had eased her through those early days on the parish council. Sharing a similar sense of humour, they had relieved any tedium with private jokes; while respect for each other's opinions had deepened the mutual liking. There had been attraction too, as much as she'd permitted – the occasional flirtatious glance, an even more rare overt compliment.

Walking slowly through to tidy the surgery, Anne admitted that once she had wondered if there might have been more. Years ago. Following his first wife's terminal illness, Malcolm had seemed to turn to her so frequently, had convinced her he needed more than her concern as his family doctor.

She had been pleased for him, of course, when Caroline had filled that dreadful abyss in his life. For herself . . . ? Anne had never denied privately that her own regret was quite intense.

Caroline was feeling good as she headed home along the motorway. The sea air had, as always, freshened her attitude as well as her lungs. Her mother's injury seemed quite minor, scarcely worth considering alongside the triumph of her part in the banner-waving protest. Perhaps she is the one from whom I inherited a bit of spirit, she thought, an idea which hadn't seemed obvious in the past.

Tonight, she had decided about her own future. The thought had occurred repeatedly over the past few months, only to be quashed by the eternal round of being busy. It was seven years since she had worked anywhere else than the farm office, yet in all that time she had not lost the yearning for the satisfaction of being on top of her job. A demanding job, at that. Managing director of a Public Relations Consultancy in London, she had learned from the start that promoting herself was as needful as promoting clients. *You cannot promote something that you do not understand.* This self-knowledge had given her a special kind of power. The power which would now enable her to start up again, on her own.

Running the business from home would be ideal. What could be more suitable than the elegant barn conversion for which she had supplied so many of the ideas? This motorway that Malcolm abhorred would facilitate access for clients. And she would still be to hand if he should need someone to cover his rare absences.

Leaving the M20 outside Ashford, Caroline took the A road instead, already looking forward to turning up the lane towards their village which spanned the Pilgrim's Way and provided magnificent vistas over woodland, sloping fields and Kentish orchards.

If Lucy Forbes at seventy-five could prove her active worth, her younger daughter could show that she merited more than working as general dogsbody. Kate would disapprove, of course. But her sister's opinion could be discounted. What did Kate know about anything – except keeping a model house for Graham, Malcolm's brother?

Anticipating her sister's reaction to returning to her career reminded Caroline of how differently she had visualised her own life seven years ago. She should have expected fewer surprises, considering the way in which the Forbes and Parker families were intermingled.

She had preferred Malcolm to Graham long before that – when she first encountered the Parker brothers at Kate's engagement party, and actually was astonished that Kate had chosen the high-flier rather than his younger, more amenable brother. Caroline herself had been attracted by Malcolm's earnest attitude to life and all the warm qualities which seemed appropriate in a gentleman farmer.

Malcolm had met and married Sue during his brother's lengthy engagement, Christopher and Nicholas were born, charmers both, who enchanted everyone on the day when Kate and Graham finally married. Evidently eager to catch up, Kate flung herself wholeheartedly into caring for her husband and his substantial house, and produced a boy and a girl, in that order, as if confirming her ability to oblige.

Visiting her sister's home for family gatherings, Caroline had found both Malcolm and Sue pleasant company, and their boys still so agreeable that they made her long for a son.

In those days she had been married to Julian whom she had met through her PR work. Maybe his hard-nosed editorship of a glossy countryside magazine was even then inducing her longing for a less abrasive partner. Certainly, their relationship was beginning to founder. Motherhood seemed disillusioning as well, having brought her Amanda, a fey child idolised by Julian to the detriment of the girl's character. *Intractable* had become Amanda's second name. It was only more recently that Caroline had begun to see how she might have coped with her. She now felt appalled that she had actually consented to Julian's application for custody at the time of their divorce.

Caroline's liking for Malcolm had deepened while she witnessed his caring for Sue during that swift terminal illness. Her own fondness for the boys had turned to love and she had needed little persuading when, after six months of struggling to manage alone, Malcolm had turned to her.

His proposal had been as realistic as she had supposed him to be. The down-to-earth presentation of the facts had seemed apt from a man whose living was so bound up in nature. He had bared his soul, and shown her it had tender roots, and was as straight as a row of trees in his well-tended orchards.

"We have a good life together," she asserted now. And was disturbed that the statement was necessary. Of course it was good. They would survive this bad patch, Malcolm was no more a victim than she herself. Returning to her career would help financially and, fulfilled, she would be better equipped for providing stability.

Becoming so enmeshed in running the farm had not been good.

From the early days of being willing to do anything to help had developed this uncomfortable situation. Now neither of them ever got away from the problems. When she returned to PR work the differing daily challenges would refresh her mind rather than wearying it. Each evening she and Malcolm would come to each other with minds (and hearts) receptive. All the old interest would resurrect. Their love for each other would no longer be crowded out.

Driving the last few yards uphill Caroline was, as always, delighted to be approaching her home. The terracotta shade of their herringbone brick drive complemented lawns and ancient trees, creating the perfect foil for the earth-brown tones of The Sylvan Barn. With an interior equally pleasing, this was no place for feeling down.

Steering towards the garage, Caroline stamped on the brake pedal when Christopher came dashing from the shadows, startling her with urgent signals to stop.

"Hello, darling, something wrong?" she enquired gently, opening the car door, hating the hurt in his blue eyes behind very evident anger.

"You'll never believe this, Mum. Dad's given me the bullet!"

"He's done what?"

"Given me the sack. All I did was ask for an advance on next month's salary. Had a scrape with the MG, got to get it fixed."

Her heart raced. "A scrape? Tonight? Are you all right?"

"Yes, fine. It just needs a bit of paint. I was only asking for what's due to me, for Christ's sake, nothing to evoke a tirade."

"Just hang on while I put the car away, we'll go indoors and you can tell me all about it."

"No. Really. I'd rather talk here. He's in there."

Caroline stifled a sigh, opened the passenger door. "Get in then, Chris. I can't stand around." Suddenly, she felt drained, her upbeat plans smothered beneath the appalling shock of her stepson's news. "Now tell me everything, exactly what your father said."

"He just got on to me, as if he'd been waiting to pounce. First of all it was the usual stuff – how I shouldn't always assume that he had the funds to bail me out. That was uncalled for, anyway, as I'd explained that all I needed was an advance. Then he demanded to

16

know if I thought he was made of money. How could anyone think that, living here, with the heating turned down so low in winter that your balls go numb . . .?"

How indeed? thought Caroline wearily, feeling that she ought to prompt Chris to elaborate on the rest of his grievance, and could not bring herself to do so. Hadn't she already had as much as she could take?

Christopher needed no prompting. "We were in the drawing-room and he pointed towards the nearest orchard. 'Money doesn't grow out there among the pears and apples, you know,' he said. Then he went on about the farm losing money. That was when he said it."

"That he can't continue paying your wages?" Caroline felt sick.

"That kind of thing, yes. I finish at the end of June."

"But that's . . . only another few weeks."

"You don't have to tell me. I can't bear it, Mum, becoming unemployed."

And nor could she bear that for him. His eyes were gleaming with unshed tears. She grasped his arm. "I'm sure it won't come to that, darling. Leave it with me, I'll speak with your father."

Malcolm heard them come in together, willed himself to remember all that Anne had said about stress, and steeled his will further to withhold recriminations.

They were passing the drawing-room doorway. He watched Caroline give his son's shoulder a squeeze, heard her murmur, "Best go straight to your room, Chris."

Good intentions overruled, Malcolm rose, came striding to meet her.

"He's told you, of course. And naturally you are taking his side."

She couldn't face their taking sides. "All I want is to get at the truth. How bad things are, and if such a drastic step is necessary."

Malcolm ached with the need for her to understand. Couldn't she see how unhappy this made him?

"It's necessary, all right. You help with the books, you know how we're placed. That if we're to turn this around we must make sacrifices."

"But not to sacrifice your own son. He, surely, is a part of what

17

the business is about. he is the future, your future and mine, as far as this farm is concerned. I've always been so thankful that Chris took up fruit growing. That he wasn't like Nicholas, yearning for a different career. You can't destroy him this way, Malcolm."

Disappointment threatened to choke him; disappointment because she really was failing to see that there was no alternative. If he continued paying Chris they would not last the year out. The truth was that simple.

"You're tired and overwrought," she told him gently. "I think you should let this rest. Just for a while, wait and see. Things should pick up soon, we keep being told about the green shoots of recovery."

When he said nothing, Caroline went to a sofa, a talk seemed to her long overdue. She had been right, she couldn't work with him like this, it hurt too much when they disagreed. Quelling a sigh, she drew in a long breath.

"You're letting worries about the farm take you over completely, you know, Malcolm. I can't help noticing. It's not good for you, and it isn't exactly comfortable for the rest of us."

He gave her a look, but neither spoke nor came any nearer to where she was sitting. Caroline longed to be in his arms, to be hugged with assurances which in the old days would so readily have come from him. She wanted the original Malcolm back, their original life. It seemed to be up to her to convince him how drastically things were altering.

"This isn't in the least like you. Look at you tonight. So wrapped up in it all, that you haven't even asked after my mother."

"You're no better yourself. Where's your concern for me? Why aren't you asking how I am?"

"I can see that. Pulling everything on top of you until there's no getting through."

And killing myself in the process, according to Anne, thought Malcolm. Since coming home he had wondered how serious this trouble really was. His father had died at fifty-seven, from arteriosclerosis. He felt like facing Caroline with the shock he'd been given today, but hadn't the heart to watch her confront it.

Sighing, Caroline turned a little away, and noticed the diet sheets discarded on the coffee table. "What's all this, darling?"

18

"The diet I must follow if I'm to live much longer."

His bitterness evaporated as she came running to hold him to her.

"We're in this together, darling," Caroline assured him. And hated the way her own words pressed down upon her. Their future seemed no better than struggling to avert catastrophe, healthwise and in business. But she was scared, badly scared, whatever could she do to help Malcolm, to make him well again? She hadn't needed a fright like this to make her understand how much he mattered to her.

Two

I n the twilight the tamarisk swayed, its pink fronds fragile as the feather boa that Lucy had hoarded from girlhood. Caroline was thinking of her mother, couldn't help wishing that she lived nearer to The Sylvan Barn. Today, the place felt far less idyllic than its name suggested. Her own spirit seemed sorely in need of an injection of Lucy's optimism. Resolving to win through didn't make succeeding less of a battle.

The morning post had brought their council tax charges which proved to be even higher than Malcolm had anticipated. An hour ago he had returned from Anne Newbold's evening surgery with a grim expression and her directions on following a stern dietary regime.

"If I don't," he had told Caroline gravely, "I can expect to be put on medication to lower cholesterol. According to her, that doesn't always work and it can even accelerate the very heart problems we're striving to avoid."

Caroline had tried hard to be reassuring, quelling her own dread while she spoke of how they would *make* the diet succeed.

"I'm going into all this with Mrs Dacre, she's got into her stride again after her holiday. She'll be only too glad to be cooking the sort of meals you're supposed to be eating, darling."

"If we can keep her on." Malcolm had sunk on to the sofa.

"Not that, please." Thinking things couldn't get worse had only invoked further crises to prove otherwise, and challenged her determination to smooth their future for him. "Isn't axing Christopher's job enough?"

"One of us has to face facts." His tone had implied that she herself hadn't sufficient acumen to grasp their financial situation.

They had argued then in a manner totally opposed to Caroline's intention, about the possible departure of their housekeeper, about further stringencies. The wretched business had upset her greatly, and left her feeling that Malcolm believed her incapable of running their home herself – and that this estimation might well prove correct if she were to be denied Mrs Dacre's help.

The middle-aged woman who had come to Kent with Caroline seven years ago had been her mainstay for even longer. During the dreary period after separation from Julian, Florence Dacre had tended Caroline and her immaculate flat as though they were family, and without a natural mother's impulse to interfere.

God, but it would be dreadful here without her! Even with Mrs Dacre and the help of their good daily cleaner, Caroline struggled now to slot in household matters alongside administering the farm office. If, as she hoped, she was to return to PR work as soon as Malcolm's health was stabilised, time would become even more scarce.

Somewhere behind her as she sat near a window in the entrance hall, Caroline heard Malcolm's footsteps. She felt frozen by their disagreement and did not turn, acknowledging his presence only when both hands came down on her shoulders and he bent to kiss her ear.

"Pax?" he asked in his little-boy-lost voice which once had seemed to jolt her heart.

"Yes – fine," she responded. Relieved, she smiled up at him. "Just look at that glorious tree," she exclaimed. "I was watching it changing with the light. Join me for a few minutes . . .?" Some impulse was insisting that the peace they sought might be found out there.

"Wish I could spare the time. Just had a call from Graham, he wants to discuss our estimated yield of strawberries. Seems to think he can find a better market."

"Can't that wait? The first crop's nowhere near ready yet, is it?"

She was seriously concerned about this artery trouble. Anyone less than blind could tell Malcolm was exhausted. She ached with love and the need to help him regain his health, yet she felt at a loss, too disturbed to be certain how to begin.

"You know Graham, always wants everything yesterday."

Yes, Caroline thought, *and perhaps if you, my love, had been more like your brother when you were younger, we might have had the farm on firmer ground where it would survive a few difficult months.*

"Give my love to Kate, if you see her. Tell her Mother's ankle is improving." Before the Jaguar had driven out of hearing Christopher came bounding down the stairs.

"Did Dad tell you Nick's coming home this weekend?" he asked, striding across to lounge against one of the dark wooden beams that intersected the white plaster of the walls.

Caroline frowned. "No, I expect he forgot."

"He's bringing a girl – Bianca Something."

"I say! So – your father communicated for long enough to pass on that information to you?"

"Afraid not. I was the one who took the call. While you were chatting with Flora Dora before she went off home."

On the day that she arrived in their household, Chris and Nick had adopted this pet name for Mrs Dacre, whom Caroline hesitated to call Florence. The housekeeper, in turn, had adopted them, loving them with a devotion which even vied with Caroline's.

They would miss her terribly, as well, she reflected, and was compelled to exert considerable will over the urge to share her fears with her stepson. Instead, she had to use the opportunity to explain his father's health problems. Malcolm needed more understanding.

Chris appeared unmoved by the news of the high blood cholesterol confirmed by the results received that evening.

"So, that's what all the fuss re diet was about," he said calmly. "Well, no one can pretend he doesn't need it. One look and overindulgence shrieks at you."

"Chris, you might at least have said you're sorry."

"Oh, I am – that he's let himself get into this state. It wouldn't be logical, would it though, to regret that Dad is being brought up sharp in time to try and effect a remedy?"

Christopher's sentiments, if phrased more gently, were echoed by Lucy on the glorious second Tuesday of May when Caroline drove over to Folkestone.

"I'm just very thankful that they've discovered this in time, as you must be, Caroline. Now you'll be able to tackle the problem together. You've always been so devoted, you must be feeling it's a privilege to be able to help."

From anyone else, the words might have seemed over the top, but Caroline knew her mother had idealised the relationship since the day she had learned of their engagement.

"It's not going to be all that easy," she told Lucy now as they sat up to the window of the sun room. "You know the kind of meals that Malcolm enjoys. And then there's the possibility that Mrs Dacre might have to leave."

"Oh? You hadn't said, darling. Does she have some kind of trouble?"

"The trouble's ours – this recession's hitting hard. And things look like getting a hell of a lot worse once construction of this rail link is confirmed."

"I remember, you told me about the way it could slice through your land. But you'll be compensated, surely?"

"That's what everyone says. Apparently, it isn't at all certain. Still, I didn't come here to burden you. How are things? Have you managed to get out at all now the ankle's improving?"

"Yesterday, and the day before. I can manage the stairs, so long as I do so in my own time."

"You do take care, I hope?"

"Naturally, my dear. I know you think I'm an old fool damaging myself in the first place, but I really am quite sensible. And people have been very kind. I've had help two or three times to manage that horrid lift."

"Have you now, you didn't say. From one of your whist drive cronies, was it? Or someone in your residents' association?"

"Not at all. From that nice Paul Saunders, the end flat right opposite the lift."

"I don't know him, do I?"

"Rather naughty, is Paul," Lucy confided, her brown eyes lighting conspiratorially. "Keeps a dog. And you know how strictly that is forbidden. Quite a large dog, too. Got to admire his spunk. Not that he's here for long, only took the flat temporarily."

Although pleased that someone had assisted her mother with using the lift, Caroline was less than riveted by this account of the man concerned. It was serving only to delay the purpose for which she had returned here today.

"Are we going out then?" she enquired, rising and offering her mother an arm. "We can call on Vinnie if you wish. I imagine Scamp will be ready for a walk."

She and Vinnie had agreed that Lucy should not attempt to exercise the terrier on her own until the ankle was completely healed.

Over to the west, the sun was dropping towards the horizon, and the evening air was cooling before the breeze sweeping in off the sea.

Beside Caroline, Lucy walked slowly but with hardly a limp as they crossed towards her friend's cottage. Vinnie's welcome wrapped them in warmth while her darting glance prompted them for news of a world that she so rarely penetrated. Lucy was happy to enlarge on the previous day's announcement that their demonstration had resulted in a rethink on road signs. Folkestone's name would not be replaced by Eurotunnel.

"You see what can be achieved, Caroline," Vinnie enthused. "You must tell Malcolm. If Lucy and her crowd can challenge bureaucracy, I'm sure something could be done where you're living."

When Caroline suggested that they might walk the dog conflicting emotions appeared on the little woman's pain-etched face. Hastily, the idea was amended to having Lucy remain with her friend while Scamp was exercised.

"Sure you don't mind going on your own, Caroline?" Vinnie enquired, anxiety troubling misshaped hands which clutched at her chair.

"I'll be quicker that way while Mother's not entirely fit."

She saw him as she had previously, out on The Leas where the breeze was increasing, encouraging several aged strollers to walk more briskly. They paused again to chat, initially about the dogs now exploring each other with more enthusiasm than their disparity of size seemed to warrant.

The surprise came with his sudden introduction. "Paul Saunders," he said, a smile lighting his fine, rather serious face.

Caroline beamed back at him. "And you know Mother," she exclaimed and added: "From the flats. She was telling me only just now of the way you so kindly helped with the lift."

"It was nothing. And so you are – Caroline or Kate?"

"Caroline. Kate's the beauty."

"Then she must be a stunner."

Caroline gave him a look.

Paul persisted nevertheless. "Really, I mean that. It isn't just a line."

Strangely, she believed him. Meeting him earlier, she had sensed a straightforwardness that in no way detracted from his appeal. This evening, however, she was too aware of him for feeling completely at ease. Being appreciated, all too rare in recent life, induced a sparkle between them almost as visible as the lights now appearing in windows and on vessels out at sea.

Walking on again, their arms all but brushing, she let him talk, while her own emotions ran like the tide surging on shingle far below the cliffs.

Paul was speaking of his work, making her see with his eyes the thrill of construction, the satisfaction which so evidently grew out of watching his plans develop into reality.

"Love or hate this Channel Tunnel scheme, no one should underestimate the skill it entails. You've not visited the exhibition, I take it?"

Her brown eyes rueful, Caroline shook her head. "Nothing would induce me, just as no one ever will get me to use that tunnel once it's completed."

Imagination filled her nostrils with the stale stench of submerged workings where urgent machines hauled further examples of man's invention, contrary to the instincts of his more liberal nature. She shook her head, as if to readmit the scent of newly mown grass, a distant hint of the stirring sea.

"Afraid you'll never convert me."

"Maybe you have your reasons. A lot of people in Kent are facing disruption of their lives on account of what we're doing."

25

"Yes," she said heavily, and did not enlighten him further. She could like the man without approving his work, was relieved to be with someone whose motivation need not perturb her.

"I love these Channel coast towns, especially for their views over the water which I try to paint when time allows," Paul told her.

"Really? I used to dabble years ago, when I lived at Hythe. Pictures of the sea are quite a challenge, aren't they?"

The dogs dashed and teased, making them laugh as neither Yorkie nor German Shepherd seemed prepared to relinquish ideas that they really were well-matched.

Caroline smiled. "I almost wish Scamp were mine. His indomitable will to prove he's the match of your fine dog would make me a proud owner."

"You don't have a dog then at home?"

She shook her head. "Surprisingly, for we're farmers. Fruit-growers on a large scale, not livestock."

"That's right – I recall your mother saying. You married brothers, didn't you, you and Kate?"

Caroline nodded. "And not very alike – either Kate and I, or Malcolm and Graham. More interesting perhaps, that way. Are you married?"

"Once, I was. One day I'll tell you."

She did not believe there would be an opportunity for that. Yet, after she had seen Lucy safely home and was driving back to The Sylvan Barn, Caroline began to wonder what had happened to Paul's wife.

"My mother would like to see you, Caroline, it's ages since she has. Kate would, as well. I told them you'd go over there tomorrow."

They were in bed, side by side in the four-poster that Caroline had coveted from the moment she began planning the barn conversion. She felt herself go rigid and struggled with recently developed dread that if she opposed Malcolm he might become ill. Stress-related meant what it said. Pausing helped her to rationalise her anger and compromise.

"I'll try and make time to drive over."

"I can spare you from the office for a few hours." The smile in his voice penetrated the darkness.

Big deal! Caroline snapped, but only within her head. Silently, she approved her own growing ability to avoid contention.

With daylight, however, immediate resentment surged. Had she become merely this adjunct – someone to detach and despatch to pacify Malcolm's mother and her own sister? Two people who, more than anyone she knew, could exist admirably well without her intervention. Where had her own persona become lost, submerged so completely that she now lacked the skill to remind them she was busy attacking problems here?

Following wholegrain cereals with brown toast, they sat at the breakfast table, each of them hedged behind resentment. Malcolm's refusal to admit to enjoying these different foods allowed his mistrust of diets to extend to the person who had placed them on the table. Caroline was feeling oppressed by these reminders that this sudden threat to Malcolm's life created additional reasons why she should be more accommodating. Whatever she did could never be enough.

"Did either Isabel or Kate say if this morning would be convenient?" she enquired meekly.

Malcolm shook his head. "Up to you, Caro. Although Mother does claim to be at her best in the morning."

Good, Caroline thought, *get it over and done.* "Don't know how long I'll be," she announced, clawing back some time for herself in compensation. "I'll do the shopping while I'm out. When Mrs Dacre arrives she'll prepare you a salad lunch, with cottage cheese."

"I don't like cottage cheese."

Caroline smiled, brilliantly. "It is on Anne's list of things you're permitted." She wondered fleetingly if she resented Anne Newbold's being so certain about what was best for Malcolm.

Half an hour later she was driving between high hedges a mile or so along the hillside. Through the open window wafted the scent of hawthorn from branches dragged down by their blossom towards swathes of red campion. Passing a copse, massed bluebells raised her heart on memories of childhood picnics. Life had been so simple then: Daddy often at sea though never farther away than the cross-channel ferry of which he was master, Mother always at home, herself, and Kate. She had relied on Kate a great deal, for companionship, as a prop when starting at a new school. When had Kate turned into such an everlasting *challenge*?

Her sister's home was extremely old, its white walls were rather less than straight, embraced by black beams like arms whose fingers extended to hold the house together. The windows were leaded, with panes, here and there, of slightly imperfect glass. Beside the dark oak door, wisteria twined from amid aubretia to clamber between and above windows, clutching the walls in its march towards the russet tiled roof.

Had she not been allowed her head when planning her own home, Caroline might have envied Kate the Parker family house. There could be no denying its beauty, greatly enhanced by gardens matured through centuries of Kent's balmy summers.

Parking in the wide space that was set to one side before stables, outbuildings and the large cold store, Caroline got out of the car to stand for a moment, just looking. The view from here was superb: the expanse of downland slopes scattered with trees, an occasional farm, distant oast houses, and the land contoured fortuitously to conceal the near by M20.

Renewed by so much that pleased her eyes, Caroline began walking briskly towards the side entrance of her mother-in-law's apartment.

Happy though she had been to settle in her own portion of her old home, Isabel Parker would no more accept its being termed a grannie flat than she would permit the children to call her grannie. No one would dare to label her a martinet – or, if they had done so, none of the others had ventured to substantiate Caroline's opinion. Over the years Caroline had noticed that, rather than address Isabel as grandmother, as requested, the children never addressed her by any name, and hesitated to make a direct approach. Life could be made very difficult.

The bell beside the well-preserved door rang somewhere in a room beyond, but evoked no response. Caroline paused a while (she must not appear impatient) and rang again.

So much for being summoned to attend, she thought, smiling wryly as she went carefully along narrow paving that led between lawn and herbaceous border to the front of the house. Kate did not welcome visitors who came in by her kitchen. For the life of her, Caroline could never fathom any reason forbidding entry through a room which – for somewhere so well used – always looked immaculate.

Kate answered the door, reaching up to kiss Caroline who was two inches taller than her own five feet six.

"So glad you could make time to come," she exclaimed, then turned away to stride along to the drawing-room overlooking the rear garden.

Isabel Parker was sitting in state, straight-backed as she might have been forty years ago, splendid in lilac twin set and pearls which on her appeared no less elegant than when they were first established as the right thing to be worn by English gentlewomen.

Caroline's kiss was received, as always, on the cheek and with less enthusiasm than a gnat's bite.

"Caroline," she murmured and, judging this sufficient preamble, gestured towards the sofa where Kate was already arranging her clearly expensive skirt.

Before her younger daughter-in-law was seated, Isabel was in full spate. "I thought we should have a little talk. About Malcolm, of course. Naturally, we are all gravely concerned that his health is causing that nice doctor of his such anxiety. Kate and I have put our heads together, and we're going to give you all the assistance you will need."

Caroline swallowed down her groan, tried – and failed – to retrieve her smile, and fixed her gaze on Isabel's cool grey eyes. "That is so kind of you," she began firmly. "As you may not have heard, though, Anne Newbold has issued masses of information regarding diet."

"But not recipes, I think," Malcolm's mother persevered. "You may not be aware that in the old days I was famous for my table. Susan always came to me for advice. And, of course, Kate is *au fait* with all manner of interesting—"

"Recipes," Kate put in eagerly.

Caroline marvelled that evidently her sister had become so acceptable that she was permitted to interject the occasional word.

"We have been through all the books you see here," Isabel went on, a lined hand heavy with diamonds indicating the coffee table. "Kate has been so good, inserting markers against every dish that would be suitable."

"How thoughtful," Caroline responded, "of you both. I knew you'd be as worried as I am about Malcolm, and only too glad to help."

Kate smiled across at Isabel and then towards her sister. "We thought it might be as well if I go through these with you while we have coffee."

"That's right, my dear. In order that Caroline may understand—"

This time, Caroline was the one who dared to interrupt, uncaringly, because limits do exist and today were being exceeded. "I only wish I had the time. But you do see our situation. Grateful though I am for the help you're both giving us, my first concern must be getting back to Malcolm. I have to be there, you see, in good time for lunch just to ensure that he is eating all the right things."

"But surely you still have Mrs Dacre," said Kate witheringly. "Doesn't she attend to all your meals?"

Caroline did not answer. "I promised I would be home," she lied swiftly, and began reiterating her concern for Malcolm. Still babbling, she rose and scooped up as many volumes as she could carry, then staggered towards the door.

Her sister gathered together the rest of the books and sped after Caroline, catching up with her while she was unlocking the car boot.

"You can't leave like this, Caro. You must at least hang on for a quick coffee. I wasn't the one who decided you needed this lot, you know."

Caroline helped her stow the recipe books then turned and grinned.

"I can believe that! How on earth have you survived this long here?"

Kate's smile was quite wistful. "I love Graham," she said simply.

Caroline nodded as they walked together towards the house. No doubt Kate's love for Graham and dread of the old girl had always been the twin motives for perfecting her role.

As Kate led the way indoors again Caroline thrust her mind into

30

overdrive. No matter what was said, she could chatter obligingly over coffee; providing escape was imminent.

Driving away, Caroline felt compelled to admire her sister. No one, not even Isabel, could fault Kate on either behaviour or her ability to cope. No matter how tense things seemed at The Sylvan Barn, Caroline could only feel immensely thankful that they lived their lives unfettered by intrusive opinions.

I shall avoid using those wretched recipes, she vowed, even if it kills me. If it kills . . . God, no! she thought, horrified. Not that, please God, not Malcolm. I'll do anything.

She drove into Maidstone, queued to park the car while she struggled to recall where she might find the nearest health food shop.

Her first call, though, was in Smith's where she spent an hour poring through every book offering low cholesterol recipes. She left the shop with five, and restored determination. *She* would find the right kind of meals to correct Malcolm's condition. And even if Mrs Dacre did most of the actual cooking it would be she herself who was in control.

Malcolm abandoned his depressing ledgers at two fifteen. He had returned to the office shortly before two. Suddenly, he felt overburdened by anxiety too powerful to ignore. He had coped, or flattered himself that he had, while worries about the farm crowded in. This fresh trouble concerning his own health seemed to have upset the balance.

Walking slowly at first, uncertainly, he went along the earthy path between apple trees now casting blossom that settled on his everyday sweater. Passing through this nearest orchard he skirted the next and the one beyond. Before him lay strawberry fields, their plants in rows, immaculate following Christopher's faithful weeding.

Chris was a good lad, his love of the land inborn, intensified as well through his years at agricultural college. Letting him go was heartbreaking, however obligatory.

A voice from beyond the fence startled him with his name, and there was Anne, smiling as if she offered him a cure for all his ills.

31

"You're not brooding about that diet, I hope?" she asked lightly. She was fond of Malcolm, hated to think her verdict had induced this solemnity.

"I was earlier," he admitted with a grin. "Not the diet, but its cause. Seems like the proverbial last straw."

"That broad back won't break so readily."

"It was Chris making me think just now," he continued, glad to be able to talk. Somehow, with Caroline, her partiality prevented him from saying much about his sons.

"I was taking a half-hour stroll," Anne said. "Can't the farm spare you . . .?"

Side by side, they headed along the Pilgrims' Way, saying very little now, as though being there had become sufficient. In a way that he never had in the past, Malcolm envied those ancient pilgrims their ability simply to walk, to take their time, making towards their objective. He told Anne his thoughts, received a smile.

"Hang on to that, Malcolm. There are means still of recapturing that spirit, however briefly."

"You sound very sure." Her certainty was a magnet, drawing together the feelings diffused by anxieties.

Anne laughed. "My professional face? A large part of my job consists of sounding convincing! Seriously, though, it's often enough just to want to slow down and check on our direction."

"That's easily said. By someone whose whole life is geared to making everything better. Where do I stand – amid the struggle to make the farm pay its way? Can I justify that as motivation?"

"You're not doing it for yourself, there are your sons, your wife."

"Christopher and Nick would survive, without me, with no farm." About Caroline, he was unsure. He wished that he knew.

"They'll survive in better condition with the stability you provide. I meant what I said, though – taking a break needn't always consist of frittering time away."

"No. It can be a few minutes philosophising with someone who's in tune." Ordinarily, he'd not have dreamed of uttering such words.

"Exactly. My door's always open, Malcolm, remember."

They parted eventually where a footpath led off through woods, in the direction of Birch Tree House. *I could walk over this way for my next check-up*, Malcolm thought. *I could do so next week.*

Mrs Dacre was relishing the introduction of new menus. Always in the past, Caroline had stocked the fridge and freezer and left her to organise their meals. These fresh ideas meant they sat together at the kitchen table, selecting things that looked tempting, adapting slightly if all the required ingredients were not to hand.

Privately, she had always considered Caroline the daughter she might have had. Cooperating like this, then being entrusted with the preparation which was her especial skill was invigorating.

It seemed, too, that being able to have this daily discussion was lightening the load for Caroline. Florence Dacre's grey-green eyes lit with a smile this morning when she saw how energetically her employer sprang to her feet.

"I'll leave that with you then, Mrs Dacre. Time I was on my way across to the office."

The housekeeper patted greying hair which she wore scraped back into a French pleat. "That's fine with me, yes. I'll do that vegetable dish for tonight, like you said. Then tomorrow when Nicholas is home we can have the Turkey Tettrazini."

"He loves pasta, as you know. And just for once Malcolm will have no cause for complaining he's still hungry."

In the office Malcolm was preoccupied, wearing his all too familiar exasperated frown which these days made Caroline anxious for him.

"At times like this I wish I'd kept my place on the parish council," he said, turning the folded newspaper towards her. "That way, I could at least have fought this wretched rail link."

From Boxley to Hollingbourne and in other villages all along its proposed route, men and women were gearing themselves to avert the raw deal in prospect.

"You can still fight," Caroline observed. "You only resigned because you claimed the powers that be take too little notice of village councillors. You could widen publicity for the campaign, a short piece every so often in a local paper is nowhere near enough. If this fight was something I was promoting . . ."

"You'd achieve no more than we have already. We've had good calibre people working on this, not for months but years."

"That's no reason to stop trying. Go for publicity in some of the glossies . . ."

Malcolm gave her a look. He loved her like this, brown eyes aglow with purpose, golden head erect with determination; but she also made him rather afraid. This splendid woman was going somewhere, and he could not quite submerge the dread that her destination might be away from him.

"You can't just give up," she was insisting now. "If you won't have another go then I will." She was nursing an idea that had returned frequently over the weeks. "Julian might be able to help – you know he's only semi-retired."

The Sussex vineyard run by her ex-husband didn't preclude him from remaining on the board of the magazine competing well with *Country Living* and others of similar substance.

"Spare me for half a day from the office and, if need be, I'll catch up on the paperwork this evening," she suggested, already planning what she would wear for meeting Julian.

In their bedroom Caroline threw off her office suit, and crossed eagerly to the large fitted wardrobes concealed beyond mirrored doors.

The honey beige suit had been new last summer, of pure wool finely woven to complement the designer's skill. The skirt was plain and to her knees, slit to facilitate walking and reveal legs that would do credit to a woman half her age. The jacket was closely fitted, its line the perfection that came with expensive clothes. She would wear her Gucci loafers, more appropriate than courts for visiting a country vineyard.

Sitting before her mirror, Caroline appraised her reflection. She wore minimal make-up about the farm and would add little more before setting out. A touch more lipstick, a further coat of mascara, she needed no blusher. Since phoning to check that Julian was at home warmth was flooding her cheeks with colour, and only when they were partying, had her ex encouraged her to apply make-up more heavily. She reached out for her perfume. Poison by Dior echoed her identity – if not, she trusted, in its name.

Her hair needed treatment. If only she had planned ahead, allowing opportunity for a visit to the genius who kept her hair up to standard . . . She must do what she could. Off-the-face styling designed to appear go-ahead revealed the hairline only too clearly. Today, she detected darker roots, a dappling of grey.

Smiling at her ingenuity, Caroline located a gold-tinged eyeshadow and began camouflaging. She didn't mean to have Julian even suspect that she might have aged a little.

Three

"No one told me you were coming."

At the door of Julian's long, luxurious bungalow stood Amanda, the daughter who throughout her nineteen years had generated in Caroline every emotion from besottedness to bleak despair. Today, all her defences were roused, but Caroline struggled to withdraw them. She loved the girl, needed to show her how much.

"Your father might have said, but no matter. You and I have always got time for each other, haven't we?"

"I was practising, your car disturbed me." Her daughter was staring back, the eyes as brown as Caroline's own looked cold.

Amanda played the violin, declared she would become a soloist. Caroline had feared all along that she possessed neither the talent nor enough determination for the dream to be realised. It seemed to her that Julian's ability to support such notions was their daughter's misfortune. Caroline always felt she was the only one to consider the girl could benefit from addressing more practical ambitions.

"Is your father in his den?"

Amanda shook her head, stirring dismal locks the shade of mouse which nature – before therapy intervened – had decreed should be her mother's. A clinging black-and-white print dress reached almost to the ankles that emerged from dusty black leggings. From the cap sleeves and above the wide, frilled neckline straggled a striped jersey, also of black and white, badly laundered. Her dainty feet were disguised in stout boots which might have been her great-grandfather's.

Evidently this was the "grunge" look, whose very name expressed this unappealing fashion, the effect appalled Caroline. She yearned to take her in hand. Yet she recognised that this waif-like appear-

36

ance represented a great deal of Amanda's fey personality. Mother-love surged, her heart and arms literally ached to hug her.

I will try that one day, she resolved, hating her own inability to do so on impulse. Sadly, long years had established the minimal contact that her daughter accepted.

As if confirming this mode, Amanda turned and rushed ahead, along the wide hallway that ran through to the rear where gardens sloped down over the Sussex hillside towards Julian's vineyard.

Caroline followed more slowly, willing away regret concerning her daughter's attitude and her own responsibility. Gazing to either side, she concentrated on glimpses of expensively furnished rooms, and on a garden no less well-designed, confirmation that in these standards, at least, Julian permitted no deterioration.

Sturdy and dark haired, he awaited her on the outer steps of the rustic building accommodating office, shop, and the hospitality room where vineyard visitors sampled his wines. Amanda was motionless on a lower step, leaning backwards into her father, her head slightly to one side, nestled affectionately against one of his arms which were linked about her. Caroline had never felt more alone.

"Hello there," she called, quickening her pace while she quelled the instinct to hang back until encouraged.

"How are you, Caroline?" Julian released Amanda to offer his right hand.

His grasp was firm, as of old, so firm that she hardly noticed that it no longer produced even a hint of a tingle.

"Fine, just fine." She recognised her "morale raising" voice from those PR days. Amanda's attitude was turning her ego fragile.

"And Malcolm?"

"Busy as ever, but great, thank you." This was not the place for admitting she could let her husband develop high blood cholesterol. Even alone, she was barely able to face the fact that her care of Malcolm had been less than good.

"Shall we go into the house? You sounded as if this visit's more than social."

"Oh, it is." She wouldn't have Julian believe anything else would bring her here.

Again, Amanda dashed ahead. Caroline jumped when an inner door closed with a slam as they approached the entrance.

The sitting-room was half-familiar, despite new, evidently costly wallpaper. The pale, impractical sofas and armchairs remained from her day, as did the bookcases of dark wood. Side tables and a modern display unit had been added more recently. They looked to Caroline as out of place as she was feeling. Somehow, she felt reassured because Julian's home wasn't as ideal as a first glance conveyed.

Julian had offered a drink and was pouring Cinzano without asking. Caroline bit back the desire to ask if he believed she hadn't changed at all over the years.

She stifled a private smile when he apologised for there being no ice. His never marrying again had been a surprise, any little reminders that her absence might have left a gap were welcome. Her smile died quite quickly. *That is so sick*, she thought: *why am I seeking proof of inadequacies?*

The spicy Cinzano tasted good anyway. She sipped, sorting her words in silence.

"So – Caroline, what's brought you here?" Julian prompted.

"It's an idea we have for publicising our opposition to this wretched rail link. Malcolm would have seen you himself if he weren't pressed for time."

The merest flicker of a well-groomed eyebrow revealed Julian's disbelief.

Caroline contained a wild desire to laugh. Julian knew, and she knew, Malcolm's contentment with distancing himself from his predecessor! The men had met only rarely, the last occasion being Amanda's eighteenth birthday. The celebration had not been greatly enhanced by their recognition that Caroline provided no bridge between former and present partners who could not be more unalike.

"You want me to give space to a feature criticising the rail route? Am I right?"

"Well, yes. Please."

"Have you got something written up?"

"Not yet, no. I – *we* only thought of this today."

The vehicle halting behind startled her. If she'd been less shattered she might have feared for her own safety, but realising that she didn't care finally triggered tears.

Dimly, she noticed the other car door opening, shutting . . . A voice called, "Stay, Captain." And then Paul was beside her, leaning in through the open window.

"Caroline? Thought I recognised this car, from the times you've parked outside the flats. What's happened? An accident?"

She shook her head, its pulsing nearly blinding her. Swallowing, she slowly straightened up, looked at Paul.

"Nothing like that. I – I've just had enough. Got a splitting head."

"Taken anything?"

"There isn't a thing that will help this. It's me – make such a mess of things."

"I'm sure you don't. But wouldn't a tablet help? Hang on, just for a minute."

Paul returned from his own car with painkillers and water. "Always carry a bottle for Captain, he'll spare you a gulp to down a couple of these." He was in the passenger seat now, dispensing tablets and water, smiling. "Fast-acting, I'm never without them. Sometimes when I have to go underground the atmosphere gets really oppressive."

"Thanks," she said, handing back the bottled water. "What're you doing here?"

"Worked an early shift, then I couldn't resist Captain's urgent appeal for an outing. What's gone wrong, Caroline? Want to talk?" His arm came round her.

She wasn't sure, not about talking to *him*. Paul was the one who provided her light relief. And she didn't want him to know, not how badly she'd always failed with Amanda.

"I'm exhausted, I guess. And – oh, what the hell . . . I've just seen my daughter. From my first marriage. Each time, I come away more convinced that anyone on this earth could have handled our situation better. I let her go, you see, agreed to her remaining with her father."

She was weeping copiously now, messily. Paul drew her to him, her face was pressed into his shoulder.

"The proverbial sympathetic shoulder," he said.

Caroline tried to laugh, and coughed. He held her for what must have been half an hour. It felt so good just to stop being busy, to cease worrying. The pain in her head was easing when he spoke again, stroking her hair.

"From what your mother once said, I'm sure your ex provides your daughter with a good life. And, knowing you as I'm beginning to, I believe you'll work at re-establishing better relations with her. You'll not rest until you've succeeded."

"I wish I knew how."

"Maybe the time isn't right yet. Could be she needs a period with her father."

"They have always been close."

"Didn't mean that. Only away from you will she recognise what she's missing. Meanwhile, you already wear yourself out caring for others. Her turn will come later. And you will know how to cope."

"You must think I'm completely wet!"

Paul smiled. "Only around your face, and a few bits of hair."

He tucked a moist strand behind her ear, his arm tightened around her.

"Paul," Caroline began, thinking. "Don't tell my mother, will you? Not about me being upset. She'll only worry."

"Shan't say a word. Promise." He kissed her cheek.

"I'm so glad you came along. Thanks, Paul."

"A cliché, I know, but – what're friends for?"

All the way home she thought of how much she needed his friendship, his affectionate concern. She could still feel his arm about her, his warmth.

Malcolm seemed pleased that Julian would help publicise their campaign.

"If he does send a journalist over, we could ask some of the parish councillors to the interview. I'll have a word with Anne, she'll know what's best," he added.

"I would have thought . . . well – she's always so busy, isn't she?"

Malcolm's smile was bland, appeared rather secretive. "Ah – but never too busy for making time for the things that count."

He himself would make time this evening for strolling through the woods as far as Birch Tree House. He'd been delighted when Anne told him that he must feel free to call at the side door where she welcomed friends rather than patients.

Malcolm was ready to leave the house when he heard the familiar sound of a very old car stuttering to a halt.

"You're early aren't you?"

Nicholas had surged through into the hall and dropped a sports bag from one hand, and an oily sweater on to a priceless Sheraton chair.

Nicholas beamed at him. "Right, Dad. Gave Bianca a lift most of the way, she wanted to be home by tonight."

"Bianca . . .?"

Before Malcolm received a response, though, his son had turned slightly, an action that revealed the coil of long hair tied at the nape of his neck.

"What on earth possessed you to grow a bloody pony-tail?"

"Fashion?" Nicholas suggested mildly, turning back to his father. His grey eyes were glittering with amusement.

"Time you tailored your appearance to your smart words, my lad. What sort of impression do you imagine you make?"

"Among my friends, a pretty good one."

"That's no recommendation. Anyway, what's so special about this – this Bianca that makes you think you're justified in skipping lectures to drive round the countryside?"

"Wait till you see her. She's brilliant, you'll adore her."

"We'll see. But I'm not amused, Nick, not by any of this. I made sacrifices to subsidise you through university, don't forget."

"I've come home one day early, Dad. It's no big deal."

"I hope you let Caroline know to expect you tonight."

Before Nick could reply, Caroline came hurrying down the stairs, drawn by their voices.

"Nick darling, what a lovely surprise."

She crossed swiftly to be hugged by her stepson, and then she stood gazing up at him, smiling into the eyes so like his father's.

"So, he didn't let you know he was arriving today," Malcolm observed.

43

"And it doesn't matter in the least. Are you hungry, Nick? Mrs Dacre cooked heaps more than we could eat. I can soon pop something into the microwave."

Heading arm-in-arm towards the kitchen, Caroline and her stepson turned to see Malcolm slam the front door after him.

"You're looking ruffled, Malcolm, and you know what I said . . ."

Anne had welcomed him into her pleasant, rather disorganised sitting-room, and was settling into the armchair twin of the one she had offered him.

"You want to try letting difficulties slide off you when you've reared a son who misses lectures only to arrive at the house looking every inch a Sixties hippy!"

"Oh, dear." Anne concealed a smile. "Do I take it that Nicholas is home?"

"A day early, as I said. He's twenty-one, for God's sake. Time he learned the meaning of responsibility."

"Did you – er, was it to tell me all this that you came over?"

Malcolm grinned, awkwardly. "I am going on a bit, aren't I? It was just – disappointment, I suppose."

"You could be even less pleased if your sons showed no signs of individuality."

He gave Anne a look but relinquished regrets concerning Nicholas in favour of discussing plans which could involve more contact with this charismatic doctor.

"Wanted a word with you, actually. About action against the rail link. Caroline's been speaking with her ex. You may recall he has some influence with one of the glossies. He seems prepared to include a piece about our campaign. I thought you might be happy to be interviewed. Local councillor, village doctor – that kind of thing."

"Sounds all right, Malcolm."

"Might come better from you – you could put forward all the arguments against the line . . ."

"Yet without having an axe to grind."

"My point exactly, Anne. So many of the rest of us speak from the angle of our personal potential losses. Whereas you would voice the common good. What's best for the patients in your care, for the community."

She chuckled. "Don't make me out to be entirely the philanthropist!"

"But you see what I mean?"

"Yes, indeed. But you must find out if they want to interview more than one person. Meanwhile, I'll get a few thoughts together, have a word with some of the others who feel very strongly."

Malcolm arrived back at The Sylvan Barn feeling infinitely more at peace than he had when he left. From the drawing-room *News at Ten* murmured its nightly dose of world events which always seemed designed to convince everyone in England that elsewhere circumstances were even less favourable.

Walking through from the hall, he was surprised to find his wife sitting alone. He had expected his favourite chair to be occupied by Nicholas, intent on bending Caroline's all too willing ear. Before he had crossed a couple of feet of carpet the loud drumming of some unidentifiable pop tune hammered forth from above their heads.

"You've just missed Nick," Caroline told him. "He's only this minute gone up to his room."

"I've gathered that," said Malcolm, his grey gaze tilting towards the lofty timbered ceiling.

"I'll turn up the television."

"No need, I'd rather talk. Unless—"

Caroline shook her head as she pressed the button eliminating the sound, and struggled against a sly smile. Malcolm often didn't even think to enquire before either switching channels or actually turning off the set.

"What is it, darling?" she prompted, her voice raised over the din from upstairs.

"Just wanted to tell you Anne's all for going into print in Julian's magazine. She'll be happy to be interviewed. Did he say if they wanted more than one person to express our views?" He was all but shouting to be heard.

Caroline began to rise from the sofa. "I'll tell Nick to lower the volume."

Malcolm shook his head. "I think I'd prefer bellowing like this to coming heavy parents again. I did rather have a go earlier, and it is his first night home."

Caroline's relief that Malcolm's annoyance had rationalised became tempered as the weekend progressed. Along with the customary armfuls of dirty laundry, Nick had brought home an appeal for further funding.

"It's for my digs, you see. Had to find a new place, the old girl at the other couldn't cope any longer."

"Nick, how awful." Caroline felt quite shaken. "Do you mean you've already had to move in somewhere different?" She had always insisted that they must know where Nicholas was living.

"Afraid so," Nick admitted.

His brother grinned across the table. "Wouldn't she have you taking Bianca back there? Or was it all the boozing?"

"I trust it was neither," said Malcolm heavily.

Nicholas avoided his glance while he toyed with the salmon salad they were eating for Sunday lunch. Bianca was joining them for a meal this evening, the reason for having something light now – and the cause of the abnormal restraint which he must employ when answering.

"To be honest, Dad, I think it was no more than the old girl finding lodgers too much for her."

"If they were all like you," Christopher began, and was suppressed by his brother's glare.

Malcolm decided to let the subject lie fallow. He had been tough with Nick in the past. Refusing to relent over this request for a larger allowance would need supporting with all the reasons. Talking to Christopher about their financial difficulties might have been handled better. He must not repeat that with Nick. And as for his son's behaviour, he had no means of controlling what he did whilst away from home, laying down the law would only generate antagonism.

After the meal was over Nick helped Caroline clear away salad bowls and plates, then began stacking the dishwasher. Flora Dora never came in at weekends, and he was glad of the opportunity to work on his stepmother.

46

Caroline was ready for him. She had already thought out her solution to the need for additional funds. She might be able to help Nick through Cambridge. The moment for discussing this with Malcolm hadn't presented itself, she could even have to wait until after the weekend to speak. Speak, she would, though, with all her persuasive powers. She checked Nick now at the first mention of money.

"Leave it with me, darling. I have something to put to your father, but it must be when the time is right. Just try not to annoy him before you set off for Cambridge, will you? Partly for my sake, but also for your own. You know how generous he can be when the occasion demands."

Only an hour or so later Caroline was seizing the opportunity to put her scheme to Malcolm. She was preparing the beef for the fatless roasting that had proved delicious the first time they had tried it. Rubbing in garlic and combining wholemeal flour and mustard for a coating, she was surprised to see Malcolm coming in from the office.

"While you're here, you might open up that bottle of red wine for cooking this," she suggested and then, seeing his expression, asked what was wrong.

"Don't know really, Caro – just a general unease. Could be about this evening. Not quite sure what to make of Nick's friendship with this girl."

"Nor I," Caroline said, her smile rueful. "Give me the uncomplicated days when both boys brought masses of friends home."

Malcolm grinned. "Oh, I don't know about that. Finding sleeping bags all over, each bathroom engaged, and ten extra for breakfast!"

, "I never thought you noticed. Didn't you always escape to the orchards?"

"And leave you to cope? I wouldn't have dared. Seriously, though, I just hope this evening goes smoothly. I might have done more for Nicholas as it is."

"If you could have afforded. I understand. And I was coming to that." Caroline rinsed flour from her hands and faced him while she dried them. "I've thought of a way of raising enough to help Nick – maybe to keep Christopher on at the farm as well."

"Don't see how, I've discussed finances *ad infinitum* with my accountant."

"But you haven't heard my idea, Malcolm. I want to work again."

"You work already, with me."

Caroline sighed. "I wish you'd listen first. I could set up a PR company here. It's what I really want, and it would soon be bringing in far more than the original outlay."

"So you have thought this through sufficiently to realise you can't set up even a small business without capital. Good. What do you propose then – selling the shares your father left you?"

"Not if that can be avoided. I thought perhaps—"

"I could fund you? You still haven't taken it in, have you? I – *we* really are strapped for cash, seriously strapped."

"It should only take a couple of thousand, darling, at most."

"If I had two thousand to hand, I'm afraid it wouldn't even cover the overdraft."

"But – the farm isn't doing that badly, is it? And we should have a good yield this year, we're experiencing none of those ruinous May frosts."

"So far. The real trouble's been this place, not the farming side. You should realise that."

"You can't be having regrets. The barn's turned out a beautiful home, you know it has – out of this world."

"And costing the earth as well," Malcolm reminded her grimly and strode out of the kitchen.

Caroline wanted to scream. He always refused to understand. She gazed around the kitchen where its oak cupboards gleamed golden in the afternoon sunlight. Every wall space not occupied by cabinets wore pale butter-yellow tiles, their glossy surface enhanced by wild flowers in groups, proof of a ceramic artist's skill. Through the open door the mahogany dining table reflected back silverware and cut crystal glasses. She loved it all, everything in this house, her home. Whatever Malcolm said (and over the years he had said a great deal) every penny it had cost was justified.

Having the barn converted hadn't been merely a whim – although a friend's fine conversion had induced rare pangs of envy – it had removed the unacceptable feeling of being a victim. The need for a new home had grown from her inability to live in her predecessor's.

"You must be insane!" Malcolm had exclaimed on the day when Caroline finally admitted that she could not settle in the exquisite former oast house. Insanity was a threat which to her at that time had seemed only too real. His first wife Sue had caused the problem. Caroline had seen too much, long before Malcolm became more to her than Kate's brother-in-law. She had watched Sue serving meals, caring for Malcolm and the boys, sewing curtains to increase the loveliness of the home furnished with her impeccable taste. Long after the sweet young woman had died, Caroline was seeing her still, moving from room to room. Sue, whose death had so distressed, and whose life lingered on, was an example Caroline could not match. She had felt inhibited before alongside Kate, who with her Aga, inexhaustible energy and skill, always did everything so much better. Only Kate did not really count, not in this way, Kate was not the one who had cared for Malcolm.

Creating The Sylvan Barn out of the neglected ruin on the edge of Malcolm's farm had been exhilarating, fun. Caroline wondered now if fun had found any space in their lives since its completion, if they ever would have fun again.

Malcolm was in their room when Caroline went up to change. He looked drawn yet rather flushed. Aided or otherwise by gulps of whisky, he was struggling to insert gold cufflinks.

Regretting the need for introducing the subject of her work, Caroline smilingly crossed to assist.

"I can easily cash in those shares," she told him lightly. "I don't want you worried."

His frown deepened rather than subsiding, as she expected. He sighed, had another drink of the whisky. "I don't want you working, other than with me."

The unmistakable sound of Nick's car in the drive prevented further discussion.

"I'm not even dressed," Caroline wailed. "You'll have to let them in."

"Chris'll do that. He's around somewhere."

"Please, let's do this properly," Caroline persisted. "I'll be down in a second. Don't know where the time's gone."

Malcolm headed towards the stairs. "Nick did say he wouldn't be long when he went to pick her up," he called over his shoulder, leaving Caroline to wonder if she ought to have set a timer for their arrival as well as for every stage of cooking dinner.

Bianca was in front of the stone fireplace, sitting back on her heels while she examined the arrangement of flowers that Caroline had placed in front of the brass firescreen. Sensing the approach of her hostess she turned her head, then rose but quite slowly as though a little unsteady.

"You must be Bianca," Caroline said, offering a hand and finding it grasped as if the girl needed support. "You must call me Caroline. But where's your drink . . .?"

She glanced over her shoulder to where her husband, flanked by his sons, was busy at the sideboard.

"I'm only having mineral water, thanks," Bianca said swiftly.

Her voice was light, though not colourless, perfectly matched to her delicate features and graceful arms. Her frock was white, full-skirted and long, lending an ethereal quality in keeping with pale hair that fell in a profusion of waves about frail shoulders.

She reminds me of an Ophelia I saw at Stratford, thought Caroline. But she suspected Bianca could be far stronger than she looked. A girl who, despite first appearances, would be sure what she wanted.

Leaving the men to entertain their guest, Caroline took a good measure of gin and tonic with her to the kitchen. *I like the girl, thank goodness*, she realised, and hoped the sense she perceived might influence her stepson. All Nicholas needed was someone to temper his enthusiasms. She prayed that, for this evening at least, consideration of Bianca might make him more widely circumspect.

The meal progressed quite well, Bianca proved to be something of a healthy-eating fanatic who appreciated each course selected from Caroline's new stock of recipes. Although obviously a little shy, the girl did converse when Nick or his brother introduced a topic. Caroline noticed Malcolm's occasional approving nod. He never had liked girls who were too pushy in new company.

They happily reached the stage where Nicholas carried in the tray of coffee, smiling as he demonstrated a helpfulness which he hoped might seem customary. Everyone appeared to be smiling as well.

Caroline could relax now, she had provided both a meal and an atmosphere to please them all.

Bianca shook her head, refusing the coffee which Caroline was pouring. "I won't, if you don't mind, thank you," she said, sounding like a little girl who has triumphed over the desire for a forbidden sweetie. "I've stopped drinking coffee."

"Because of the baby," Nicholas blurted. "You've got to know some time."

He stared down at the table as though the action might conceal a face competing for colour with the Super Star roses in their silver bowl.

Caroline battled to haul back her gaze from the linen napkin daintily tucked into Bianca's pink velvet sash. Malcolm was swallowing hard, his neck puce while the skin around narrowed lips turned greyish. Caroline was struggling to find even one appropriate word when Christopher guffawed.

"I say, Nick, you sure know how to spring surprises."

Bianca smiled dazzlingly in his direction. "But how can it be a surprise? This is the nineteen-nineties, Chris. Nick and I love each other."

Malcolm recovered his voice. "It isn't that simple. Forgive me," he began, and paused. Why the hell was he apologising in his own home to this slip of a girl? She and Nick were responsible for delivering the blow. The pair of them ought to have enough sense to know that if they had been so stupid as to indulge in this sheer folly they must now, at least, impart the news more gently.

"You must admit, both of you, that you have been irresponsible. Extremely irresponsible."

"That's hardly fair, Dad," Nicholas put in. "You know nothing of the circumstances. For months, we were most particular. It wasn't until we were both really sure of our feelings that we stopped having safe sex."

Caroline felt that both eyes were revolving in her head. She blinked them, twice, to no real effect.

Nicholas had turned to her. "Mum, no! You're not going weepy on us? You never cry."

Caroline was too amazed to be feeling any other emotion, but she was compelled to swallow in order to speak, which would only reinforce his supposition.

"Oh, no – I'm not going to cry, not over the two of you. Like your father, I feel you could have behaved with more consideration – and not only of our reactions. But since it is late in the day for recriminations, we must be more practical. When are you getting married?"

Nick sighed. "I'm afraid that sounded rather like Bianca's mother."

He glanced towards Bianca, encouraging her to say something.

She smiled. "It isn't that we're thinking we'll never marry. When we do, though, it will be because we need to commit ourselves completely, not just for the sake of the baby."

Nick's sudden statement that it was time they left for Cambridge came as a relief. Caroline was thankful for a respite, if nothing more, and she managed with a glance to quell Malcolm's move to have his say. She would talk to him, as soon as Bianca and Nicholas were out of the house.

Malcolm was resolved to talk to *her*, and did not wait until the noisy engine of the old car announced their departure. "You've let them off too lightly," he began while Chris was striding after the other two, helping with his brother's baggage.

"We can't like what they've done, Malcolm, I know that—"

"Too bloody true we can't!" he fumed, rising from his seat at the head of the table. He seemed slightly unsteady, grasped the back of his carver chair.

He's had too much wine, Caroline thought: their fault again, making him need something to stiffen him in order to accept what's happened.

"Let's just sit quietly somewhere and discuss what must be done."

"This is no matter for a quiet little chat," stormed Malcolm, still clutching the chair. "You've been altogether too lenient with both my sons, look at them now. Nick's taken to swanning round Cambridge, impregnating girls—"

"Come on, Malcolm – that's not fair," Caroline interrupted. "So far as we know, Bianca's the only one. And she seems a nice girl."

"So far as we know," he echoed pointedly, then sank back on to the chair. He massaged his chest. "That beef you served gave me indigestion. You want to go back to cooking it the old way."

"Sure it's that?" she said gently. "I'd have thought the bombshell we took with the meal—"

Malcolm sighed, gave a shrug and winced. Sweat had broken on his forehead, he eased a finger around inside the collar of his Savile Row shirt. "God, this pain!"

Caroline pushed back her chair and dashed to him. "Just stay there quietly," she urged, stifling her own alarm to call in the direction of the front door which she heard closing. "Chris, quick – it's your father. Ring Anne Newbold, I'm sure it's his heart."

The speed with which the doctor arrived confirmed the likelihood that Caroline's suspicion was correct. Opening her bag, Anne took a hurried glance at Malcolm and spoke calmingly.

"Now I'm here there's no reason to panic, Malcolm. I'm giving you something to ease that pain. Then we'll get you into a more comfortable position."

Intensity of chest constriction had forced him out of the chair when he could no longer sit still. He had reached the far end of the table, but had been compelled to stop, and remained leaning over the residue of their meal, holding on to one of the other chairs.

"Just give me a hand, Christopher, will you?" said Anne. "Caroline, phone for an ambulance. Say it's heart—"

Malcolm slumped as soon as they tried to move him. Between them his son and his doctor struggled to support the eighteen stone which couldn't have been much less than their combined weights.

"We'll lower him gradually to the floor," said Anne; "Best place, anyway. I want his back raised slightly, against the side of that armchair will be fine. And we need a cushion under his knees."

"The ambulance is coming," said Caroline, wishing fervently that she didn't feel so useless.

She stood watching as Christopher stepped back, making more room for the doctor to loosen his father's clothing at neck and waist.

When she finally turned away from her patient, Anne smiled reassuringly. Yet there were tears in her hazel eyes.

"I don't believe this is much more than a warning," Anne began carefully. "Although, of course, no one can be certain. But because you acted so promptly we may have averted any lasting harm. The medication will be easing the pain already, and he'll soon be in hospital now, with everything that might possibly help to hand."

Caroline nodded, cleared the throat that ached with anxiety. "Thank you so much for all you've done."

"Only my job. For old friends like this, though, you can't help feeling special concern."

The soul-churning note of the ambulance was heard in the lane outside, and then its halting in the drive.

Anne sighed with relief, smiled again. "We'll soon have him there now. If you two would like to lock up and make sure you have keys, we'll follow the ambulance in my car."

Four

"Are you quite sure there's no one you wish me to contact?"
Anne was gazing concernedly from where she had turned just
inside the doorway of the waiting room. *She cannot bear to leave*,
thought Caroline, recognising the doctor's sudden feeling of helplessness now that care of Malcolm had been taken from her hands.

Caroline pasted a smile on to lips that felt stiff with the need to
contain her panic. "No one, thanks, for the moment. And thank you
so much for all you've done."

Anne smiled back, wearily. Her hazel eyes appeared green as they
reflected the shade of her olive suit. "I'll keep in touch then," she
said. "If there's anything I can do, don't hesitate to ask."

After the bustle of arriving at the Intensive Care Unit had settled
and she'd begun to accept that Malcolm was receiving the attention
of all these experts, Caroline had developed the feeling that Anne
Newbold was intruding. She was not a part of the family, and even
being immensely grateful to her did not preclude the wish that the
doctor would go about her business. They needed to concentrate
their minds on willing Malcolm to survive. Suspecting that such
sentiments regarding Anne were unjustified increased Caroline's
unease, and the need to be alone with Christopher.

Perversely, their doctor's absence soon induced another rush of
the terror that Caroline had experienced during Malcolm's attack.
She swallowed hard, and tried to calm herself. There was nothing
she could do but *be here*. No more was expected of her.

Christopher smiled slightly, his strained blue eyes searching her
face. "You all right, Mum?"

"I will be." Suddenly, she felt she needed to lean, almost as
though she had aged tremendously and must find succour in

55

younger family members. Christopher had coped brilliantly already. It was he who had traced Bianca's home through directory enquiries, and called her parents just in time to prevent Nicholas driving off from there to Cambridge.

Nick was on his way to the hospital now. Caroline was surprised to find she was hoping Bianca would come with him.

"It's going to be up to you and me now, Chris," she said. "To look after him *properly* once he's . . ." Her voice trailed off.

She dared not challenge providence by expressing confidence that Malcolm would survive. But anything else was too dreadful to contemplate.

"I know." He squeezed her wrist. "We make a good team, it'll be all right."

"He may be in here for weeks. Even after these crucial first days of tests." She was convincing herself really, accustoming her own mind to the idea of Malcolm needing professional care. Intensive care.

However would she endure this anxiety? She couldn't bear the prospect of returning eventually to their own home, of being obliged to wait there, aware that each telephone call might be the one most dreaded, dreadful. Full of dread, that is how life would be. *Always* perhaps . . . Now that Malcolm could die.

"I'll be there," said Christopher simply. "There's nothing I have to do that will take me away from the farm."

"I know, darling, don't think I'm not appreciating that. It's just—"

"While we're here, it's easier to believe they're not going into a sudden panic about Dad's condition. I imagine we'll remain here all night, anyway, don't you?"

Caroline nodded.

Chris squeezed her wrist again. "Don't go worrying yet about what being at home might be like. If he's heaps better by morning we'll both feel differently."

When will they let me see him? she wondered, *how soon*? The instant the ambulance had reversed up to the doors here Malcolm had been trolleyed away out of sight. Anne had assured them he was in no immediate danger since being connected to the machines

56

monotoring his heart, but Caroline needed to see him. During all
these tense minutes that had passed that need had grown more
desperate. *If I can't hold on much longer,* she thought, *if I scream out
that I have got to check that my husband's still alive, will I be
banished?*

"You may come through in a moment, Mrs Parker."

The double doors to the ward had whispered open, releasing a
male doctor who looked far too young to have the remotest idea
how to treat a bruised finger, much less a damaged heart.

"I'll just explain, if I may, what we believe about your husband's
condition, and what we are doing for him. I understand Dr Newbold indicated that the heart attack seemed slight . . .?"

"That's right." *God,* thought Caroline, *he's about to break it to me
that Malcolm is much worse.*

"So far, we concur with her opinion. Naturally, however, we are
taking every precaution. You must not be alarmed by all the wires
and so on – the elaborate equipment we use here is only to ensure
that we remain aware of the slightest change in a patient's state." He
smiled widely, as if to make his optimism catching.

It was not. Feeling quite unlike her normal capable self, Caroline
noticed her steps were meandering when she followed towards the
ward.

The doors were still swinging slightly behind her when Christopher glanced towards the outer entrance as his brother rushed in.

"How is he now?" Nick demanded huskily. "He is still alive?"

Christopher nodded. "Sit down, you look worse than Dad did!
They seem to think he's going to pull through. We'll soon know
more. Mum's just been allowed in to see him."

"It's all my fault, I know. They'll neither of them forgive me,
ever." His eyes were staring with alarm, red-rimmed from tears that
he'd scarcely tried to conceal.

"Don't be more of an idiot than you must, Nick! It wasn't only
you."

"Me and Bianca then. Should have thought to prepare them, give
them the news more gently."

"Oh, come on . . . You weren't to know they were that far
removed from the nineteen-nineties. Especially Mum – you look

at her and you think she's totally up to the minute. No one's going to blame you for failing to see that she's enmeshed in antiquated notions. And Dad takes notice of her, tends to believe she's *au fait* with life as it is."

"All the same, the way we spilled the beans was crass."

"Anyway, it wasn't only that. There's the farm, as well . . ."

"What do you mean, the farm?"

"Surely you knew? Losing money. Seriously losing money." He paused, swallowed. "Like I'll be out by the end of next month."

"Rubbish, Chris – Dad would never—"

"Dad has, already. Bit of a facer, must admit. Suppose that might be shelved now, at least till he's out of here."

"He will come through this though? How long will he stay in here, any idea?"

Christopher shook his head. "Don't think anyone has, or will have – not until after the next day or two. That's what Dr Newbold said, anyway, and that they'll most probably hang on to him after that for tests. She was brilliant, arrived at the house and took charge almost as if she'd been waiting for us to call her in."

"Do you think she had – expected this to happen, I mean?"

"Well, she did insist on that diet. Pity Dad didn't consult her earlier." Christopher grinned, suddenly. "Oh, do sit down, Nick. Makes my neck ache staring up at you. And take that dismal look off your face. Forget what happened over dinner, this lot's been building up for ages. It wasn't just you and Bianca." He glanced around. "You haven't left her sitting in your car, I hope?"

Nicholas shook his head. "With her parents. I promised I'd ring as soon as I have any news. They'll drive her to Cambridge first thing tomorrow, and let my tutor know what's happened. Can't believe I'll make it back there."

Caroline went to hug Nicholas as soon as she emerged from the four-bed ward. For a few seconds, she remained with her face pressing into his chest. Holding back tears while she was sitting beside Malcolm's bed had been all but impossible, but she had managed to contain them. Seeing Nick had brought a surge of relief that dissolved her last dregs of will-power.

"Glad you've made it, Nick," she said at last, gazing up at him, trying to smile.

"I'm only thankful we hadn't set out for Cambridge. How is Dad now?" he asked and his brother echoed the question.

Caroline sank on to one of the chairs and the other two sat either side of her. Simultaneously, they each grasped one of her hands.

"Well – the staff here seem cautiously optimistic. It looks quite alarming, as they said, because he's connected to all that machinery. But the pain's a lot easier now. He's very drowsy, in fact. They want him to rest, that's why I came out again."

"Can't we go in there?" asked Nicholas. He desperately needed the reassurance of seeing for himself how his father was.

"You'll have to enquire, I suppose," Caroline said. "And I'm afraid they won't want you to chat away to him."

"Of course not," said Chris. "I'll just find out what they think."

"Are you staying here all night?" Nicholas wanted to know.

"I've got to," Caroline replied. "Can't bear the thought of not being here if . . . One of the doctors said there was no reason for stopping here, but going home is just not on."

Chris and his brother were allowed into the ward, very briefly, on condition that they did not disturb Malcolm by so much as a murmur.

The night seemed intolerably long. While her stepsons dozed, Caroline remained sitting upright, her mind rushing ungoverned in countless directions. If Malcolm didn't survive how ever would she exist without him?

I blame myself, she thought repeatedly, *I should have seen the signs long before this, should have taken him in hand when there was still time for providing more care to have some effect. I should have given him more of my attention. I love Malcolm wholeheartedly, why on earth couldn't I have devoted the whole of my caring to him? Some of those trips out to see Mother might have been unnecessary. I ought to have understood his worries concerning the farm earlier – to have shared the burden.*

Just let this be no more than a warning for me as well, she prayed. *Only give me a chance, and I'll do anything. Any mortal thing that I can. Malcolm must not die, not at forty-one, not while we have so much life, so much love, still ahead of us. I'll never stir from his side,* she vowed, *if he can only come home to me.*

The hands on the wall-clock had dragged towards three in the morning when Caroline experienced the worst stabbing of guilt. She felt overwhelmed with remorse. How could she have laughed and talked out there in Folkestone, how could she have relished the stimulation of fresh company? Why had those occasional meetings with Paul Saunders seemed so important? Why – when here at home she had the man who was the dearest in all the world to her?

I'll never even spare Paul another thought, much less see him, she resolved. Guilt was flushing her face, her entire head, guilt because she had savoured the company and the compliments of this man who was a stranger. If she had thought at all about the way in which she had kept silent at home about meeting Paul, she'd explained the reason to herself as his having no connection with her family. And why had she felt so thankful just because Paul had listened sympathetically?

There was so much more between herself and Malcolm – so much love that they both had grown confident in it. Wasn't this how they had begun speaking less about their feelings? As long as he lived she would make certain he understood how desperately she needed him.

Caroline was glad of the stirring about the hospital when day nurses hastened in to take over from the night staff. At last, she might have some direction on which to fix her mind, maybe even something positive that she might do.

"Did you let Uncle Graham know?" Nicholas asked when he was the first of the brothers to awaken.

"No, I shall do so shortly, just as soon as there is someone around to give us an up-date on your father's condition. It seemed too late last night, once we got him here. In any case, they wouldn't have permitted anyone else in that ward."

Wasn't her being here enough for Nick? She didn't relish the prospect of having Graham present, well meaning though his assistance would be. He was too much the elder sibling who always knew what everyone ought to be doing. Much like Kate, she supposed, though perhaps in all honesty with more cause to be assertive.

And as for her mother-in-law . . .! Caroline stilled a shudder, silently acknowledged her thankfulness that she had not added to her night-time cares the realisation that Isabel must be informed. And be included here in this circle of everyone concerned for Malcolm.

Lord, but I wish she was more like my own mother, she thought, and wondered how many occasions over the years had created the seed of that particular sentiment.

She telephoned Graham's number at eight o'clock.

Kate answered. "Caroline – whatever's wrong? Something is, isn't it?"

"I'm afraid so. Is Graham there?"

"I'll fetch him, in a minute. Is it Malcolm?"

"Yes. But it's not as serious as it might have been, thank goodness. It is his heart, though – a minor attack, they're saying."

"I'll bet it doesn't feel minor to you! God, if it was Graham . . . I'll get him, shall I?"

"Or you can tell him yourself. Because at the moment I don't really know any more than I've just told you. I shall hang on at the hospital until the consultant has done his rounds, then we might learn a bit more. All they're saying so far is that Malcolm seemed fairly comfortable through the night. You might suggest Graham should stress that when he breaks the news to his mother."

"Have you been in touch with Lucy?"

"Not yet, Kate. There isn't a thing she can do, and she'll only work herself into a frenzy of anxiety." And there are enough of us doing that, Caroline thought grimly.

Graham arrived just as the three of them were being assured by the consultant that Malcolm was in no immediate danger.

"When's he being discharged then?" asked Graham briskly.

"Ah – now, that is something to which there is no ready answer," the consultant told them. "I explained last evening that there will be certain tests that must be carried out. And we must take radical steps to reduce that blood pressure. I gather that our patient was not overkeen on his new dietary regime. I'm afraid he is about to find that our methods are even more stringent." He beamed from one to the other of their little group, as though delighting in this information.

Graham went in to see his brother, followed closely by Caroline. Malcolm was hardly in a state for saying very much, but being able to hold his hand was something, and just to look at him a relief. He certainly appeared more himself than he had the previous night, his colour was almost normal, and he managed a smile or two.

If he gets over this, I'm not sure that I ever will, she ruefully reflected when her brief spell beside the bed was terminated by an assertive little nurse.

"I'll drive you home," said Graham quickly. "And then we must talk. Make a few plans, about running the farm."

"Thanks, Graham," Caroline began as the four of them trooped out to the car park. "But I'm sure Chris and I will be able to manage."

"Ah, but will you manage to recoup some of the losses? That's what you should have in mind, you know – getting the business on its feet again. Then when Malcolm is discharged he'll be taking over something that is less of a burden. Makes sense, yes?"

Getting into the car after hugging each of her stepsons beside Nick's car, Caroline tried to focus her thoughts. Did Graham not understand that with her brain somehow contriving to be both overtired and overcharged she would make sense of very little?

She realised afresh during the journey to The Sylvan Barn that Graham was one of those exhausting people who supposed any silence existed only to be filled with conversation – preferably generated by himself. *I can't take this in*, she found long before their lane was reached, and settled for letting his words rush over and away from her.

"Well, don't you agree?" he demanded, assisting her from the car outside her front door.

A smile seemed to be expected from her, and a nod of the head at least. Caroline obliged. "Of course," she said firmly.

"Got to dash just now, I'm afraid," said Graham. "Someone I must see. But I'll be round later on. Say, about midday. You won't be going back to the hospital until after that."

Caroline tottered up to the door on legs turned to gel by weariness. Slotting the key into the lock required a second try. And then she was inside her beloved great entrance hall. Suddenly, though, it seemed impersonal rather than impressive, anything but welcoming. Tears welled in her eyes, thickened her throat, and made her feel even more wretched than she was already.

Impulse took her rushing towards the stairs. If she locked herself in the bedroom she could at last indulge in the weeping that over so many weeks she had tried to keep below the surface.

She was less than halfway up the staircase when she heard Nick's car halting briefly before driving away again. Christopher called cheerio to his brother, then his key was inserted in the lock.

Swallowing, Caroline turned and walked slowly down the stairs to reach the foot as Chris closed the front door behind him and looked towards her.

"Uncle Graham didn't stop long, we passed him in the lane."

"Think he said he's meeting someone. He's coming back, though, later on."

Christopher groaned. "Does he think we can't cope without him to supervise?"

"Don't start that, darling, please. Graham has offered to help, we can't throw that in his face."

"Suppose not. What time's he coming? You look all in, Mum. Better lie down for a while."

"I'll be fine when I've had a shower. You and I will have to get across to the office before long. And Mrs Dacre will arrive any minute, I must put her in the picture."

"I'll go and fill the kettle. Make some toast."

Caroline had thought that under the shower might be the one place where she could give way to tears. Somehow, though, she felt unable to let go now, was rather afraid that if she once started she would lose control permanently. Tonight, she promised herself, in bed. Until then she must keep going, attend to whatever needed doing in the office, and gear herself to paying more heed than she had just now to Graham's suggestions.

Her brother-in-law arrived while she and Chris were taking a short break for a sandwich lunch.

"Have you eaten?" Caroline enquired, hoping he wouldn't expect her to rustle up a snack for him. Mrs Dacre had been badly shaken

63

by Malcolm's illness but had cycled off unsteadily to collect the shopping.

"Far too well, as a matter of fact," Graham admitted. "That's if I'm to avoid Malcolm's problem. Although I do take plenty of exercise."

Of course, thought Caroline, recalling Graham's insistence on regular tennis on the court to the rear of his home. Glancing at him compelled her to acknowledge that he did appear very fit. Roughly the same height as Malcolm and of similar colouring, the resemblance ended around the middle regions where Graham's flat stomach was proof of a maddening degree of self-restraint. Or of Kate's even more maddening ability to provide only the most sensible of foods.

I'll show them yet, she resolved; when I get Malcolm home I'll show them what healthy eating can do. I've got to save him.

"Well, shall we take a look at that storage space I mentioned earlier?" said Graham swiftly.

About to ask whatever he meant, Caroline checked herself, and quelled her sigh before it surfaced. Graham was obviously referring to the conversation they had had that morning, the conversation to which she had given less than half an ear. Panic soared through her as she realised the extent of her neglect. It wasn't even twenty-four hours since Malcolm had been taken ill and she was already making a hash of keeping things running.

"Right," she said, rising from the table. "Just leave that last sandwich, will you, Chris, and come along." If she was capable of such a gross misjudgement she needed someone present to stand up to Graham, should the need arise.

While they strode across the entrance hall and around the side of the house towards the farm offices, Caroline trawled her memory for fragments of that morning's journey from the hospital. Beyond her own relief that Malcolm seemed to be stable and her longing for home where she would be permitted some silence, she recalled nothing of any import.

"Since Chris wasn't in on what was said earlier, Graham," she began, "I'd like you to outline what you have in mind."

Graham cleared his throat. "It's perfectly simple – I want us to utilise some of the space here which is normally used only when your pears and apples have been picked. As I said, Caroline, I'll pay the going rate for storage. These days, that's quite an item. You should find it offsets some of the recent poor results."

"That's great," Christopher exclaimed. "If we can reduce the overdraft for Dad that'll give him a real boost when he comes out of hospital."

"My sentiments exactly," said his uncle firmly.

Caroline felt less enthusiastic, she was indoctrinated with her husband's misgivings about Graham's business. When she unlocked the storage building, though, she noticed how huge it was. It'd be foolish to let this lie empty during most of this year.

"You do see this as a temporary measure, don't you, Graham? Only until Malcolm is back in harness. All decision-making then will revert to him."

"That goes without saying. I only want to assist you during this difficult period, Caroline, and if that helps my outfit to function more effectively it's all to the good."

After inspecting the fruit store, they adjourned to the office next door where Graham set down the figures which he had calculated.

"Feel free to check these rates, but I guarantee they are charges currently applied in our area. You'll see that even one month – given that the store is used to the full, and I intend that it shall be – will recoup a sizeable amount for you."

"Yes, indeed," Caroline agreed, she didn't feel up to arguing. And Christopher supported the idea. She didn't doubt that Graham meant to store here some of the imported fruit that he distributed, right now helping to keep Malcolm's business afloat was more vital than considering his reservations about importing.

"The initial load will be here tomorrow first thing," Graham announced. "It will be palletised, and naturally my men will do all the handling. I'm arranging to have my spare fork-lift round here well in advance of the delivery."

"So, we don't have to do anything?" asked Chris.

"Just open up the store, take your copy of the delivery notes, and make sure the place is locked when they drive off again."

The prospect of money coming in like this cheered Caroline

considerably, although she emphasised to her stepson the importance of keeping the scheme from his father.

"Do me a favour, Mum – do you think I haven't heard enough from him on what Uncle Graham's importing does to the local growers? Dad's prejudiced, we know, but where's the harm in us saving the farm by refusing to be quite so dogmatic?"

Caroline and Chris were having a hasty cup of tea in the early evening when the doorbell rang.

"That'll be Nick, I suppose," she said. "He's always mislaying his key."

When Christopher returned from the door he was preceded by Lucy.

"Mother," Caroline exclaimed, her eyes filling as she ran to hug her. "Am I glad to see you! But who told you, and how did you get here?"

"Kate rang me, of course, darling. And then I simply had to get ready at once and catch the next train."

"Bless you, that's wonderful. We're just about to go to the hospital, you must come with us, naturally. Although I can't say for sure that they'll let you see him."

"That's all right, Caro. You mustn't worry about a thing. But how is Malcolm, what's the latest?"

"When we left this morning he seemed much easier than when he was admitted. I rang early this afternoon, and they appear to consider he isn't in any immediate danger."

"But the next few days will be crucial," Lucy put in. "Don't think I don't understand, my dear. I'm afraid several of my friends have experienced similar attacks. And most of them have recovered. Malcolm's being so much younger and stronger than they are will stand him in good stead, I'm sure."

Having her mother with them felt marvellous. For the first time since the previous evening Caroline began to feel that they might approach the hospital in a more optimistic mood.

Nicholas was just emerging from the Intensive Care Unit as they arrived, and he immediately confirmed that optimism was justified.

"Dad looks a whole lot better, and the nurses say he's proving a model patient. I bet he'll be on his feet in no time."

Caroline's opinion was tempered with rather more reality when she saw her husband was still connected to the machinery which, despite her understanding of its being essential, perturbed her. But his smile was genuine enough and his grasp on her hand reassuringly warm.

"Sorry to put you through all this anxiety, Caro," he said as soon as he'd affirmed that he was feeling better. "How are things at home, coping all right?"

"Yes. Chris and I are managing very well between us. Have to admit we've had hardly any queries to deal with, but I'm sure one of us will find an answer if problems should arise."

"You can always refer to Graham, don't forget. He told me he will keep an eye on things, not that I expect you to require help from anyone."

Caroline smiled, and hoped her eyes did not say too much. "Yes, he popped over during the day, seems geared to help if we need him to. You can forget about the farm – just give your mind to getting over this."

She asked if there was anything he wished her to bring from home.

Shaking his head, Malcolm's grin was rueful. "We're not allowed much in the way of individuality on this ward. Not even flowers are permitted, have you noticed? All to do with keeping the place sterile."

Caroline glanced around her, and was glad to return her gaze to Malcolm. Ill though he seemed to them, all the other patients in the unit looked infinitely worse.

"You'll be thankful when you're up to being transferred to a normal ward."

"I shan't be really thankful until they allow me home."

"I know. That's how we all feel. But they think you're being a good patient, don't spoil that already by becoming restless."

When Caroline asked the staff nurse about the chances of her mother being permitted to see Malcolm she was disappointed by the answer.

"I'm sorry, Mrs Parker, but your husband's already had his son in to see him, hasn't he?"

"Yes, and his other son has arrived with me."

The nurse frowned. "Oh, dear. Well, don't turn him away, but you must tell him that his father has really had quite enough excitement."

Nicholas was speaking earnestly to Lucy when Caroline came through the swing doors to give Chris the nurse's instructions.

"Well, darling, that is good news," Lucy responded. "And I look forward to meeting Bianca next time you come home to Kent. You did say she's on her way back to Cambridge now?"

"With her father, yes. I'll most likely follow tomorrow, now I know Dad is showing signs of improving."

"Well, I hope her father takes the journey steadily," Lucy went on. "In her delicate condition all this riding up and down the country can't be very comfortable."

"Oh, she's got ages to go yet," said Nicholas lightly. "She's only just missed the second time."

Caroline resisted the impulse to stare in amazement at her mother who seemed to be taking the news of Bianca's pregnancy extremely calmly. *I suppose I should be thankful that she is*, Caroline thought, *I'm certainly far too exhausted for tackling family repercussions.*

"You must let me know when there's anything you want for the baby," Lucy was saying impulsively. "I know you and Christopher aren't my natural grandchildren, but I think of you both as though you were."

"That's very nice, you know, Mother," Caroline said, and hoped that Lucy's attitude might be compensating Nick for the reactions within their closer family.

Despite her tiredness, she and her mother talked that night, sitting on the bed in the spare room which, with Lucy's possessions around them, reminded Caroline of her girlhood home.

She had thought she was too old to need her mother's support, but she was very glad that Lucy was willing to put herself out and come here so swiftly. Did all daughters continue to need this sort of contact? she wondered. What was she doing to Amanda? How deeply was the girl suffering because of their separation?

*   *   *

Lucy planned to stay for several days and, after her first visit to the Intensive Care Unit, professed to be certain that Malcolm would recover.

She remained a constant source of reassurance, her optimism making Caroline feel that the weight of Malcolm's illness was diminishing.

At the beginning of her mother's visit, oppressed by too many worries, Caroline had fussed about finding some means of keeping Lucy occupied whilst she herself and Chris were busy in the office.

Lucy soon proved that she needed no one to entertain her. She and Florence Dacre had always got on well, and often spent an hour or more chatting over cups of tea in Caroline's elegant kitchen.

It wasn't long before Lucy was provided with her most stimulating company. She had already spoken of ordering a taxi for the drive over to see her other daughter when they met Kate one day at the hospital. With her was Isabel Parker.

From what was said, Caroline and Lucy gathered that Graham had persuaded his mother to wait for a few days before going in to see Malcolm. Now, though, the old lady evidently had decided she had delayed quite long enough and had demanded that Kate drive her there.

"I was going to come, anyway, of course," Kate assured her sister. "It was only that Graham had emphasised Malcolm should not be exhausted by too many visitors."

Isabel had greeted Lucy with the tight little smile that Caroline always believed was reserved for herself, and in a surprised voice which implied Lucy was intruding.

"Take no notice, Mother," whispered Caroline as soon as Isabel had swept through into the ward. "You know you belong here with us."

"Caro, you don't have to worry," Lucy interrupted cheerfully. "Don't forget Isabel Parker has been Kate's mother-in-law for a very long time. Hasn't she, Kate darling?"

Kate's smile looked quite wan, full of reservations.

"The three of us have always got along," Lucy asserted. "I'm looking forward to spending some time over there, catching up on all their news."

And imparting ours? wondered Caroline uneasily. Her lips would remain clamped while Kate was here beside them, but she must engineer a quiet word before Lucy was able to relate all that she had learned about Nicholas and his girlfriend. Although now able to accept that Bianca's pregnancy had been only one of the factors possibly contributing to Malcolm's attack, Caroline was well aware that skill would be needed when conveying the news to Nick's grandmother.

I must *remember tonight to warn Mother against passing on that particular piece of information,* Caroline was thinking when the doors swung open as Isabel returned to them.

"Malcolm seems much as I expected, not too bad at all," Isabel announced. "And I have always had a certain ability to judge a person's state of health."

Caroline felt Kate stiffening and willed her own composure to remain unfaltering. For the first time in recent years, she could sense what her sister was feeling. It would not do to display their clear recollections of the way in which Isabel Parker's husband had died whilst she was away from home, and following her assertions that his constant complaints of feeling unwell were sheer malingering.

Afraid that her still fragile self-control might let her down, Caroline began hurrying towards the ward entrance. She had a hand outstretched to push the doors open when she heard Lucy's firm voice.

"Well, Isabel, what do you make of Nick's announcement? Aren't you delighted you'll soon be a great-grandmother?"

Five

A fterwards – so long afterwards that she'd recovered from her initial anxiety about her mother-in-law's reaction – Caroline began to see how funny it was that Lucy had unwittingly caused so much turmoil.

Relieved though she had been to escape and sit chatting with Malcolm in the ward, Caroline had felt that she ought not to have left the rest of them to battle without her.

Battle, it seemed, had been the only word for the scene which had developed so spiritedly that the nursing staff were obliged to ask Malcolm's visitors to lower their disruptive voices.

"Would you believe it was Kate who had the most to say?" Lucy had exclaimed eventually, hurrying out to the car as though she might explode if expected to contain the excitement for another moment. "Anyone would think that Nick and Bianca were the first couple in England to anticipate marriage. I soon told her that Nick had explained what a marvellous girl Bianca is. I certainly shall not withhold my blessing. I told Kate straight that I have every intention of giving the pair of them every assistance I can manage."

"What did Kate say to that?" Caroline had enquired, her heart plummeting. Kate and Graham's two were both being groomed for the future, and introduced among what Caroline privately considered the snobbiest ranks of the county set.

"Naturally, she was quick to point out that neither of her offspring expected help from anyone. I was about to assert that I was *offering* to give them a bit of help, not reacting to any request for a hand-out, but the harridan cut in with her opinion."

"I'm only surprised that Kate got a word in first."

Lucy had grinned at Caroline. "You wouldn't have been surprised if you'd seen Isabel's expression. For once in her life, words had drained from her along with all her colour. She compensated quite fully, of course, when she finally found her tongue."

"Go on, Mother, tell me the worst . . ."

"I'm going to, don't you worry. Isabel drew herself to her full height, and gazed disdainfully towards me. 'I trust, Lucy, that my ears are deceiving me – and that I did not hear you say you intend encouraging these foolish young people . . .' It doesn't sound much, I know, but the iron-hardness in her eyes and in that mean mouth made her look quite ludicrously stern."

"Was that all she said?"

"Oh, Caro . . . ! Do you need to ask? Of course it wasn't. On and on she went, about the lenience both Nicholas and Christopher had always been shown."

"*Always?*" Caroline enquired, surprised.

"Well – well, if you must know, Isabel did say something about that having been since – since you married Malcolm."

"That's more like it."

"You won't behave any differently towards Isabel because I'm telling you this, will you, darling? I don't wish to be the cause of any trouble. But I do consider that you ought to know what she has been saying."

Caroline laughed. "Oh, Mother, you are a gem! You may be sure that Isabel will withhold no scrap of her opinion when we meet. In fact, she'll no doubt have embellished every detail of her reaction to the news. As for my attitude towards her, I've never been other than in awe of Malcolm's mother, there is nothing existing between us that you might ruin."

Despite saying all that, Caroline experienced several uneasy days and even more uneasy nights anticipating her next encounter with her mother-in-law. Amid so much family anxiety concerning Malcolm, this was no time for conflicting with Isabel. What she didn't expect was that her own mother would take matters in hand.

Between keeping the farm office going and dashing back and forth to visit Malcolm, there had been little time for more than checking that Lucy was filling her days with something of interest. It wasn't until she greeted them with a beaming smile one evening that they learned that she had called on Kate and Isabel not once but twice.

"You two may congratulate me," she remarked, resembling a snowy haired kitten who'd been plundering the cream jug. "I had to have two goes at it, but I've won Isabel Parker round."

"What do you mean?" asked Caroline.

"Have you dared to telephone her?" Christopher enquired.

"Better than that – I've been over there. The day before yesterday, and again this morning."

Lucy went on to describe her first visit which conjured up for Caroline a scene much like the one that had greeted her on the day when Kate and Isabel had combined to daunt her. Lucy had not exactly been daunted.

"Must admit I gave them a bit of a lecture – beginning with Kate. After all, she is my own daughter, I can feel free to express my opinion. Told her she'd become bigoted and stuck-up, that she lacked understanding. I was surprised to notice that Isabel was listening, even though Kate appeared to be giving me only about as much attention as you two girls generally do."

"Mother," Caroline began to protest, but Lucy waved aside her interruption. And really Caroline had no desire to wait before learning the rest.

"After a while, I got Kate to recognise that she failed to comprehend how difficult it must be for youngsters when they are surrounded by their peers, all sleeping around quite freely. At that point I thought Isabel looked in danger of gagging. I added very swiftly that I was only thankful that Nicholas had stuck to the one partner."

"Not literally, I hope?" Christopher put in.

Lucy gave him a look. "Remind me later to reprimand you for talking dirty." She took another breath and continued; "Kate had begun nodding in what I assumed to be agreement. I didn't expect she would voice such sentiments, though, not in front of Isabel. That was where I left the subject, until today."

"And how did you carry on from there, Gran?" asked Christopher. "Must say you've more pluck than any of us, even daring to tackle those two."

73

Lucy smiled appreciatively, her brown eyes warm. "I know Kate too well to be seriously anxious about her opinion, so I decided to concentrate on the old girl. She's the one who is capable of damaging the future for Nicholas and Bianca."

Her smile grew reflective. "Over the years, Isabel and I have always enjoyed the occasional spat. Can't help thinking she relishes someone standing up to her. I caught her on her own this time. In that room of hers which always looks uncomfortably tidy. Rather as though it belongs to a dead person. Anyway, she greeted me with that chilling *politesse*. That was when I thought, *Oh, to hell with it – I've been determined for long enough to stay on the right side of her. Time I said what I'm really thinking.*"

Caroline shook her head at her. "Trust you, Mother. Was life becoming too dull again, since you'd recovered from all the banner carrying in Folkestone?"

"That's quite unkind of you, darling. Especially when I was only working to establish better relations within the Parker family."

"And having a high old time, Gran – admit you were . . ." said Chris.

Lucy grinned. "Well . . . As I was saying, I tackled Isabel head-on. Told her I was glad we could have a private chat, that I was surprised that she hadn't shown her usual grasp of a difficult situation. I wasn't surprised, of course. But she was not to know that her initial reaction had been one I could have foretold. Still, that got her listening. I went on about our generation quite a bit – and how we are the ones who *ought* to have the wisdom to see beyond the irrelevances to what really matters."

"I'm sure Isabel enjoyed that," Caroline observed.

"She did give me a searching look. But I carried straight on to indicate that we should be the ones who, because of our experience of life, are capable of accepting that it so often falls short of the ideal we might visualise. That was when she laughed – a positive chortle."

"But Grandmother never laughs," Chris protested.

"She does with me, once every five years or so. This was one of those occasions. 'That makes them look up to us, does it?' she snapped. Suddenly, I was nodding and laughing too. I must admit I quite forgot myself and gave her a hug."

"Yuk!" said Christopher, miming the sickness that he generally described as a technicolour yawn.

"Isabel really was rather a lamb after that," Lucy continued. "She called Kate in to listen while she delighted in announcing that she personally would show Nicholas how tolerant his family could be. Before I left Isabel had begun murmuring possible baby names aloud."

"Christ," said Christopher. "When you see her next, Mum, she'll be so mellow you'll not recognise her."

Caroline shook her head. "Oh, I don't think so. Knowing her, she will still display martinet tendencies." Good though it was to believe Isabel would be less likely to cause Nick unhappiness, she suspected she knew who might be made to pay for his actions.

Isabel was at that moment addressing Malcolm with all her customary aggression. Hearing that he was out of Intensive Care, she had insisted his brother must drive her to the hospital. Malcolm had frowned as soon as Graham mentioned that he was keeping an eye on The Sylvan Barn farm, a frown that didn't go unnoticed by Isabel.

"Just look at you. Too mean-minded to thank your own brother for taking a load off your shoulders. I'm not surprised you're laid low, Malcolm, with all that sourness inside you."

"And who do I inherit that from?" Malcolm muttered.

"Hardly from me, I think," his mother retorted. "I am always most judiciously fair. You never were one for counting your blessings, I know, but I would have thought this should be teaching you that lesson. It is in your own interests, surely, to acknowledge that you could use a little help now?"

"It's times like this that draw families together," Graham put in. "You know I run a tight ship, I can delegate occasionally to free myself for popping over to your place."

"All right then, thanks," said Malcolm, mustering a smile. He was feeling so much better today that he believed he'd soon be at home again, taking charge.

"Could be more gracious," Isabel began murmuring, but was distracted by Malcolm's widening smile as he looked towards the ward entrance.

"It's Anne!" he exclaimed. "You two remember her, of course, from Sue's illness . . ."

The doctor was beaming as she hurried down the ward to greet Malcolm. "Good to see you're out of Intensive Care. This is great."

"Knew you'd be delighted, Anne. You remember my mother, don't you, and Graham?"

She chatted with the two of them before turning back to her patient.

"I've got some news, about opposition to the rail link plans. Several action groups, including our own, walked out of the meeting with Union Railways."

"The meeting you'd told me about, to be held at the Boxley House Hotel?"

"That's the one – I've never seen anyone more staggered than the Union Railways' officials. Three of the parish councils joined the walk-out as well."

"Which three were they?" asked Malcolm eagerly.

"Let's see if I can remember, with so many people present it's difficult to recall. Thurnham and Boxley . . . and Detling, that's it."

"And which were the other action groups?"

Before Anne replied Graham and Isabel interrupted to say good-bye to Malcolm.

"Come on, tell me all about it," he prompted, the second that the others moved away from his bed.

Anne grinned. "My word, you are better! Well, the meeting was attended by groups from right the way along our hillside and beyond. And all the rail line officials were offering was some sort of cosmetic exercise – mounding of earth, tree planting, and such. Boxley and Penenden Heath Rail Action already had a petition of close on three thousand signatures. It stated that only a long tunnel, taking the route underground, was acceptable."

"But the rail link chaps weren't having that, I suppose?"

"We were told that that idea was not under discussion, having been rejected by the government. That was when others handed in submissions in favour of the long tunnel scheme, and as a body swept out of the meeting."

76

"Did no one stay to hear the Union Railway people out?"

"Very few, according to the *Kent Messenger*. We didn't wait to find out. You should have heard the buzz while we were heading for our cars."

"Wish I'd been there. Still, it's good to know there are plenty of you with the guts to protest so forcefully."

"You want to join us as soon as you're out of here, Malcolm. I'm sure it would do you no harm."

"It'd certainly provide an interest. The doctors here give the impression that I shan't be allowed to do very much about the farm for some time."

Anne nodded seriously. "Afraid I'm inclined to agree with them. But I'll have a word on that with your consultant before you're discharged."

"So, what's the next step regarding the rail link?"

"Our group has a meeting tonight, I'll know more next time I see you. And I've asked for a couple of volunteers to be interviewed along with me for that magazine. Several sounded only too eager to see themselves in print – don't fancy weeding them out. Especially as they all seem to be patients of mine."

Malcolm laughed.

"Good to see you in such good form."

"That's only while you're here, cheering me up. Otherwise, it's all pretty dull."

"You had visitors, though, when I arrived."

"The kind I have to steel myself to endure. Mother never was a very comfortable person. Graham's worse still."

"Oh, dear. No doubt you can look forward to Caroline coming in this evening, though?"

Malcolm nodded. Suddenly he was compelled to quell a wayward thought. He glanced towards the clock, then leaned against his pillows letting relief surge through him. Caroline would not arrive for another hour at least, she'd not be here to dilute Anne's company.

"Do you still take that walk through the woods to Birch Tree House?"

"Not as often as I would like."

"It was good that day, talking."

Anne's smile lit her hazel eyes. "Exercise is one thing you will need to maintain once you're over the worst of this."

Smiling back, he nodded. The possibility of repeating that stroll with her seemed one of the few things to which he'd look forward.

"We'll have to make that my reward for accepting the stringencies here."

"Are they restricting your diet very severely?"

"Not too badly so far – apparently, I lost quite a bit of weight during the early days after the attack."

"So they're striking a balance between restoring your strength and keeping an eye on what you eat?"

Malcolm nodded again. Discussing it all with Anne was making him far happier about everything. Enticed with plans, however undefined, for after his return home, Malcolm's will to cooperate fully and be out of hospital was increasing.

"You're a bloody good doctor," he said suddenly. "Perhaps most of all for my morale."

After she had twice visited Malcolm following his move to a general ward, Lucy told Caroline she felt the time had come for going back to Folkestone.

"You have Florence Dacre, after all, as well as Chris. You're not coping on your own, and I feel certain now that Malcolm is unlikely to have a relapse."

"So do I," her daughter agreed, and marvelled that the day had finally come when this dreadful anxiety might subside. "Of course you must get back home if that's what you wish. It isn't as if we were so far away that you couldn't pop over here again and cheer us all up."

Cheering, however, had not been the undiluted effect of Lucy's stay, although Caroline would never reveal this to her mother. The trouble had grown from Lucy's repeated visits to Kate and Isabel. Much as Lucy herself might never suspect such a thing, her constant relaying of events and attitudes in the other Parker household had increased Caroline's misgivings concerning the way things were done in her own.

If those two weren't proving their super-efficiency in the home, she had reflected, they would be asserting their greater ability to cope with serious illness. She had lost count of the occasions when Lucy had arrived back at The Sylvan Barn fortified with their ideas on how Caroline should ensure that Malcolm regained his health.

"We're managing quite well, Christopher and I," she asserted now. Silently, she added that it would be good to be able to concentrate on matters no more disturbing than farm routine and fitting in hospital visits.

"Yes, I'm sure you are, darling," Lucy agreed. "I know you have your own way of working."

"I'll run you home whenever you're ready, Mother. How soon did you have in mind?"

"Is this evening convenient? Could Chris go on his own to see Malcolm?"

All the way to Folkestone the breeze through the open windows freshened the heat shimmering from the road surface ahead. By the time Caroline was parking the car she felt so enlivened that she might have been embarking on a holiday. Almost, she wished that she were. Even now that Malcolm was stable and improving she seemed to have lost the ability to relax properly for more than a moment. Wishing for escape seemed wickedly selfish, though, ungrateful as well when she considered how their situation might have been much more grave.

"Are you going to have a little snack with me?" Lucy invited when Caroline had brought in her case and helped her to go around opening windows.

"No, I'm fine, thanks."

"And you want to be getting back. I understand, Caro."

"Well – thanks once again for rushing over to us, Mother. It was really heart-warming. I shan't forget. And nor will Malcolm."

They hugged and kissed and Lucy walked with her to the door.

Out in the open again, Caroline inhaled deeply, savouring the sea air, and the scent of nearby roses. She couldn't go straight home, could not face going back to the farm, not without seeking the renewal that somehow always occurred whilst she was over here.

Guiltily aware that she was avoiding the area visible from her mother's windows, she strode out along the road that skirted houses and hotels until she reached the westward edge of The Leas. Pausing, she gazed out to sea where the dying sun dazzled back from calm water.

Below her on the beach strolled young people in their teens and twenties, arms about each other, reminding her of Nicholas and Bianca.

Nick had telephoned again today, checking on his father, offering to come for the weekend. His relief when she said there was no real need had been engagingly evident. Despite what Malcolm supposed, she believed Nicholas worked quite hard at Cambridge. If he chose to play hard as well, that was no more than he deserved. She had gathered that for him and Bianca a day out with friends was scheduled. *I hope they make the most of it*, she thought. For too many years her own friends had been crowded out. She hadn't known how much she would miss them.

Captain, the now-familiar German shepherd dog, came bounding towards her, recognition in his urgently wagging tail. Paul followed more slowly, ascending one of the paths that snaked between trees up the steep cliffside.

"Good to see you again," he called.

"And you," Caroline responded swiftly. And was jolted to discover that since Paul had listened to that outpouring of anguish he now seemed a very close friend.

"How's your husband now? Improving, I hope?" said Paul as he reached her.

"Much better, thank you. I've just brought Mother home actually."

He glanced all about them while his dog settled affectionately across Caroline's feet. "She's not out here with you?"

Caroline shook her head. "I imagine she's unpacking and so on. I didn't wait to see. Should be on my way back, only . . . well, never could resist a walk here."

"Care for a drink? I was just thinking of finding somewhere."

She sighed, torn between sitting over a drink with him and recognising that going to a pub would feel too much like a date.

Paul was smiling. "It doesn't matter. You must be considering the drive home."

Below the foot of the cliffs the rush of an incoming tide was stirring shingle, echoing for Caroline her own inner disturbance. He asked where she was parked, and seemed pleased that they would be returning in the same direction.

Halfway back to the flats they halted and stood side by side to watch the darkening sky and the sea with its occasional glint of light from a passing boat. Caroline listened to his urgent breathing.

"It's so good to be here . . ." She had spoken unthinkingly, and felt Paul's gaze on her. She met his glance, gave a tiny shrug. "Don't know what's got into me. It isn't that I don't love my home, it's a very nice house in a beautiful village."

"So Lucy told me."

And Mother wouldn't understand or forgive this, thought Caroline, any more than she herself could. After all her resolve, those urgent promises.

Approaching the flats, Caroline glanced upwards instinctively, was relieved that her mother was nowhere near the front windows.

"You look exhausted, you know. Why don't I make you a quick coffee?"

Startled by Paul's suggestion, she hesitated. The desire to prolong their meeting was as strong as ever. A cup of coffee was harmless enough, and if she turned the offer down how would she explain to him? He'd only ever been kind, there was no reason to suppose he'd even suspect how much she had attached to their friendship.

"I don't really know," she said, still doubtful. "Should have been on my way."

"Is your husband out of hospital?"

"No, not yet."

And, Caroline realised, *this could be my final opportunity to spend any time away from the house.* She still wanted a friend, someone who wasn't caught up in the family's traumas.

In all the years since ceasing her PR job she had worked so hard for the farm and Malcolm's people that she'd had little time for seeing anyone, and certainly none for making new acquaintances. But she had survived without them, she concluded ruefully, no doubt she could ensure this was her last meeting with Paul.

"I always go in the back way," he announced, grinning conspiratorially. "Because of Captain," he added, stroking the dog's head.

The service stairs seemed dark as they came in from the street.

"Watch your step," Paul warned in a whisper. "I never risk switching on the light."

Captain padded ahead of them, reached his own floor and waited until they had crept up the last few steps.

"He knows to check the coast's clear," Paul told her, grasping her hand and slipping his other fingers through the dog's collar before hustling them both across to his door.

When they were inside Paul's flat with the door closed behind them Caroline began laughing. "Talk about conspirators! Have they really never found you and Captain out?"

"Never, so far! To my eternal astonishment. Mind you, several of my fellow residents are in the know. They're very good."

Captain was prowling around the room. He completed one circuit and headed sharply for the kitchen where he could be heard urgently lapping up the water in his bowl.

"Coffee," Paul announced decisively, then chuckled. "I don't mean that's what he's drinking."

Suddenly Caroline was laughing again, light-hearted enough to relish enjoyment of the ridiculous.

"This is fun," she declared, following Paul to stand in the kitchen doorway while he found coffee and cups.

"Not a lot of it around."

Watching him, Caroline thought of his marriage that no longer existed and felt concern replacing that brief good humour.

But Paul did not mean their earlier mood to escape them. Facing her while he stood there waiting for water to heat, he grinned.

"Living alone, I can hardly spend too much time laughing my head off, or I'd be labelled as even more peculiar than I am already. Must confess some of the people here have concluded that developing constructions like that tunnel is a more than unfortunate eccentricity."

"And you daren't have them discover that you're also so Bohemian that you paint pictures!"

Together they laughed again.

When their coffee was ready, Paul carried the tray through to the sun room twin of her mother's. Caroline experienced a curious mixture of sensations – interest because the place was *his* and gentle relaxation as it had enough familiarity for her to feel at home here.

Beyond the windows daylight had drained away, leaving only street lamps, the glow from other homes and a scattering of stars. Deep within her Caroline felt an insistent tugging pulse, a steady awareness of coming alive – to an experience that could be pleasurable. The look in Paul's blue eyes from across the tiny table was warm confirmation of his own awakening to her.

"I shall have to go before long," she told him, knowing she ought to run.

"I know." There was regret in his words, but a reassurance that he understood their parting was inevitable.

Very briefly, as Caroline rose to leave, she felt his grasp on her shoulder. Each finger seemed to be pressing individually, marking her with his touch, increasing the forbidden yearning.

All the way home to the village Caroline felt she was encased in a silence more real than the engine's thrum or the swish of passing traffic. Paul had given her a break from that dreadful reality of Malcolm's illness. She hadn't had the heart to indicate this must be the last time. Only she herself knew that it would be so. But their friendship could have worked, she could have lived with this need, knowing it to be undemanding. She might have been content to recognise that it was to remain unfulfilled.

What a strange world they were in, where fun could matter so much. But she had quite desperately needed to divert her mind from the ever-present threat that her husband might die.

Nearing The Sylvan Barn she felt assaulted by the light shining out from just about every window, streaming across the neat patterning of the drive, shadowing the grass with restless images of tamarisk branches.

Christopher was hovering near the foot of the staircase, hands in the pockets of his jeans, a severe expression darkening his blue eyes.

"Where the hell have you been? I've been out of my mind with worry!"

"Whatever for? Chris darling, I'm sorry. I had a walk, that was all, over in Folkestone. It was such a lovely evening."

"Night, more like, by the time you'd dropped Gran. She rang, thought she'd left a book somewhere in her room here."

"What time was this?" Caroline asked – guiltily, for she was guilty.

"Don't know for sure, seems ages ago. Certainly long enough for you to have driven home twice over."

"I went for a walk, I said." She could almost dislike Chris for spoiling that all too brief peace, for making her feel yet again that she had been doing wrong.

Her stepson followed as she turned to enter the drawing-room. When she sank on to a sofa he crossed to stand before the fireplace looking down at her, the archetypal English male, accusatory. *One day I might laugh at this*, she thought, and knew that day was way ahead in the future.

"I really wouldn't have worried you for worlds," she said, and noticed every last scrap of quiet had evaporated.

"How was your dad?" she enquired, bringing into the room the only concerns admissible in her future.

"Still improving, badgering the doctors now about coming home. Though I gather that will only be to some effect one he's shed sufficient weight. And evidently the blood pressure still keeps rocketing."

Caroline was standing again, eager to escape to her room before she became too depressed by this removal of all her calm.

"There was a call for you a while ago," Chris told her. "Your ex – he wants to bring someone over, something about an interview."

"Regarding rail link opposition, I know. I'll ring him back in the morning. You'd better remind me."

Tomorrow, she would be immersed again in the everlasting round of lurching from one crisis to the next. She had to talk to the doctors about Malcolm's erratic blood pressure, find out just how serious the prognosis really was.

On her way towards the bedroom Caroline experienced like the stab of a sudden pain the understanding that no matter how upsetting life became she must never again seek comfort in turning to Paul. From this day she had got to exclude him from her mind as well as from her life.

Six

This time, Caroline was able to visit her hairdresser before seeing Julian, and although the scattering of grey and duller roots were beginning to show she wouldn't allow them to matter. Her hair was gleamingly clean, its style flattering.

Returning from Folkestone to Christopher's reproof had been salutary. Ever since that night she had been resigned to relinquishing even her bit of personal vanity in order to concentrate on family, and family concerns.

Malcolm's returning strength was making this prospect more inviting, and sacrificing her wayward longing to see Paul was producing its own strange satisfaction. *I might end up as immaculately intentioned as Kate*, she reflected. And laughed privately, at herself.

She had contacted Anne Newbold. Between them they had decided to see Julian and his journalist friend at The Sylvan Barn. Any doctor was liable to face interruptions in her own home.

"And it'll be easier since he knows his way here," Caroline had added. The only difficulty was the absence of the two stalwarts chosen by Anne to express village opinion regarding the rail link.

"Would you believe there's a parish holiday abroad at present – just about everyone who attends the church is away on that," she had told Caroline. "I suppose I could approach some of the others, although I must admit that might be a touch embarrassing. We had a bit of a spat, merely because I couldn't choose everybody."

After a brief discussion, Anne had put forward another idea. "We could, of course, have Christopher in on this. He'd be pleased, I'm sure, and Malcolm certainly would."

"But how much of a grasp does Chris have of all the potential threats from the rail link? What does he know of the various proposals?" Family problems had prevented them from discussing the scheme.

"Quite a lot, Caroline. He surprised me only the other evening when we were at the hospital together. The night you'd driven your mother home, I think. And my nephew who plays squash with him always maintains Christopher is well indoctrinated with his father's ideas on the matter."

"Fine then, Chris it is. And what about this nephew of yours as well?"

Hazel eyes lighting with amusement, Anne shook her head. "Hardly. He works at County Hall, the Planning Officer's department. No one could expect his opinions – if he were allowed to voice them – to be unaffected by his work."

Caroline was glad that the meeting would be in her home, and glad also that it was giving Malcolm and herself a subject to discuss which appeared to bring them closer together. The guilt she had experienced over enjoying Paul's company had developed into such ridiculous proportions that she often felt quite awkward with her husband. She seemed to need something to remind her how much they had in common.

Some visits to his ward could be difficult. Malcolm had realised now that the medical team really did mean business, and had no intention of discharging him before he was showing substantial signs of responding to their regime.

"I'm out of my mind with boredom," he would insist, so irritated with the way of life forced upon him that he scarcely heeded Caroline's efforts to alleviate the tedium during the time that she spent with him.

Upset because she could not think how to tackle this, she'd been driven to ask Anne for advice, as well as to learn more about the significance of erratic blood pressure.

The doctor's response had been just as confounding as his attitude.

"Oh, I'm sure there's no cause for you to be so anxious. They will stabilise him before he's discharged. Meanwhile, Malcolm seems quite happy and well adjusted whenever I see him."

And just how much of that is due to your presence? wondered Caroline. But that was one question on which she must not dwell. If Anne was good for Malcolm, so be it. Despite his understandable longing to be discharged, he *was* infinitely better than he might have been. She herself could only be grateful to anyone who was contributing to that progress.

Caroline awakened early on the day of Julian's visit and relished the fact that those first few moments of awareness were not filled with unease. She had told Julian to be sure and bring Amanda along as well as his journalist friend, and she was looking forward to seeing her daughter. If nothing else, the traumas of the past few weeks had generated the feeling that she could cope with anything so long as it wasn't life-threatening.

She had been planning the day ever since speaking with Julian over the phone. They were invited for eleven o'clock by which time any urgent farm business ought at least to be organised. A consignment was due into Graham's store, but that would be here soon after eight, and such deliveries really were creating very little work for either Chris or herself. Caroline was enjoying the prospect of showing Julian the store; it did look impressive, stacked as it was with so many different kinds of fruit.

She was planning to give Amanda a more leisurely tour of the farm. With Christopher engaged in this interview as soon as Anne showed up after morning surgery, she herself would be able to concentrate on her daughter. Caroline was determined to make up for all the shortcomings of the past. She would use this opportunity to begin founding a better mother/daughter relationship.

They might start with a tête-à-tête in the office. Amanda should be interested to see how the farm was organised. At present, there was little real activity out of doors, the strawberry crop would not be ripe for another week or more and the hard fruits were only now forming on the trees. Although routine work of keeping down weeds and pests was hardly likely to fascinate Amanda, Caroline was hopeful that just seeing such an expanse of orchards and strawberry fields could arouse some feeling for the land. From the start, she herself had experienced an upsurge of satisfaction that they were working alongside nature. It had seemed a great antidote for all those years amid fierce commercialism.

There was the house as well, and Caroline had always been distressed by the fact that her own daughter had never visited The Sylvan Barn. Today, she felt sure Amanda was going to fall in love with the place. Even though, here in Kent, conversions of barns were appearing faster than those of the oast houses once so very popular, theirs was beautifully done and sufficiently original to interest someone so evidently artistic.

Following an invigorating shower, Caroline dressed and sped down the stairs, picturing as she went the moment when she would introduce her home to Amanda.

Christopher appeared without the calling from her which normally preceded his dash to the breakfast table.

"Isn't this exciting?" he exclaimed. "I'm *almost* glad Dad's not here so I can put our case." Malcolm had primed him the previous evening with all the points that he felt ought to be made. Having heard his father's views had not, however, precluded his own.

Caroline was pleased that her stepson seemed only too eager to enlarge on the ways in which the proposed rail route could damage their local environment.

"I know lots of people are fighting on behalf of their homes and businesses," he added. "But we've also got to consider this countryside we've inherited."

"Seeking to preserve that should look well in print," she agreed.

Anne called them before beginning morning surgery, just to say what time she hoped to come along and that she was looking forward to seizing this opportunity which Caroline had organised.

Graham's fruit arrived to time, and Christopher was glowing with excited anticipation when it was all stacked in the store and he brought through the documentation.

"We seem to be doing quite well out of Uncle Graham. Is that showing in our figures, Mum?"

Caroline smiled across at him from behind her desk. "Certainly is! I got him to pay us on a weekly basis, you know. We're already seeing an upturn. Once those strawberries go to market as well, we shall be in a far healthier position – get the bank manager off our backs for a while."

"Will we be making a profit by the time Dad's back home again?"

"It's early days yet to say that, but we should be reducing the overdraft. And certainly by the time he actually returns to work we should have overcome most of the problems."

"And of course, with a farm like ours, so much of the income is seasonal. It's only really on a yearly basis that its viability can be assessed."

Smiling, Caroline nodded. Chris had a sensible head on him, and a good grasp of the business. This endorsed her belief that he would be equally adept at putting forward all the salient rail link factors.

From the office she had a view of the lane, and spotted Julian's car before it turned in at their drive. "They're here, Chris," she said, smiling again as they went out, locking the office door behind them.

The journalist Julian had brought stepped from the front passenger seat, looking for all the world as though she needed only a hat to fit her for Ascot. Her linen trouser suit seemed to be a MaxMara with its Nehru-collared jacket and slender-fitting pants. *I hope that that daughter of mine has noticed how smart she appears*, Caroline thought, and wondered how Amanda was dressed.

"All right if I leave the car here, Caro?" Julian enquired before getting out.

He was wearing pale casual trousers and a silk shirt the shade of bronze that echoed the glints in his immaculate hair. He seemed overpowering. Only when he was standing beside her to introduce his companion Sarah Dwight did Caroline realise that Amanda wasn't in the back of the car. Chris was beside them now.

"Has Amanda got something else on today?" she asked the instant all the greetings were exchanged.

Julian shrugged. "Just said this wasn't quite her thing, I think."

Caroline swallowed, warning herself not to voice her suspicion that Julian might have discouraged their daughter from coming. Somehow, she beamed towards both of her guests and invited them into the house.

"This certainly is an elegant home, Caroline," Sarah remarked.

"And I understand from Julian that you yourself came up with many of the ideas for its design."

Caroline smiled brilliantly again. "Thank you very much. Yes, I did contribute quite a bit to the end result." She urged them to sit as soon as they reached the drawing-room, then offered coffee, and all the while all that she could feel was devastated. Amanda did not wish to see her.

Chris helped to pass around cups and explained that Anne Newbold would arrive as soon as morning surgery finished.

"And how is your father?" asked Julian.

"Oh – vastly improved, thanks. He's only kept in hospital now because his blood pressure has to come down a little further."

"And his weight," Caroline added.

Christopher grinned. "That as well – if it will. Although Anne tells us that getting the weight down is more of a long-term aim – mostly to be achieved once he's home."

Though still too perturbed about her daughter's absence to feel sure of anything, Caroline wondered if she had missed something Anne had said previously. She'd no recollection of this particular view regarding Malcolm's condition. Shelving a nagging feeling that she was more out of touch than was desirable, she resolved to concentrate. Or risk proving as inadequate a wife as she was a mother.

Normally, Caroline would have relished meeting a fresh journalistic face, and enjoyed exercising her old skills of dealing with media people. Today, she seemed all too aware of how young Sarah appeared and how extremely capable. *Damn Amanda*, she thought, *she's diminishing my ability to tackle anything.*

Her ex, Caroline noticed, was entranced, watching Sarah's expressive face even when she was not the person who happened to be speaking. Everything was conspiring to increase her own dismal feeling of inadequacy.

Hearing Anne's car in the drive, Caroline felt relieved that the attractive doctor was someone who would hold her own in any company.

"This journalist woman oozes youth and power," she murmured as she greeted the doctor on the step. "I'm glad you're not the kind who's easily daunted."

Anne laughed. "And what about Chris, how's he reacting?"

"Too early to say, but if he follows the example of my ex he'll be enslaved within an hour!"

They laughed as they walked through to join the others and, after Anne was introduced and served with coffee, Sarah began telling them that the interview would be quite informal.

"I've brought my little tape machine. I hope no one objects, but it is the most efficient way of getting thoughts down accurately."

And can be the most damning, Caroline thought, recalling interviewees who regretted off-the-cuff remarks preserved unequivocally.

The telephone rang before Sarah had reached the climax of her introductory preamble. Graham was on the line.

"Would you hang on?" Caroline asked him. "I've got someone here. I'll take this in the office."

"Sorry about that," she continued to her brother-in-law after running across and unlocking the office door. "We've an interview going on – a journalist from one of the glossies, we're expecting her to do a piece about the rail link."

"Look – if you should be in on that, I'll ring back later. It's nothing imperative."

Graham's suggestion jolted Caroline into realising no one had said she ought to be included in the discussion. Feeling hurt, she sighed.

"Actually, Christopher is speaking up for us. And Anne Newbold's here on behalf of the village as a whole. She's still on the local parish council, of course."

"Fine. Well then, Caroline, I'd like you to consider continuing to store our fruit. I believe we've given it a fair trial, and from our point of view it's working very well. What are your reactions?"

Caroline hesitated uneasily, she hadn't expected Graham to require any commitment from her regarding the future. Surely it was only agreed that this should be a temporary measure? She put this to him, and soon noticed his annoyance.

"Are you saying the deal is creating problems your end?"

"No, not at all. But I did emphasise this was only to remain in force until Malcolm could reach a decision himself."

"That's all very fine – but unlike you I have got to plan ahead. I do need to know what space I'll have available before I clinch anything with contacts abroad."

Caroline saw the sense of this. "All right then. But how far ahead precisely?"

They discussed details and then Graham digressed to say how well Malcolm was looking. "We're all greatly relieved, Caroline, you should know that. And you're doing a tremendous job over there, you mustn't worry about anything he might say once he's discharged from hospital. Just leave Malcolm to me, I'll square this business with him."

Caroline hung up wondering if Graham understood his brother at all. Did he really not know how opposed Malcolm was to handling imported fruit? She would have to give this one considerable thought – try and find some means of making the scheme acceptable to Malcolm. Perhaps the need to slow down and take life steadily might have made him more realistic about obtaining maximum potential from all aspects of the farm. She hoped, without any real foundation, that this could be so.

The conversation with Graham had added to the distress of learning Amanda had no wish to join her. Determined to leave herself free for entertaining her daughter, Caroline had caught up on any outstanding paperwork and ensured that all outdoor jobs on the farm were up to date. Until Graham had made her conscious of what was expected of her, she might have assumed that the others would think of her returning to the interview. She was growing uncomfortably aware now that they might expect nothing of the kind.

Lunch was being prepared by Florence Dacre who'd been in- structed to serve it at around one o'clock. It was now eleven twenty, the rest of the morning stretched ahead, a blank chasm. *Damn Amanda*, Caroline thought again, and picked up the receiver in- tending to ring her.

Slowly, a sigh rising from her chest, she replaced the telephone. The relationship with her daughter was tenuous enough, she mustn't vent the anger that could only enlarge the gap between them.

Think positively, she willed herself, drawing in a calming breath.

Being left out of this magazine interview is your own fault for not expressing your opinions, but you do possess the ability to put them across. It is up to you to take action in the future.

Caroline knew in her heart that she had never fully supported Malcolm's opposition to this wretched railway line. She could blame no one but herself if other people neglected to see what she might contribute. She would put that right. For the present, all she could do was adopt a pleasant front and resolve that no one should sense how ridiculously miserable she felt, so left out of things.

For the rest of that week Christopher remained on a high generated by partaking in the interview. As soon as they had all sat down to lunch it became plain to Caroline that Sarah Dwight had taken to her stepson and allowed him as much of a say as Anne Newbold. Anne later commended Chris when their visitors were driving away. It seemed to Caroline that such praise from the doctor sealed his delight.

During their hospital visit that evening Malcolm naturally demanded to hear all that had been said, and he quickly expressed satisfaction over the way his son had handled the occasion. "I'm certainly looking forward to reading that article. How soon will it appear?"

"They haven't given us an exact date yet, may not be for a month or two – Julian warned us. But Sarah promised to get it in earlier if humanly possible. She realises just how important the timing is."

"Quite. We mustn't lose sight of the fact that these months through to September are the crucial ones, while meetings continue between the planners and interested parties. Thank goodness I shall be out of here before very long. Anne feels I can play a valuable role in coordinating some of the local feeling."

"I can help you there," Caroline insisted. "My PR experience will show us the best way of presenting our case."

Malcolm gave her a look. "We'll see," he said. Caroline had never before appeared to have any strong motivation to oppose this wretched scheme. He remembered her insistence that she must return to her career. Was she perhaps considering working for their action group as a means of making people notice her skills?

He decided to say nothing now. The indications were that he would soon be at home. There would be time enough then for sorting out the situation. Anne was quite capable of speaking up before then if Caroline began interfering in ways unlikely to advance their aims.

Studying her expression, Malcolm thought that Caroline looked quite uneasy, these days. *Could* she be preoccupied with making use of any publicity that might be coming their way?

Conscious of his scrutiny, Caroline shifted on the hospital chair. For the twentieth time she wondered how much longer she would have for finding good reasons to prevent Malcolm from hitting the roof when he learned how their farm store was being utilised.

The day, which had begun so badly with Amanda's refusal to visit her, had turned out so full of difficulties. Caroline hardly knew which problem to consider first. She'd been hurt by their doctor who seemed dismissive of any suggestion that her PR expertise might be useful. All Anne had promised was that she would put the idea to those she represented. Something in the way that she reacted left Caroline feeling that she was the last person Anne Newbold wanted around. Could it be that Anne wished to exclude Malcolm's wife?

I hope I shall feel differently once he is home again, thought Caroline; this abnormal way of life might be contributing its own unease.

On the day that Malcolm was finally discharged, excitement swept away all of Caroline's negative emotions. She felt as though Malcolm had been away for an eternity and just wanted to see him back at home.

The call came late that morning, and even the fact that it came through Anne did nothing to dilute her delight or her relief.

"You keep an eye on things here, Chris, while I go to pick him up," she told her stepson, refusing his eager offer to drive over to the hospital. This was one time when no one on this earth would be permitted to deputise for her.

Dressed in outdoor clothes again, Malcolm already seemed much more like himself as they walked side by side towards the car.

"This is one thing I've got to tackle Anne about, driving. So far, they are advising me not to even attempt it, but we mustn't let this continue indefinitely."

Caroline smiled at him. "Just try to take one step at time, darling, eh? I know you want to get back to normal, but this is only your first few minutes out of that place!"

He laughed with her as they got into the car. "As you can tell, I'm back to my usual self. Maybe you'll be sorry there isn't more of an improvement . . .?"

"Idiot! You should know I'm simply very thankful that this day has at last arrived. And that you look in such good shape. Extremely good shape," she emphasised, pressing at his waistline.

"I've shed a stone since that first consultation with Anne. Pity that's not enough."

Thinking of all the menus she had been planning whilst he was in hospital, Caroline smiled contentedly. "I think we've found a way of ensuring that you continue to bring down that cholesterol without feeling deprived."

"Actually, it will be so good to be home that I can't imagine being dissatisfied with meals or anything. I've been in here far too long."

Chris ran to greet them as soon as Caroline drew up in the drive. He was very aware of the doctors' warnings that for some time yet Malcolm should avoid being troubled by farm problems. Keeping him out of the office from the start was, he believed, the only way they might distance his father from potential traumas.

For several hours Malcolm was, in any case, so delighted to be back in The Sylvan Barn that he was content to roam from one room to the next, reacquainting himself with the feel of his home.

He had hugged Caroline close the moment they arrived indoors and he did so again after returning to the drawing-room.

"God, but it's bloody marvellous to be here with you again," he exclaimed between kisses. "I'll do everything they tell me from now on, just to ensure that I never again end up in that place."

"They saved you from something far worse, though, darling."

"Anne did that, in those first few minutes after the attack. I owe her a very great deal."

Caroline felt her heart grow weighty again, disappointment raced through her. Seconds ago, she had believed that Malcolm was fully restored to her. But was he? Would she always have this feeling that she was obliged to share him with the doctor towards whom she felt this far from pleasing indebtedness?

As the day progressed she willed such emotions to fade. She had arranged for Chris to run the office, freeing her to be with his father. They lounged around and talked, about family, especially about Nicholas who had to be telephoned later that day with news that the hospital stay had ended.

"I've thought a lot about Nick, you know," Malcolm confided. "And about this girl of his. Bianca's seems sensible, and they're genuinely fond of each other."

Caroline agreed. "My sentiments too. We're going to give them our support then, are we?"

He nodded. "Got to, haven't we? Time we took an adult attitude, I think – showed them that we're not so hidebound by tradition that we have to insist on a wedding."

"That's good. They're only young, after all, Malcolm. They will need to feel that we're behind them."

"Pity we can't do much financially as things stand at present."

"I don't think they'll mind that. And Mother's promised them some help."

"Has she really? Good old Lucy – very generous of her, considering Nicholas isn't strictly her grandson. Must have a word myself – tell her I appreciate that."

Caroline was delighted that Malcolm appeared quite happy with life. She wished she knew how best she might influence him regarding Christopher's future. Chris had been such a reliable person to have around these past few weeks, she couldn't face the prospect of his being compelled to find employment elsewhere.

She was pleased as well as surprised when Malcolm suddenly referred to the matter.

"From what you've said from time to time, I gather that Chris has more than pulled his weight while I've been incarcerated over there. Seems wrong to let him go. Maybe I ought to rethink. Especially if you are intending to set up again in public relations."

"You mean – if I go ahead with that, there'll be one less taking money out of the firm?"

"Right. Well, that's how it'll be, won't it?"

Smiling, Caroline nodded. "I'm so glad you're thinking this way, darling. Though I must confess I haven't given my own plans serious thought for ages. All I want first and foremost is to make certain that you recover completely."

"Still – I will have a chat with Chris. Don't want him feeling he's not appreciated."

Delighted that Malcolm also seemed to have accepted all her ideas about setting up a PR business, Caroline wallowed in a satisfaction which for weeks now had been all too rare.

Once Malcolm had settled down into a routine she would begin listing potential clients. Several from the old days had remained in touch and always *said* the people they had taken on instead were less effective. It would be up to her to make them see the sense in returning to her. And then there was Julian – through the magazine, he possessed several business contacts who would benefit from being presented more forcefully. His vineyard might also have provided a wider circle of acquaintances. She must let him know as soon as she visualised a firm date for freeing herself from the demands of the farm.

Suddenly, she felt revitalised, as though looking ahead was ridding her already of the weight of Malcolm's illness. And he really did appear infinitely better than he had for a very long time. Provided with the sensible diet that she and Mrs Dacre had worked out, he soon would be as fit as any man of his age.

Caroline had persuaded Malcolm to leave farm matters aside for at least twenty-four hours and was glad that he seemed happy to do so. By the next evening, however, he was showing signs of longing to take a hand in the business. She wasn't surprised when he interrupted their meal that evening with questions about how the day had gone. Nothing exceptional had occurred in the office or around the orchards, there wasn't much to tell.

Malcolm grinned at their non-committal replies. "Am I to take it that you're running the place so smoothly that I can't even offer any advice?"

Caroline smiled. "Don't be silly, darling. Neither Chris nor I have anything like your experience. But we do appear to make a reasonably good little team."

"Ah – yes. I was coming to that." Still smiling, he turned to his son. "I'm proud of the way you've shouldered so much responsibility, Christopher, very pleased that Caroline has been able to rely on you so greatly. That's one of the reasons why I want us to have a little chat."

When Chris said nothing a tiny frown passed fleetingly over his father's forehead, and was erased almost immediately.

"From what you both tell me, the farm is on a better footing than it was a few weeks ago. I shall need to look into that, of course."

Caroline felt Christopher's gaze seeking hers but kept her attention on the food her fork was spearing. This was not the time for going into the cause of their financial upturn.

Malcolm was continuing, and relieving her by speaking of her own plans and their earlier discussion. "And so, Chris," he finished, "I'm very glad to say that I shall not, after all, feel obliged to economise so drastically as I feared. There should be no need now for you to find alternative employment."

Caroline looked up at this and smiled at them both. She could think of nothing else that should seal their happiness so effectively.

Christopher swallowed, twice, looked down at his plate, reached a decision and faced Malcolm.

"Thanks, Father, for saying that. I'm only sorry it's too late."

"Late? Too late? What do you mean?"

Caroline saw that her stepson was fumbling for words. The awkward pause threatened to become prolonged; and then Chris sighed and began speaking again.

"You may as well know – I've got another position. Rather a good one, in fact. I'm to start there as soon as you're back in harness."

"Are you, by Jove? Then I suggest you rethink pretty smartly. This isn't just any job I'm offering you. This is the family business – the business that you stand to inherit. Or a major share of it, at least. Think about that."

"I have thought, Father. You compelled me to consider my position here with you. Frankly, I decided it was no longer for me."

"Not for you? What're you talking about, boy? Where's the sense in what you're saying?"

"You wanted me out, Dad. Only the other week you wanted me to go."

"Correction – letting you go seemed inevitable, at the time. It never was something that I wanted. Not at all. Now I've explained – after due consideration I feel we can keep you on. I don't see where the problem is. If you have something else lined up, all you've got to do is tell them you're staying on here. Anyone can see it's the better option."

Christopher shook his head. "I'm afraid it's unsettled me, made me wonder what would happen next time we hit a bad patch. I can't live with that degree of uncertainty. Excuse me," he muttered, rose from the table and left them.

Malcolm glanced towards Caroline, smiled reassuringly. "Saving face, that's all the lad's doing. You'll see, he'll be glad to accept my offer and stay on here: everything will revert to normal."

Seven

At least Malcolm didn't immediately make everything worse. Caroline was relieved when he didn't pursue the subject of Christopher's job before his son went off to play squash. She was even more relieved when it wasn't raised as soon as Chris returned that evening. Both men would benefit from letting the matter lie. She was becoming confident that, in time, they would reach an agreement.

Malcolm's convalescence was supposed to involve plenty of rest, and she and Christopher continued to have an early breakfast together before going across to the office.

"I meant it, you know," her stepson asserted the minute he reached his desk the following morning. "I'm not staying on here, I can't, not after what he did to me."

Caroline felt her heart plummeting. Chris had not been saving face then, nor bluffing. She would have to do something. She couldn't just let everything collapse about them.

"But you heard what your father said, darling, he regrets that he ever thought your leaving might be necessary."

"Tough for him. Sorry, Mum, but I simply wouldn't be comfortable here long term."

Caroline needed to understand in order to talk him round. "You mean – you think he might reach that conclusion again if times became equally hard?"

Christopher sighed. "No. At least – partly, it might be that. It's the reason I gave Father. Mainly, it's that he's made me think. The farm's as much family as – well, as *we* are and if it should go to the wall I'd be as distressed as anybody. If I remained tied to the farm completely I'd be doubly shaken, wouldn't I? So disturbed that I might not be able to function. This way, I'll always have one bit of security, whatever. And besides, it's all experience. Be great to tackle something different."

"You have somewhere else in mind then?" Caroline was shaken, quite appalled. The chances of Chris ever changing his mind grew more remote by the minute.

Christopher nodded. "So he hasn't said. I wondered."

"He?" When had Malcolm and Chris talked again? *Why had no one told her?*

"I'm going to Julian, as Vineyard Manager."

"Julian?" Caroline was horrified, instantly felt afraid she might be sick.

"What's up? You haven't got a thing about it, because he's your ex?"

"No. It's not that at all. You know I've always remained on quite amicable terms with him."

"Well, he certainly understands what he's about, you needn't have qualms on that score. Julian knows all there is to know about viticulture."

"I'm sure."

"What then? Mum?"

She shook her head. Where was the point in anticipating the fury Malcolm would experience when he learned the identity of his son's new employer? There would be friction enough – she mustn't prepare Chris for speaking up for Julian.

He smiled at her, his eyes lighting in the way that Malcolm's had whenever he'd been certain that he was right. Christopher possessed all his father's old charisma; pity they didn't use that on each other.

"Trust me. This isn't some appalling mistake. Working for someone else, I'll be free to mature, to have some of my own ideas *considered*. Seriously considered."

Caroline could say nothing. She knew exactly how Chris was feeling. However reluctantly she had come to admit it, working with Malcolm was stupefying. He never permitted anyone else to handle interesting decisions. And now Chris was leaving – wouldn't she herself feel obliged to continue on in the office here?

Keeping the matter to themselves lasted barely as long as Caroline supposed it might. That evening Malcolm tackled Christopher again, beginning by softening him up.

"I've decided to make you Assistant Manager of the farm," he announced over dinner. "It's no more than your due for the way you stepped in for me. Initially, I'm afraid there'll be no substantial salary increase. But I'll put that right as soon as feasible. In the meantime, I shall ensure word gets around that I'm promoting you."

Caroline prayed that Chris might have the grace to seize this final opportunity and accept.

"Sorry, Dad, this is simply not on," he interrupted. "As I said, I can't remain here."

"Can't, or won't?" Malcolm's eyes were anguished.

"Whichever suits." Christopher's struggle to be firm was making him brusque.

Caroline ached for both him and his father, longed to hug the pair of them. Something held her back. She wondered dismally if her inability to make any physical contact with Amanda was spreading to her response to her family here.

"I resent your tone," Malcolm began and Caroline cringed, but he said nothing further, and when her stepson responded his voice had modified.

"Yes, well . . . I'm afraid I resent your implying that I'm in the wrong – you were the one who broached the subject of my leaving."

"Only when compelled."

"As I am compelled now to go elsewhere."

This time, Christopher didn't leave the table before the meal was over. Caroline almost wished that he had while she watched his father shovelling down fresh fruit salad as though it had caused him injury, and hastily enough to ensure it generated an internal disruption to compete with this family conflict.

After his son went up to his room Malcolm followed Caroline out to the kitchen. She and Mrs Dacre were clearing away dishes.

"Can't you leave that, Caro?" he asked wearily. "I need to talk."

"You go on, I'll soon have this lot put to rights," Florence Dacre assured her willingly. "Doesn't matter if I'm a few minutes later getting home."

In the drawing-room Malcolm crossed to pour himself a drink. "Yes, it is all right to have this," he told Caroline tersely, anticipating a protest. "I'll explode if I don't have something. He's doing this on purpose, of course. Ever since he was little Chris has loved cocking a snook at me. Don't think I'm unaware of that."

"Oh, Malcolm – credit your son with a bit of intelligence! Chris isn't likely to risk his entire career just to see you put about. He is doing what he feels he must. And you really cannot blame him, darling."

"Because I started it all, I suppose?"

"Well, there can be no denying that, can there? Perhaps this won't be quite the catastrophe you seem to think, though. Let him go, and with a reasonably good grace, if you can. Give him time to sample working for someone else, and he could decide to come back."

"He won't. I know Chris, he'll never admit he might have reached a wrong decision."

"Well, we'll just have to see, shan't we?"

"Wish I knew who the sod is who's offered to employ him. Must be somebody local. Don't know how they could have the gall to . . ." As he paused something in the careful composing of Caroline's expression alerted him. "You know, don't you? He's told you who."

Dreading his reaction didn't mean she could prevent it. But Caroline still hesitated before replying.

Naturally, Malcolm persisted: "You'd better tell me. I do have to know."

"It isn't somebody local, you needn't worry on that score. It's Julian."

"Julian who? Oh, not . . ." His complexion changed colour several times within seconds. "Not your bloody ex?"

"You mustn't let it matter. You'd have hated the person whoever they might have been. You dislike Julian already."

"Too right I do. But whatever I've felt towards him in the past is nothing to the way this makes me feel." He paused, a sigh travelled up from deep inside him. "Why, Caroline, why? Why are you doing this to me?"

"Me? I? Darling, please – I had nothing whatsoever to do with this. It was entirely between Julian and Chris. I didn't know anything until a few hours ago."

"He'd never have met the man except through you. Wouldn't even have known that Julian existed. I just – can't take this in. Cannot believe it is happening."

"You'd have felt this way no matter who chose to employ Christopher. And I cannot regulate the actions of your son, of either of your sons."

His eyes narrowed sharply. "You surprise me. I was sure you'd always taken good care to encourage them to take a stand against me."

Caroline flinched, bitterly hurt. She had worked for so long to do what she felt was best, for Malcolm and for Nicholas and Chris. All she was receiving in return from this man she loved were reproaches and an absence of understanding.

"You've said that before," she murmured, unable to contain her disappointment.

"Only because it's the truth. But I do think common decency should have prevented you from finding Christopher employment with *him*."

Caroline had exhausted every possible thing that she might say, and had exhausted herself to the degree where summoning justification of her position seemed beyond her. She was still struggling to gather her wits when Malcolm swung away from her, strode out through the hall and opened the front door.

"Don't go off like this," she began.

The door closing behind him drowned the last of her words.

"Have you walked all the way over here?"

Anne was standing beside an armchair into which Malcolm had lowered himself. His face was flushed, except for the area around his mouth which was pale and drawn. His lips had a greyish tinge.

"I was in no state for driving that car. Far too vexed."

"Besides which, you've been cautioned against driving yet. I shall have to get Caroline to cooperate and ensure that you don't attempt it."

"She'll comply only too readily. These days, she relishes interfering."

"Over your lifestyle, you mean? Oh, Malcolm, you know she's the one responsible for what you eat, and for . . ."

"I don't mean that at all. It's other things, about the farm. Or – well, really about Christopher."

"I thought he was set to leave, anyway, as soon as you're up to taking a more active role again?"

"That's just it. I was going to prevent his leaving. Business seems to be improving slightly, I told him he would be staying on, promoted. Stupid fool says he's going anyway."

Anne smiled sympathetically. "I see. He's thrown the job back in your face. Poor you. Still – not the end of the world, is it? He could well discover which side his proverbial bread is buttered . . ."

Malcolm groaned. This was exactly what Caroline had suggested. "He'd never admit it if he did. Especially considering where he's going."

"Where's that?" she asked lightly, and then thought for a moment. "Oh."

"Don't tell me you knew as well. What is this – a confounded conspiracy?"

"There's no reason to become paranoid. It's only that I've just remembered something that was said on the day when Julian brought that journalist over."

"And to think I was actually glad Chris was involved in that interview, that by all accounts he acquitted himself very well."

"So you should be. That young man's got a lot of sense in him. You could afford to be proud. No matter where he works."

"Julian is making him Vineyard Manager."

"There you are then. Now, shall we discuss something else – something that might bring your blood-pressure within the accepted register? I've got news again, from our action group."

"Go on . . ." Malcolm said with an effort. He would please her by showing an interest, even though he was too disturbed to arouse any real enthusiasm for anything tonight.

"This should be reported in full in Friday's *Kent Messenger*. There's nothing absolutely concrete, as yet, but it's a step in the right direction. Roger Freeman – the Transport Minister, of course – has given the action groups a measure of support."

"Really? Sounds promising . . ."

"It follows on the occasion when so many people walked out of that meeting with Union Railways. Evidently, Mr Freeman has told Andrew Rowe, the MP, that he will only accept as proper those consultation meetings which include issues like the long tunnel option we put forward."

"So – we could end up with the rail link going underground?"

"In areas of outstanding natural beauty, yes."

"It's a start, certainly."

"Knew you'd be pleased, Malcolm. Gives us cause for a little optimism."

He was nodding, though still looking serious.

"It was intended to lighten the load," said Anne. "You might allow yourself to acknowledge that not everything is doom and gloom."

"But can't you see, Anne? All the bother at home concerning Chris makes me feel that I don't really care, that nothing matters any longer."

"You'll get over that. You're not long out of hospital, remember. You are holding back and letting them cope with the day-to-day running of the farm, I hope?"

"Oh, yes. I'd enough of a scare to heed that warning."

"Then shelve this set of problems. We know they won't go away, but it'll do you no harm to concentrate on matters other than personal issues. Like the rail action group. There's a lot you can do there without sending your pulse racing. And I'd be around to keep an eye on the amount of pressure."

"Sounds tempting. Stagnating in that hospital made me realise how highly I value the opportunity to exercise the grey cells."

"And other kinds of exercise?" Anne enquired. "Apart from hurrying over here in a paddy, which would do you no good at all."

Malcolm grinned. "Haven't quite worked out a routine."

"Then we'll start tonight at a suitable leisurely pace. Now you've got your breath back. A walk won't hurt me either."

As it had on that other occasion, retracing The Pilgrims' Way seemed to bestow a particular form of peace. The summer evening was warm, yet with sufficient breeze stirring the grain in a nearby field to make walking a pleasure. Beneath the sky from which the sun was slipping birds hovered, their song all but obliterating the distant thrum of a lawn-mower. When they reached the wood Malcolm took her hand, was glad when it wasn't withdrawn.

You mean so much to me, he thought, *not only since saving my life – for always accepting me as I am, for continuing to give me some sense of direction. It isn't that I love Caroline any the less*, he realised, *but I do need you in my life somewhere.*

"You're good for me, Malcolm," Anne said, startling him into pausing to gaze into candid hazel eyes. Her laugh was light, he sensed he was not wrong to detect affection in it.

"And . . . ?" he prompted.

"Maybe I shouldn't say. On the other hand – for so many years, *too* many, I've felt isolated, have contained so much. The lives of my patients, all the things I'm not permitted to discuss. And here you are, making me feel like a normal human being, free to talk. To care."

Since leaving her native Yorkshire and settling here soon after she'd qualified, Anne had remained very conscious of needing to stand a little apart from people. She knew herself, the way she relished close friendships – and the danger in possessing an eagerness to chat! Guarding her tongue neither came naturally nor was it something she enjoyed.

Malcolm drew her to him, held her there, with only the trees to murmur over the scene they witnessed. Somewhere, a rabbit scuttered over grass, another small creature rustled leaves fallen last winter. His kiss was full on her lips, but restrained, he was aware of all the hazards. They both smiled as he released her.

"I needed that as well." Her voice, no more than a whisper, was barely audible. Tomorrow, he would believe this moment had grown from his own imagination.

"Will apologising, profoundly, help?"

He had walked into the bedroom where Caroline was seated before the mirror, brushing her hair.

She turned, her face impassive but Malcolm added "please".

At last she smiled. "I'm still too thankful that you've survived to have a huff for very long," she told him. "Come here . . ."

Malcolm bent to kiss the angle of her neck. It felt as silken as the robe she wore, which would usually have inflamed him. He took a backward step, experiencing the guilt which he had convinced himself he needn't feel. The kiss he had given Anne took nothing away from this relationship. And would lead nowhere. She was his doctor, for heaven's sake, he cared too much for her to even contemplate carrying their affection further. Or – to be truthful – he might allow himself to *contemplate* it. Fantasies were not forbidden.

"Did you see Anne?"

He started, but nothing in his wife's attitude or in her voice conveyed anxiety, much less disapproval.

"You know me very well, bless you. We're fortunate in our doctor. She's far more accessible than most."

"And she gets you thinking about this rail link business, takes your mind away from family matters that irk. Even from wives who do."

"But you don't."

"Come off it, Malcolm. You've always resented the way the boys became attached to me."

"I'm thankful for it, at the same time. We'd be in one hell of a mess without you. And then there's the way you help running the farm, especially since – well, you know. I count on you for so much."

Caroline felt warmed by his words, so much happier that she was prepared to continue doing all she could in the farm office for as long as she was needed. Plans for re-establishing her own career could be delayed indefinitely.

Three days later Caroline and Christopher were crossing towards the office after breakfast when one of Graham's vehicles drove in to offload at the store. She gave the driver a wave while Chris hurried ahead of her to get the store key.

After all the fruit had been unloaded the driver came in with the paperwork. He was a pleasant man, always paused for a word or two without wasting time in a lengthy chat.

When he had left, Caroline began gathering together worksheets from their own casual labour. Now that strawberries were being harvested and packed they were employing several of the pickers who seemed to enjoy returning year after year.

"I'll make a start on the wages," she told Chris. Their working week finished on Wednesday evenings, today was Thursday and wages were paid out on a Friday. "If you'll check that everyone's turned up this morning, and see if anything out there needs attention, I'll man the phone and deal with whatever comes in the post."

Fond though she was of her stepson, Caroline occasionally liked having the office to herself. Chris seemed to relish letting their domestic life spill over into this work situation. She herself, in some ways, still preferred the business scene. She felt more adept there than ever she had as a homemaker. Or as a mother.

Caroline had been alone for a few minutes when the door was thrust open. Startled, she looked up.

Malcolm was standing there – his appearance shook her more than his abrupt and sudden entrance had. Even that first glance told her that he hadn't shaved, and his sweater and trousers seemed to have been thrown on in great haste.

"What is it, darling?" she began, but he was telling her, anyway, in a voice that drowned her enquiry.

"What was Graham's vehicle doing in our yard? He doesn't collect my fruit at this time of day. What's going on, Caroline?"

Malcolm had no need to ask: he *knew*, she read that in his anger.

"Graham only wanted to help us," she explained. "To get us out of the red. It seemed like a good way of—"

"Storing his bloody imported fruit? How long has this been going on?"

Caroline swallowed, almost choked on her sigh, and steeled herself to tell him. "Since – since shortly after your attack. He made the suggestion and I hadn't the heart to throw it back in his face."

"Yet you knew full well that I'm dead against handling imported stuff."

"It's purely on a temporary basis. I made sure Graham understood it was only until you took over again."

"Because you were well aware that I would never approve."

"Because I thought you'd wish to have a discussion with him as soon as you were back in harness."

"Too right I shall! Like this morning, before I do another thing."

"Darling, please listen. Don't ruin it all before I explain. Graham's paying handsomely for use of that store, our figures are starting to come right."

"You say that as though it's the only consideration."

"You were pleased enough to learn our situation was improving."

"Maybe. What I can't abide is any upturn being at the expense of ethics."

"There's no need to get into a state, Malcolm. All you need do is tell Graham that this cannot continue."

"I shall do that, you may be certain. What infuriates me most, though, is that you've gone behind my back."

Malcolm slammed out of the office. Caroline was sickened. His final remark *was* justified. And all she wanted was to let go completely and weep. She had no notion how she might put this one right. Not least because she recalled so clearly how torn she had been about acceding to her brother-in-law's suggestion.

Moments later she was jolted out of her distress. A car was starting up. Rushing to the office door, she was in time to see Malcolm in the Jaguar as it sped away from the garage and screeched across in front of the house towards the drive.

"Darling, no . . ." she called, but knew already that if he heard he would ignore her. Oh, God – don't let anything happen to him, she prayed, and trudged back to her desk.

For several minutes Caroline sat there, willing herself not to give in to the shaking that threatened to reduce her to a wreck. Eventually, she stilled outward evidence of distress, but her inner turmoil only increased. This couldn't go on. Before Malcolm's illness she'd often felt so disturbed by all the problems that she had longed to get away. Today things were even worse. She was trapped here by being so conscious that he needed to have her around. Once Christopher went to work at the vineyard Malcolm would count on her more than ever.

But she couldn't work with him any longer, their ideas so rarely coincided. And disagreements like this upset her so dreadfully.

Malcolm tore down the hill heading towards the A20. He would see Graham, and leave him in no doubt of his opinion. He would show them all that he was still capable of handling every situation. He could trust no one else. His own wife was conniving with his brother to oppose his specific wishes.

The lane was winding, narrow in parts, and the car felt quite strange after all those weeks of not driving. Malcolm was rather alarmed by this sensation that he might not be entirely in control.

He steered round a bend, was confronted with another vehicle almost upon him. He stamped on the brake pedal. And felt perspiration douse him.

The other driver was a woman, she waved agitatedly. Indignant, Malcolm swore. His driving had been no worse than her own. He watched her door open and was astonished that she was actually stepping out on to the road. That was the moment when he recognised her.

Anne came striding uphill towards him, her usually placid features registering fury.

"How many days is it since I told you not to drive?" Anne demanded. "You really are behaving totally irresponsibly."

"But I've got to see Graham, this won't keep."

"It will have to, I'm afraid." She reached through the open window and removed his keys. "This is how seriously I take your not driving."

"You can't do that. You're my doctor, not my – my keeper determined to police my every move."

As he finished speaking Malcom registered with a shock that Anne's eyes had grown saddened, not furious.

"I'm your friend as well," she reminded him quietly. "I can't let you go ahead and risk killing yourself. Killing others as well, if you should have another attack at the wheel."

"But I'm better now, you know I am."

"Better perhaps, not cured. We need to wait a lot longer than this before we'll feel at all certain the heart won't play up again."

"This is so bloody frustrating."

"I know, love. Believe me, I do know. Now, how about we find a spot where we can leave your car, and I'll drop you off at home?"

He shook his head. "Can't go back there."

"Row with Caroline?"

"And how!"

"You really are the end. After all she's done, coping with your illness and the farm."

"But you haven't heard what she's been up to."

Anne sighed, gave a rueful grin. "I've a feeling you'd better tell me. If you explode it will help no one. But you'll have to keep it brief. I've been out on an early call, already late for surgery."

Malcolm hastily explained how Caroline had agreed to Graham's request for storage space. Anne listened then gave a tiny shrug.

"You'd been saying for ages how badly the farm was doing."

"That didn't mean I was prepared to sacrifice all I believe, simply in order to make a profit."

"So, OK – you can change things now, can't you? That way, you'll preserve your own integrity. You'll just have to be grateful for the money your brother's scheme has yielded already."

Put like that, it all sounded very reasonable, not in the least something to which he could take such exception. By the time they had found a spot where the Jaguar could be left and he was getting into Anne's car, Malcolm's chief concern was how he might make his peace with Caroline.

She wasn't in the farm office when he'd trudged reluctantly up the drive. As he turned away, he met Christopher crossing from the house.

"You've survived then, Dad? Mum's indoors. She went up to your room."

Chris had been shaken by finding Caroline in tears. He was not going to warn his father about her distress. Malcolm ought to see the state she was in.

Caroline was lying curled on the bed, her glorious hair strewn across the pillow already damp from her tears.

"Thank God you're all right," she exclaimed, her voice strained with sobbing. "Don't you ever do that to me again!"

113

"I'm sorry, Caro. Again. I am so sorry." He felt his own throat constricting with emotion. Anger he could understand, but not this tearfulness. In either of them.

He sat on the edge of the bed and drew her into his arms. "I should never have spoken to you like that."

Caroline eased away slightly. "But you did, and it's shown me again that I must leave you to get on with running the farm just as soon as you're given the all clear. We'll never agree, Malcolm, and these differences between us will make me forget how much you mean to me."

"I won't let that happen, Caro."

"We might neither of us manage to prevent it. I think it really is best that I only stay on in the office until you're fully fit."

"But it's always been an intrinsic part of our life together." He had been deprived of so much that was familiar, couldn't contemplate further changes.

"I thought so as well, once," Caroline told him, her eyes awash with tears. "It's been chastening these past few months to have precious illusions shattered."

"Then we'll piece it all together again, put it right . . ."

She shook her head. "That isn't the way, not any longer. I need work of my own where I can extend my ideas. And you must have the freedom to do what you believe right regarding the farm." Pausing, she sighed. "I did know I was going against your wishes when I said yes to Graham. But I also knew how badly we needed to have some money coming in. I was worried, realised that it wouldn't be until now when our own fruits are ripening that we'd have anything going to the markets."

"Quite."

"You didn't get as far as Graham's, did you?"

"No. Met Anne on my way there. She gave me a going over for attempting to drive."

So that's the reason he turned back, he would heed no one but Anne Newbold. "I hope you'll listen to her."

"She persuaded me to leave the car then gave me a lift back home. Will you go and pick it up? It's only down the lane."

"Sure. No problem. I was just doing the wages."

"I could calculate those. It's hardly the kind of stressful work that I'm supposed to avoid."

"All right then. And what about Graham, want me to run you over there later on?"

"We'll see."

Letting the present arrangement stand might after all be more sensible, just until their bank balance recovered. Since he himself wasn't responsible for the agreement he needn't feel he was compromising his own ethics.

Nicholas and Bianca came to stay over the following weekend. Looking forward to their arrival kept Caroline going for days. Nick's visits during Malcolm's stay in hospital had been brief and, when Bianca accompanied him, had involved sleeping at her parents' home. Their idea had been to spare Caroline additional work, and she'd tried to disguise feeling deprived of precious hours of Nick's company.

Malcolm too seemed to be anticipating this visit quite eagerly, making her glad that he'd have something to take his mind off their recent disagreements.

The pair zoomed up to the house on the Friday evening, late for the dinner which Florence Dacre had placed in the oven before going off home. Malcolm was already being amenable, sipping Slimline Tonic and talking cars with Christopher, evidence that their differences were shelved if not settled. Between visits to the kitchen to check on the meal, Caroline caught herself smiling fondly on both Malcolm and Chris. This weekend, at least, shouldn't be marred by animosity or resentment.

Bianca was looking well, the weight she had put on since their first meeting suited her. And Nicholas appeared pleased with life. During the meal he explained how they had been making plans. They were flat hunting in Cambridge, had decided to make their home there until he obtained his degree.

"You'll be staying on as well to do your PhD, as planned?" said his father.

Nicholas grinned. "That's less certain, I must admit. At this stage. When the infant's here, one of us will need to be earning."

"But he can return for his PhD later," Bianca put in earnestly. "I'm insisting that he should keep that in mind."

Malcolm was frowning slightly. Caroline discovered she was holding her breath, willing him not to disapprove openly. After a moment his frown changed to a smile. He nodded.

"Sounds all right to me. You appreciate the responsibility that will soon be yours. So long as you don't relinquish all thoughts of what you wish to achieve academically."

When they had eaten Christopher dashed off again to play squash and Bianca insisted on clearing away and stacking the dishwasher. Naturally, Nicholas helped.

Alone with his wife in the drawing-room, Malcolm grinned. "Quite an alteration to have Nick finding his way to the kitchen! I'm pleased, nice to see him willing to save you additional work."

"You know I never mind what I do for either him or Chris."

"That's not the point."

The four of them talked for a while afterwards and then Nick announced that he'd promised Bianca he'd look out the family photographs she was longing to inspect. "There are some old transparencies, aren't there?"

"In the loft," Caroline told him. "Perhaps tomorrow we'll dig those out. The albums are in the cupboard here, why don't you get them?"

As always when family photographs were to be shown to someone new, Caroline began feeling uneasy. No one, least of all Malcolm, seemed to understand how vulnerable she remained whenever Sue was mentioned. Her predecessor had had so much in her favour. And she was the boys' mother.

Caroline need not have worried about Bianca's reaction. The girl evidently was well-primed in Parker history, and tactful enough to limit her remarks to "she looked very nice," regarding Sue, and "a pretty house" concerning their former home.

"I hope you won't mind if I have an early night," said Bianca at ten thirty. Nicholas followed her upstairs five minutes later.

Caroline listened to them moving around in the room above her head, and steeled herself to accept that they were sleeping together here. She hadn't believed she was this old-fashioned. While making up the bed she had been compelled to ignore her innermost thoughts that this was all wrong, tonight she was even more determined to conceal what she really felt. Nothing must influence Malcolm's apparent willingness to live with the realities of the situation.

She was surprised twenty minutes later when Malcolm spoke, his expression rueful.

"I never thought I would see this day," he admitted. "When we would be obliged to condone one of the boys sleeping with a girl under our own roof."

Caroline smiled back, relieved she was free to express her own misgivings. "I know. That's what I've been feeling since getting their room ready. A bit of a double-bind, I suppose – it is late in the day for trying to separate them, yet you still feel you shouldn't be pushing them together."

"Time *we* grew up, darling, eh? These youngsters are always quick to indicate that we don't live in the real world."

Caroline nodded. "It's just when it's your own children that you can't help feeling this unease."

Malcolm was gazing intently across at her. "And that's the way you've always considered both Nick and Christopher. Bless you. Now more than ever, I need to know you're coping alongside me."

Caroline smiled, pleased by his admission. She tried to subdue the niggling suspicion that this understanding between them would never last.

Eight

C hristopher would have given anything to be in the farm office. He had left The Sylvan Barn before either Caroline or his father came down to breakfast. He'd no intention of being late on his first morning at Julian's vineyard, but departing this early owed rather more to his reluctance to endure an encounter with them. Once it became plain that he really was determined to go to Julian, Chris understood that his father could never forgive him completely. And when Malcolm Parker was unhappy Caroline generally suffered the most of anyone.

Chris was worried today. How would they get on in his absence? Ever since Nick's last visit home the pair of them appeared to be agreeing to a truce, but that still felt unstable. The fuse of his father's temper certainly hadn't lengthened, despite Anne Newbold's cautioning.

It wasn't that he thought his stepmother would prove any less efficient in the office than he himself. Chris believed it was *because* the love between her and Malcolm was so deep that arguments over farm problems upset her quite badly.

Crossing the border into East Sussex, Christopher tried to look ahead to his new position, and to put home anxieties behind him. He would be expected to work hard and effectively, that was for sure, he'd never anticipate less with Julian as his employer. He would also have to be careful what he said, not something he normally found at all easy.

Over the years, he had recognised that there was no affinity between his father and Caroline's ex. Daily contact with Julian would provide innumerable occasions when a careless word might convey the impression that all was less than well in the Parker

118

household. I'm not that disloyal, he thought, I'm only changing my place of work, not my allegiance.

The dismal scraping of a violin greeted Chris as soon as he turned off the MG's engine. Stifling an inward groan, he headed towards the front door of the bungalow. He glanced sideways when he first sensed, and then saw, that he was being watched from one of its windows.

The girl who eventually opened the door to him was scarcely recognisable as the person who had been so overdressed in gleaming material for her coming of age party. Even the face that had regarded him through the window just now looked drab and ordinary. *How could Mum have borne such a creature?*

"Early, aren't you?" Amanda snapped. "Dad's still in the shower. Didn't he state a time?"

Christopher's ready smile seemed to have no effect, but he kept it in place, anyway, and stilled the urge to fling back a retort. "Just didn't want to be late, I guess. First day and all that . . ."

She didn't invite him in, but pointed instead in the general direction of the vineyard. "I'm busy practising, but it's obvious where everything is. I'll tell Father you're waiting for him out there."

Amanda began closing the door, Chris was obliged to remove himself. Feeling chastened, resenting the fact that the cause was such an unprepossessing girl, he turned and stomped away. He was tempted to sit in the car until Julian emerged, but thought better of that. It wouldn't hurt to wander as far as the edge of the vineyard and take a look at the state of things. On the day of his interview he'd been given the full tour, but that was some weeks ago now and he needed to familiarise himself with how the grapes were progressing.

The fifteen minutes or so before Julian joined him felt more like an hour, and allowed too much time for thinking. Beginning a fresh job closely resembled the first day in a new school: today, Christopher felt disadvantaged by having gone straight from agricultural college to working for his father.

He remembered his early days in the orchards where Malcolm's delight to have his son beside him there tempered all that they did together. It had seemed then that his father was geniality itself, and would do all he could to make that aspect of their life successful. Christopher wished to God it hadn't all gone sour, and wondered what might have transpired if the offered promotion there had occurred first, instead of that dreadful mention of redundancy.

"You're keen!" Julian called, striding near-silently towards him. "Sorry I wasn't around when you arrived. I hope Amanda wasn't too dreadfully dismissive."

Seeing Christopher's embarrassment, Julian placed a friendly hand on his shoulder. "I'll try and convince you that you *are* welcome here. Just don't report back too precisely to Caroline, eh? She does tend to think we haven't got everything quite right with Amanda."

"Some people are a little . . . difficult in a morning."

Julian laughed. "Tactful as well, eh? You are going to make a hit with me! Seriously, Christopher, I do hope this gels. No reason why it shouldn't, of course, you've a lot to offer. But – well, I suppose I have wondered how strong the influence might have been against me."

Chris grinned. "You don't expect me to answer that, I hope."

Relaxing, he began to enjoy himself as his boss led the way through one of the vineyards, talking about the variety of grape, soil quality and structure, and the climate which today was providing an example of the necessary warmth. By the time they eventually entered the sample room with its adjoining shop Chris had lost most of his unease.

"I'm going to like it here," he announced. "It'll be good to concentrate on such a very different kind of fruit-growing." And, he added silently, to extend himself within a business unaffected by such immediate family tensions.

"As I explained earlier, I shall expect you to acquire some understanding of the wine-making process," Julian continued. "Although your primary task will be concerned with viticulture, you will need to grasp what we require of our grapes. And the essential differences between say, Müller Thurgau and Seyval Blanc."

"How many people did you say you employ?" Chris had been curious when they met no one during the whole of their tour.

"Full-time, only a handful of production staff. You'll meet them when I show you the various processes. Most of the others are locals who come in as required. Visitor tours during the week are by arrangement only, when I call in regulars who at weekends run the shop or act as guides. Of course when we harvest that is hectic, a matter of recruiting as many people as we can."

"Sounds exciting."

"I'll remind you of that before too long when you're exhausted and don't know where to turn! But I suppose you'll be used to seasonal panics, anyway."

Chris nodded. "And your method of employing regulars along with casuals sounds much like my father's. Although he does have one advantage of growing a wide variety of fruit, ripening at intervals."

When Julian told him at one o'clock that he was expected to join Amanda and himself for a lunchtime snack Christopher wondered if the atmosphere would be conducive to eating. The girl had never impressed him very favourably in the past, this morning's encounter had done nothing to improve his opinion of her.

Strangely, though, as soon as the three of them were seated in the conservatory overlooking the rear gardens, Amanda's attitude seemed to relent. When Julian continued describing what went on at the vineyard she joined in and proved herself quite knowledgeable.

They were drinking wine produced from Julian's grapes, a Huxelrebe. Amanda surprised Chris again by contributing an informed opinion on its fresh fruity bouquet.

He grinned in her direction. "I can see I mustn't underestimate your knowledge of wines."

A flush spread up from her unlovely T-shirt sitting unevenly about the neck which might – against more flattering clothes – seem elegant.

"No one could live here for long without learning something. Dad will tell you I'm always eager to try new wines when we receive them back from bottling."

"Of course – you don't bottle on site, do you?" Chris remarked.

It was Amanda who continued. "I've tried to persuade Dad that we should, but he won't have it."

121

Julian smiled. "Perhaps in a year or two, when our most recent vineyards are producing to capacity. Until then it wouldn't really be viable."

"Why do you want to see bottling here, Amanda?" Chris enquired.

She giggled before replying. "Silly, really, I know – but I love seeing rows and rows of bottles, gleaming as if it's sunlight you've trapped inside them."

Her father snorted and made a face, but Christopher wasn't inclined to ridicule Amanda's notion. Suddenly, he saw how her artistic nature encompassed far more than the expected forms of art. He could respect her for allowing that to show, especially before a comparative stranger.

Julian led the conversation away from work, commenting on the MG which Christopher drove. "Do you inherit your love of classic cars from your father?"

"Don't know really, never thought. He drives a Jag, don't remember a time when he didn't own a recent model from that stable. Can't say I'm much influenced by him at all – unless it's contrariwise."

Amanda joined in their laughter and Chris suspected that she was thinking of her own relation to her mother. From what Caroline had said in the past, and how little she *had* said, he'd always been aware that the two were not exactly compatible. He felt quite sorry for the girl. Though he did like Julian, there was no way he would choose him as a parent, and the thought that Amanda was missing out on Caroline's warmth made him sad.

Chris spent the afternoon being briefed on the various stages of wine-making. Although fascinated by something that he had never encountered in the past, absorbing Julian's rapid explanation of the processes involved was tiring. By the time he was getting into the car for the drive back to The Sylvan Barn, Christopher felt his head was reeling.

He took the journey slowly for him, willing himself to concentrate on the unfamiliar roads until the border with Kent was crossed and he felt he was reaching home territory.

Chris remained quiet that evening. Even when his father as well as

Caroline asked how the day had gone, he failed to respond very fully to their concerned enquiries. He had always been aware that Julian could be hard-nosed; that he hadn't seemed so today had surprised him. What astonished him now was his own growing recognition that it was unexpected aspects of his new job which would prove wearing.

Lacking so much basic knowledge about the vines was going to be more of a disadvantage than he had realised, he would need to study all the harder to assimilate a full understanding. And there was the personal aspect of being employed by Julian: against his will, Chris was being compelled to feel this concern for Amanda. Disliking her had lasted for only a handful of hours; he could no longer pretend, even to himself, that he was unmoved by what she was missing through this separation from her mother.

He watched Caroline now, smiling as she dispensed coffee and collected empty dishes, giving no sign that the tiredness visible in her face sprang from stress as much as from work in the farm office. For more years than he cared to count, he had taken for granted the devotion that she had bestowed on himself and Nick as generously as she had on their father. And a share of this should be Amanda's, he thought, was there a hope in hell of reconciling the situation as it was and the way that he now felt that it ought to be?

With Christopher's departure from the farm and the reallocation of their jobs, Caroline forced herself yet again to shelve her longing to return to PR work. Although claiming to be fully back in harness, Malcolm mustn't be allowed to shoulder too many of the problems. And she couldn't rid herself of the habit of watching his health. She always seemed to be alert for any sign of a relapse.

A few days ago she had been so perturbed by her own preoccupation with this insecurity that she'd telephoned Anne Newbold for a chat.

Their doctor had been at once reassuring and realistic. "That's all to the good really, Caroline. So long as you keep your anxiety within reasonable bounds. Knowing Malcolm, he can't be relied upon to take sufficient care of himself! But on the other hand he is in far better shape than he was a few months ago."

"I'm glad I rang you," Caroline said immediately. "Didn't want to display my neuroses about this too publicly, but at times I do wonder if I am doing enough . . ."

"You're there, keeping an eye on him, that's one thing he needs. And there's the diet. From his last visit for a check-up, I saw you're holding him to that."

Caroline smiled. "It's not easy, even now, though the spell in hospital did provide time in which to think up a wide range of meals which—"

"Which he enjoys," Anne interrupted.

"Did he say so?"

"Even without any prompting."

"He might have told me," said Caroline ruefully. "We still have the occasional spat about the restrictions."

"Men!" exclaimed Anne, and they laughed.

Feeling lighter in heart about her care of Malcolm wasn't quite enough to make Caroline fully contented. The farm office was no less humdrum than in the past, so many of her tasks there occupied only a part of her mind. The rest was free to roam towards her unfulfilled ambitions.

It was Lucy, arriving one Sunday for lunch, who suggested a means of getting away from The Sylvan Barn of an evening, and for an occasion that would provide quite a challenge.

"We've been talking about you, Caro," she told her as they cleared away after the meal. "At our little residents' association. You know how most of them are oldies like me – well, we're none of us nearly so informed on sensible eating as we should be."

Caroline groaned. "Can't you let me forget this wretched diet business for five minutes?"

"This delicious meal today reminded me. We need to know more. We lived through the war, some through restrictions during the difficult thirties; we concentrated on filling our families up. We didn't consider what all those substantial meals might be doing. That's why we need re-educating now."

"You're surely not suggesting I'd become involved in that!"

"Why not, darling? You've acquired this understanding of what's good for Malcolm. You could talk to us – about the right foods, and how to cook them interestingly."

Caroline shook her head before bending to stack the dishwasher.

"You need somebody professional, a dietician, someone like that."

"Not true, dear. What we want is a woman like ourselves, who'll put it across in our sort of language. Your PR experience means you know how to convey your thoughts in a way that'll appeal to all the people present . . ."

Caroline continued to steel herself to disregard Lucy's evident disappointment. Despite the seemingly endless weeks committed to Malcolm's diet, she often felt that she was still bumbling along, experimenting.

Getting ready to go out that evening, Caroline forgot Lucy's suggestion. They were all invited over to Kate's, an occasion which Christopher chose to miss.

"Tell Aunt Kate some other time, will you, Mum?" he said, and grinned when Caroline frowned. He and his younger cousins had had little in common since the day when childhood games were left behind them. He could see no other reason for attending.

"It isn't so much your Aunt Kate who will be perturbed, is it?"

Chris laughed, his eyes glinting. "But you know my absence will relieve the old lady of at least one source of contention."

Lucy turned to her daughter. "There's one old lady here who's always sorry to see so little of that young man."

Caroline nodded. "Actually, I suspect Isabel will experience more regret than she'll ever voice simply because Chris isn't with us."

Isabel certainly enquired why he hadn't accompanied them, her mouth had turned down as she watched the three of them coming through into the sitting-room at the farm. Lucy, however, crossed swiftly to give Isabel a hug, an action which startled Caroline until she remembered her mother's accounts of previous visits there. Isabel appeared pleased if somewhat surprised by the gesture, and immediately indicated that Lucy must sit beside her.

Kate was hovering behind Graham who was already talking shop with Malcolm. Feeling rather *de trop*, Caroline strolled across to a vacant chair. Eventually, Kate settled in its twin and the two brothers ambled, still talking, towards the other sofa.

Isabel was glaring at Malcolm. Only after sitting did he grow aware that he had merely included his mother in the general hello that he'd tossed into the room. Rising swiftly, he crossed to her side and kissed her cheek.

"How are you, Mother?"

"I'm well enough," she responded quite sharply. "All the better for seeing that you appear to be improving. Back at work, aren't you?"

"That's right. I've been easing myself in gradually for some time now."

"The weight you've lost has done you no harm, I'll say that for you. Look ten years younger without all that flab. Just shows how good that housekeeper of yours is, keeping you to the diet."

Caroline felt herself stiffening, compressed her lips to withhold the words that would correct Isabel's misconception concerning responsibility for organising diets.

Lucy spoke up for her, smiling disarmingly on Isabel. "I believe Caroline's the one who plans what they eat at The Sylvan Barn, you know."

Kate stared across at her mother. "Ah, but not having to do the actual preparation and cooking oneself eliminates all the hard work."

Lucy frowned and glanced towards her other daughter.

Caroline shook her head slightly. She wouldn't even remind them that Florence Dacre didn't come in quite every day. She'd no wish to prolong this discussion, however infuriating its implications might be. She had never once felt that she came off well in a confrontation with her mother-in-law, and didn't mean to use today for trying to assert herself. As for her sister's continuing disregard for the facts, she knew Kate well enough. And whose opinions would be endorsed while Isabel remained in the room!

Determined not to let this spoil the day, Caroline asked after the rest of the family. Noting that Christopher's cousins were absent she had reflected that he might have been even more bored than he'd anticipated if he had been persuaded to come here.

126

"They're both away," Graham told her. "For once in their lives, together. Weekending over near – where was it, Kate?"

"Just beyond Mersham, these friends of ours are related to the Brabournes, you know."

"Lovely," said Caroline, smiling while she tried to recall precisely how the Brabournes were connected with the Royal Family. Somehow, Kate's satisfaction only served to decrease her own interest in her niece and nephew.

With Lucy's presence, and the fact that Malcolm and Graham seemed to be in unusual accord that day, the gathering wasn't quite a disaster. All the same, when she and Malcolm set out to drive her mother home Caroline was feeling that Isabel and her own sister had yet again deflated her.

By the time they reached the motorway she had recognised that their attitude, perversely or otherwise, had influenced one decision for her.

"I'll do that talk you suggested, Mother," she said over her shoulder. "Only you must tell them to keep it quite informal."

"That's the way we always are. Darling, I'm so pleased you'll come. And the others will be delighted."

"What's all this?" Malcolm asked.

"Just something we discussed when we were clearing away after lunch, Malcolm, dear," said Lucy. "Caroline's coming to give our residents' association all her ideas on this splendid diet you're on."

Malcolm didn't even try to conceal his laughter. "You'll be suggesting next that I come to be shown off as a specimen!"

"Well, of course, if you really think . . ." began Lucy, sounding nonplussed.

"Don't worry, Lucy, nothing would drag me there! So when's this lecture to be then?"

"That's up to Caro. As soon as she can fit us in."

"Just ring me, Mother, when you can suggest dates." And I'll be glad to give this a go, thought Caroline. It isn't really a PR job, but it's closer than anything else I've been doing. I need to show that I still have it in me to present something.

*   *   *

The evening was a Thursday in August, Caroline set out with conflicting emotions churning inside her. A part of her was thrilled to be embarking on an opportunity for addressing people again. Otherwise, she was dismayed by an unfamiliar feeling that she might have been better equipped to speak on almost any other subject. She also remained undermined by her mother-in-law and her own sister. Did she really cope only because of heavy reliance upon Florence Dacre?

Maybe I'll be all right when I get there, she told herself, and was thankful that the journey was short enough to prevent too much nervous anticipation.

Caroline did, indeed, feel better as soon as Lucy met her in the doorway of her flat.

"You look terrific, Caro," she exclaimed. "But, knowing you, I suppose you'll want to freshen up. We've plenty of time, there's a clean towel in the bathroom."

Caroline was surprised that her reflected face revealed little of her misgivings, which seemed to be unnoticable alongside flushed cheeks and quite a glint in her eyes. Her hair, recently cut and coloured, looked reassuringly good, and made her smile to herself. She had always pointed out to clients that smartening yourself provided a remarkable boost, even when information was all that was expected of you.

The residents' lounge was far larger than Caroline had imagined, and was already three quarters full. She was glad to see people in comfortable chairs, grouped around low tables, and not in the rows which often felt rather daunting. But suddenly there was no more time to observe, Lucy was leading her to a distinguished looking man who rose from his seat to be introduced.

"Admiral Dainton is a great friend of mine," Lucy began while he was shaking Caroline's hand. "Because of our having so much in common, naturally – with your father being at sea."

Naturally? Caroline thought with an inward smile; *have you never mentioned to him that Dad was master of a cross-channel ferry?*

The Admiral, however, was a charmer who soon made her feel at ease, chatting as she took out her notes while more residents and their friends arrived to occupy the remaining seats.

He gave a bright introduction, referring to his own need of a healthier diet (a claim unsubstantiated by his lean, very erect person).

It was time for Caroline to speak. She calmed her nerves with a deep intake of breath.

"This all began when I received a dreadful shock, learning that Malcolm was in danger of suffering a coronary." She soon had everyone laughing over her embarrassment, rooted as it was in the belief that this reflected badly upon her care of her husband.

Caroline felt their warmth encompassing her, encouraging more honesty regarding all her early fears that she might fail to alter their eating habits sufficiently to save Malcolm.

Moving on to outline how a low-cholesterol diet was structured became easy – his doctor's forbidding of dairy produce, animal fats, and less obvious naughties like cooked meats, sauces, pickles. Caroline had gained their attention, and was finding it simple enough to go into more detail about recipes that she used, as well as embracing general principles.

She agreed to respond to questions only after pointing out that she was no dietician and spoke solely from her own experiences. The queries were few, in any case, and seemed to have been answered when a tall man, rather younger than most of the people present, rose from his seat near the back of the hall.

"May we ask perhaps how your husband is now?"

It was Paul. Caroline was so shaken that she hardly took in the question, much less was she able to do more than stumble over her reply.

"He – he's really quite well. That is – as some of you may know, he did suffer a heart attack before we really got down to tackling the cholesterol. Since then, however, his doctor assures me that the diet has played a vital role in his recovery. We've been very lucky!"

Again, she felt the audience warming to her and, rather shaken by the degree of general empathy, Caroline sank back into her chair. Lucy rushed across to her side, and congratulated her before hauling her off to be greeted by a succession of friends. Coffee and biscuits were to be served. Suddenly though, Caroline felt that even one additional eager question would be more than she could

129

tackle. Too many years had passed and too many traumas had been endured since she'd last faced any kind of public speaking.

"Would they think it very awful of me if I disappeared now?"

Lucy beamed. "Of course not, my dear. You've done your stuff. Magnificently. This way we'll have more time – we *do* have more time before you must set out? Can't have you driving home without a snack inside you."

Caroline was thanked again by the Admiral, and the generous applause already received was repeated. Smiling and nodding her thanks in turn, she headed towards the exit.

Lucy's hand was on her arm as she steered her through corridors, in the direction of her flat. They weren't the only ones leaving the hall. It wasn't obvious to Caroline until they were almost at Lucy's door that Paul was immediately behind them. And there he was beside them, overtaking.

He smiled. "Right then, come along in."

Only then did Caroline realise that the snack had been prepared not by her mother, but by Paul. Without seeming grossly offhand she couldn't decline his hospitality. And she didn't wish to decline.

"Paul insisted," Lucy was saying as he ushered them into his living-room and closed the outer door. Captain barked and began ambling through from the kitchen. He saw Caroline and padded towards her, tail swaying rapidly from side to side.

"You know Captain quite well, I see," Lucy observed and smiled.

Caroline nodded. "Scamp and I made his acquaintance while you were laid up with the ankle."

"Coffee all right?" Paul enquired, heading for the kitchen.

Captain had settled proprietorially at Caroline's feet. She fondled his head while trying to regain composure. What a fool she was to be affected so greatly, purely because Paul had wanted to provide a sandwich or two. She glanced towards the table. Segments of quiche, fingers of toast with pâté, and various other savouries nestled beneath their covers of transparent film, confirming that he had taken the trouble to lay on more than the odd sandwich.

Lucy was chatting on about Admiral Dainton, Caroline sensed that if she were less preoccupied with her own emotions she would have been wondering just how deep her mother's interest in the

Admiral was. As things stood, Caroline felt it extremely unlikely that she would be able to summon up sufficient self-possession to manage coherent conversation by the time Paul returned to the room.

When he did join them, however, Paul brought interests of his own along with the coffee, and soon was engaging them with details of a recent visit to France.

"I dare hardly admit it, employed on the Channel Tunnel as I am, but I do relish a sea trip. Have you ever indulged in them?"

Caroline and her mother exchanged smiles and then Lucy enlightened him. "My husband was a ship's master on the ferries. Have I never told you?"

"So you would have lots of jaunts across to France."

"Very exciting they were, when Kate and I were small," Caroline confided. "Being shown around the bridge made us feel very special."

"Kate used to pretend we were on a huge ocean liner," said Lucy dreamily.

"Kate would," Caroline observed.

Paul laughed. "Whilst you simply revelled in the experience. Just as I do going across there now. This last time, however, was a first for me – on the *Sea-cat*."

"What was it like?" Caroline asked, wishing she might have tried it for herself. With him.

"Rather bumpy that day. Lots of people didn't appreciate it because of the sea being so choppy. In fact, the homeward trip was by hovercraft, the *Sea-cat* had been taken off on account of the heavy seas. Luckily, I'm a good sailor, nothing spoiled my enjoyment of the food over there."

Perhaps because food had been their topic already that evening, Paul did not reveal what he had eaten. Caroline wondered what kind of meals he loved, wished that she knew more of what his tastes were in everything. But she was being a fool, surrendering to the excitement of a developing acquaintance, an acquaintance that should be allowed to progress no further.

Rendered uneasy by her own secret emotions, she rose and excused herself as soon as Lucy stood up after they had sampled

Paul's delicious food. Together they thanked him, and he walked with them to the door.

Lucy had remembered a book she had for Kate. "You'll see her before I do, darling. Take it with you, save me putting it in the post."

Leaving Lucy's flat, Caroline glanced at her watch. It was ten o'clock, not terribly late to be driving home on her own.

Paul was still at his open door. He beckoned to her. When she reached his side he stretched out a hand for hers.

He drew her with him back into his home. "Something I want you to see."

Still grasping her hand he took her through to his sun room. An easel was set up, with a worn teacloth concealing the painting it supported.

The portrait was almost completed, of an attractive woman whose high cheekbones were enhanced by gleaming dark hair drawn back from her face. Caroline noticed the photograph resting against one corner of the picture. Without being told, she knew who the woman was.

"Even copying, I can't do her justice," Paul said softly, his fingers moving restlessly over her own. "I thought this would help to – to say goodbye to her, I guess."

"Did – did you tell me you divorced?" she asked, thinking how strange it was that he should still wish to paint her picture.

He shook his head. "She died. An overdose. Intentional."

"God, I'm so sorry. I should never have asked." Caroline turned to face him.

"I wanted *you* to understand. It's not something I mention as a rule."

She could believe that. Losing a partner in any way was traumatic enough.

"It was because of me, you know," Paul went on, gazing straight into her eyes. "Because my work took me away from home so much. It was a sort of double-bind, for both of us. She hated travelling, was only really happy in our home. Not her fault, she didn't easily make new friends. Or any friends at all – though it was years before I understood how significant that was."

"What a terrible situation for you both."

"For her, certainly. As time was to prove. I'll always regret so deeply that I didn't see how desperately miserable she was."

"It's all so different for men," said Caro. "You throw yourselves wholeheartedly into your work, often enough that's the only way to succeed."

"I was determined to get on. My father was a miner, not in Kent, the Yorkshire coalfields. He contracted silicosis and died far too young. But not before he'd ensured that I got the education necessary for the job I'd chosen. I suppose, in a way, I was trapped by my debt to him."

"There are far worse reasons for pursuing a career."

"I hope so."

Caroline couldn't hold back when he drew her against him, could not turn her lips away when he covered them with his own.

"You're the first one," Paul said. "The first since – since it happened. I needed you to understand."

There was nothing she could say. She could only continue holding him, arms reaching up about his shoulders, her eyes uptilted to search his face. But Paul's eyes were closed. Long white lashes fanning across weathered cheeks urged her to touch. Caroline willed her fingers to remain where they were, and grew aware of stronger urges.

Paul's body felt lean and firm, insistent; and now he stirred and Caroline moved with him. For so many weeks she had recognised this attraction, had banned it from her mind as she could never ban it from the rest.

She had needed to sympathise, to show her understanding. Since the day he'd helped her overcome her distress about Amanda, she had wanted to assure Paul of her friendship.

Only now there was this. Her breasts were hurting under the pressure of his ribcage, her legs seemed to weaken. And somewhere in between she was smouldering, aflame.

"I know you must go home," said Paul, his voice husky. "That anything else would distress you. I'm not one for practising deceit either."

One last time, he kissed her, for one final lingering minute he curved her to him.

133

"I'll see you to your car."

Caroline's hands were shaking when she shoved the key in the ignition. She steadied them on the wheel before slipping the car into gear. She had told Paul to go back indoors, but she saw him now in her rear-view mirror, watching from the entrance to the flats. She sensed that he would watch until she had driven out of sight.

Her body had become an intensity of longing, screaming for fulfilment as it had not done for years. She smiled wryly, aware of the irony that was their need of each other.

Paul knew her, all right – well enough to believe there would be no affair. He didn't know that she had long since vowed to avoid him. These emotions tonight confirmed that she must put that vow into practice.

Nine

I t was raining junk. Odd shoes, socks, T-shirts, voluminous skirts, scarves, paperback books and CDs were falling across the drive in front of him. Christopher braked, halting the MG as the window to his left in the bungalow slammed shut.

Getting out of the car, he noticed his front wheel was pinning one of the cleaner-looking T-shirts to the stone paving. He leapt back into the MG and reversed the few inches that would free the shirt. Until that moment he had felt quite angry: arriving a second earlier, he would have caught the full impact, a shoe could have shattered his windscreen. Did the mindless individual responsible have no idea what a replacement would cost? Now suddenly he felt concerned, trapped by his inadvertent marking of that T-shirt into being involved.

Chris had left the car again when, head-down, arms and shoulders hunched around a violin and bow, Amanda tore past him. She ran around the far corner of the house and out of sight. Even without glimpsing her expression, Chris sensed her distress.

Bewildered, he shook his head. He had believed Amanda the only person capable of tossing out possessions in such a frenzy, yet everything about her now suggested she was the victim of someone's annoyance.

Christopher shrugged, took his keys from the car, secured it and strode out in the direction of the nearest of the vineyards. He and Julian were talking pest control today, seriously talking. Along with weeding, it was his least favourite aspect of growing any kind of fruit. Determined to do his best, though, he had spent most of the weekend reading up everything his college books contained on the creatures and diseases considered a threat to vines.

135

When he reached the vineyard Julian was nowhere in sight. Surprised, Chris looked to left and right of him and ahead, making certain his boss wasn't perhaps bending down somewhere to examine the crop.

After five minutes, Chris decided he should show some initiative, begin inspecting the vines himself, if only to demonstrate that he meant business.

Red-faced and with most of his self-possession absent, Julian arrived fifteen minutes later.

"Glad you've made a start. Hope you know what you're looking for . . ."

Christopher straightened his back, greeted him, and grinned. "I did swot up a bit."

"Just as well. Afraid I'm rather distracted. Are all you young folk heedless?"

Chris didn't know how to reply. Honesty would have had him acknowledge the times he'd been reproved for a television switched on and then left blaring, for sports gear rotting in a bag when it should have gone in the wash, for the perennially untidy room. Loyalty to the rest of his generation prevented even one word from emerging.

Julian snorted. "You can't have missed the contents of my daughter's wardrobe being shifted from carpet, bed, chairs and tables in her room! My doing."

Christopher smiled, suddenly sympathetic. Julian had a nice home; he had heard and seen about the place an elderly woman who came in daily. A woman too old, too detached to have a mother's tolerance.

"We'd be left to clean up and make meals ourselves if Mrs Grant departed," Julian persisted. "Amanda really is the end. It happens over and over again. First the chairs acquire a hillside of clothes, slanting from the back to the edge of the seat. Then the tables gain a heap of clutter, after that the floor."

He saw Christopher's suppressed laughter. "Now, be fair," he said. "*You* won Caroline's skill as an organiser."

The window on Julian's domestic life made Chris feel easier still with him. Chris became free to admit the truth when baffled by more potential threats to a good grape harvest than he'd believed existed. Julian, in turn, was warming to the frankness. He knew college types, tended to be wary of their textbook opinions.

This ease between them continued during lunch when they discovered a mutual interest in rugby. Julian talked about how he used to play for his university and Chris, although not participating since school, still loved to watch the game.

"Maybe you'd be interested in going to Twickenham this season," Julian suggested. "That's unless you attend matches with your father?"

"No, Dad's not really into sport. And I'd love us to go together."

Amanda hadn't come in to eat with them. Even while enjoying their masculine conversation Chris wondered where she was. He could understand she'd still be upset by her father's action. Walking back to the house, they had seen that someone had cleared every last item from the drive. Bringing in their meal, Mrs Grant had confirmed that Amanda had put everything away.

They were due to go outdoors again when Julian took a telephone call. He indicated Chris should go on ahead. They were to spend the afternoon inspecting a second vineyard.

It was there that Christopher found Amanda. Her violin and bow beside her on the grass, she was seated with her back to one of the oaks which grew among the hedge that formed their boundary. She didn't answer when he said hello, and nor did she attempt to disguise that she'd been crying. From the state of her face, Chris could believe she had done nothing else since early morning.

"You must be horribly embarrassed, I know I would be," he said gently, and wondered how to continue.

"Leave me alone, just leave me."

"Don't be daft. You want somebody on your side, don't you?"

"No one is, ever. They never have been. Even since Dad's been on his own, he's had old Ma Grant to back him up."

"He does rely on her a lot, I suppose. Bet you wouldn't like it either if she left. You'd have to clean the place and do all the cooking."

"Do you think I couldn't?"

Christopher grinned. "You'd have a shot at it. But I don't believe you'd be very happy tackling something so mundane."

Amanda stared curiously at him. She didn't smile but the expression in her red-rimmed eyes revealed rising interest.

"That violin you're guarding as if it were gold-plated evidently means a lot to you. Wouldn't you be gutted if you couldn't fit in time for playing?"

"Absolutely. But that's all nonsense, anyway. If old Ma Grant left, Dad would get somebody else in."

"They might be even worse."

Amanda shook her head. "They'd be younger, understanding."

"They might understand *him*, have you thought of that? Could be someone he'd get keen on . . ."

"Don't!" She had been afraid of that ever since she'd seen how her father's eyes followed the glamorous Sarah Dwight around.

Christopher felt a strong impulse to stroke her head. She seemed such a child, a lost child.

"D'you keep your room tidy?" Amanda demanded suddenly.

"Sort of – when I have to. We were never allowed to let things get too far out of hand."

"Is your father terribly strict as well?"

"Old-fashioned. But Caroline was always the one keeping an eye on us . . ." He let his voice trail off. He hadn't quite got used to the fact that he was speaking to her daughter.

"She was bossy with me, but—" Amanda shook her head, clamping her lips together.

"You miss her?"

"No. No, not in the least." Her eyes were awash again.

All at once Amanda picked up her violin and bow and sprang to her feet. Hearing a sound somewhere behind him, Chris guessed that Julian was approaching.

"I'm glad we've talked," he said swiftly, but Amanda went darting off, running between the rows of vines to avoid her father.

"Is she very cut up?" Julian asked with concern.

"She was having a bit of a moody when I got here, think she's getting over it."

*　　*　　*

138

Caroline was in turmoil for weeks after her visit to Folkestone. The sadness and sympathy she felt for Paul ensured that he rarely left her mind for more than a few hours. And thinking about him never failed to resurrect the longing that she had been compelled to suppress. She had reckoned without its power to disturb.

She could feel this physical need wearing her down, eroding energy and gnawing into her patience. On days when Malcolm was resentful of his diet and every other curtailment of his life, she struggled to soften her tongue. Whatever else, she would not take this out on him. Once or twice, though, she couldn't avoid reminding him that he really was extremely fortunate. He might have been dead, or severely incapacitated, instead of which he was by now reasonably fit for coping with work.

"But not for much else," he grumbled. He felt so tired – too tired for going out to socialise. In any case, still concerned that he shouldn't take on too much, Caroline encouraged him to rest of an evening. He began to suspect that he was slipping into the kind of life more suited to an old man. Not something that he relished.

The only occasions when he seemed to leave the farm were meetings to resist those wretched rail link proposals. The best part was being there with Anne, although Malcolm genuinely loved being involved in trying to control that scheme. Things had been hotting up ever since the Kent Association of Parish Councils pressed for a code to minimise the environmental and social impact of construction work. They'd also urged the appointing of a Complaints Commissioner.

Malcolm often arrived home elated, if unsure whether Caroline wished to know all that had taken place.

He didn't realise that, even while wondering if she were being ridiculous, his wife was beginning to believe he enjoyed having a part of life from which he excluded her.

If he'd analysed his deepest feelings Malcolm would have found such emotions close to the truth. Working together as they did, he and Caroline were in each other's pockets too frequently. And his friendship with Anne had grown very precious to him.

Since he was forbidden to drive, she insisted on picking him up and dropping him off at The Sylvan Barn, regardless of the venue of each gathering. Some were over near Ashford, providing longer journeys in which to enjoy her company.

They would always set out for home discussing matters that had arisen during the course of the evening, and always they ended up talking on a more personal level. Anne would ask searching questions about his health, and somehow that often turned to discussing his general well-being.

Talking in the car with the darkened countryside all around them seemed preferable to talking in her surgery. Even so, Anne startled him one night with the directness of her enquiry.

"And how are other things, Malcolm? Your sex life? Back to normal, I hope?"

"Does it matter?" he said very hastily.

"It should, to you. And I certainly believe Caroline will think so. Do I take it then that you're still not having relations?"

"Not – not since the attack."

"I don't think you need abstain any longer on health grounds."

"Who says I am?"

"You're only in your early forties, Malcolm. It's a bit soon to lose your drive. Look – if it'd help, you could see a specialist."

"I'm not impotent," he said fiercely.

"But if you're not able to—" She stopped speaking when Malcolm shook his head.

"React? So you don't realise what effect you have upon me?"

Doctors weren't entirely unshakeable. Anne fell silent while inside her head her own voice was protesting, *No! No, I don't want to know this.* Except for the drone of the car's engine, the quiet between them grew substantial, impermeable. She wished she believed she could have misunderstood, but he couldn't have been much more explicit.

Malcolm was struggling to rescue something. "I would never have told you, Anne. You're my doctor, I want that to remain so. And I do still love Caroline, only – she and I need to sort a lot of things out."

"You're right, of course, the two of you must get this sorted." *Leave me out of this,* she thought. *Don't say one more word.*

"I'll never harm your career. I've thought and thought, and that's the last thing ever."

Anne's sigh was weighty. This was more real even than she had feared. "You've realised the dangers then? Caroline doesn't deserve this, she's always been so good for you, and for the boys."

"I know, I know. I shan't take anything away from her."

"But you are already, now."

"Do you believe it's what I chose?"

"No, no." Her own taut voice revealed how alarmed she was. "So, we've got to be sensible, extremely sensible."

This was their problem, but not a problem they could share. Only – only by each tackling it separately in their own way. For her this meant avoiding all physical contact, from this day.

Malcolm felt utterly dejected. "You mean, that's it then?" Their relationship had altered. In that few seconds. He couldn't bear the prospect of a future where everything between them was different.

"I can't believe you'd wish us reduced to a bit of fumbling in the back of a car!"

Anne sounded totally unlike the person that he knew. Malcolm longed to cover his ears, but that wouldn't make her horrible words go away. "You make this sound so base."

"Basic, perhaps. That's what it is. A man and a woman who, temporarily, are finding no release. And you have a wife, Malcolm."

"And you've no one else."

"So far as you're aware."

He looked so startled that Anne was compelled to smile. "No one, at present. That doesn't enter into this."

Anne accelerated, and drove swiftly to The Sylvan Barn then parked near the entrance to the drive.

"Good-night, Malcolm," she said very firmly.

"Good-night."

She was leaving him no alternative to getting out of her car. At that moment he felt that she was making him get out of her life. It didn't necessarily mean she was, did it? Malcolm prayed there might be some way of avoiding that.

Arriving back at Birch Tree House, Anne walked from her garage to the front door on legs that felt too insubstantial to support her. The life of a GP always provided shocks, rarely any which had shattered her so completely. She had been a fool. She could see that plainly enough now – now she'd been brought up sharp by such blatant facts – jolted into awareness of the hazards.

It seemed incredible to her that she could have remained so oblivious to where the friendship with Malcolm might be leading. Weren't all members of her profession trained to recognise the signs of a latent attraction which might threaten doctor/patient relations? Hadn't she always considered herself sufficiently mature to ward off unwelcome advances?

But she was genuinely fond of Malcolm, she reflected, crossing her living room to pour a whisky. Was that affection responsible for blinding her to what could be developing between them? Even tonight, was it generating this urge to discover some means of continuing their friendship? Did these surging reminders of how she must help Malcolm recover completely spring from a need of her own, the need to continue seeing him?

From her armchair, Anne stared out through the window, trying to be honest about her emotions, about *all* her emotions. Shaken though she had been by his confession, she had experienced one moment of delight. Learning that someone found her attractive, she supposed – that Malcolm did.

At least I coped this evening, she thought. *I left him in no doubt that our relationship would never be permitted any physical expression.* Today, she'd demonstrated that there would be no nonsense between them. Did that compensate to some degree for the past, when she had been less than careful in admitting that she relished their friendship? When she had even indulged in kisses that ought to have been forbidden. However innocently intentioned those kisses had been, their potential for being misinterpreted was something she should have recognised. And avoided.

Even when she went up to her bedroom Anne felt she was no nearer accepting that she had allowed this situation to develop. No amount of rationalising really excused her part in what she now saw as a wedge gradually inserting itself between Malcolm and his wife. She had no wish to take the drastic action of asking him to find another doctor, but unearthing some other solution would be far from easy.

* * *

Caroline was sitting with Florence Dacre, recipe books open before them on the kitchen table while they planned the week's menus. Normally, they looked no further ahead than the next two or three days, but Malcolm had suddenly grown more reluctant to accept the strictures of his diet. Caroline was determined to introduce additional variety to make the limitations less evident.

"I must admit he surprised me this morning," Mrs Dacre was saying, for once outspokenly critical. "The way he turned on you over that salad, for all the world as if it was just to be difficult that everything's had to change."

Caroline stifled a sigh and smiled. "I suppose it isn't easy to accept that he's never going to go back to ham and eggs, and all those steak pies and puddings that he loved. We've got to remember that he was brought up in a family that believe in giving their menfolk hearty meals."

"Even so . . . he only makes things harder, being so tetchy, and with you, of all people."

"It's what wives are for, isn't it, Mrs Dacre? To absorb the reactions to life's hurts and irritations." But Malcolm had seemed especially prickly during these past few days, so on edge that the least little annoyance provoked a tirade. He was making her feel that she must be particularly inept at coping.

The telephone rang for several seconds before Caroline hurried to answer it. Malcolm was busy with someone from the Ministry of Agriculture, and even yet she wasn't quite accustomed to there being no Christopher around to deputise.

The call proved to be for herself, anyway, and surprisingly it was from Anne Newbold. Hearing her on the line, and bearing in mind Malcolm's recent edginess, Caroline's heart began thudding. Was this bad news concerning his progress, or lack of it?

Anne soon reassured her. "Nothing like that, Caroline. I was just wondering if you could see your way to coming along with Malcolm to some of our rail link meetings. We could use your PR expertise, you know . . ."

"Really? Are you sure?"

"I've just been re-reading the report of an action group whose leaders delivered a petition to Downing Street in July. Somehow, we never learned what was going on or our lot would have participated. We can't afford to have our village interests overlooked."

"And you want me to help ensure that they aren't?"

"Would you mind? I thought if you attended with Malcolm for a meeting or two, at least, you'd get the feel of things. Could come up with some ideas . . ."

Later that morning Caroline went over to the office, and told Malcolm Anne's suggestion. His reaction was difficult to fathom. He looked pensive initially, then a slight smile appeared and he nodded.

"Why not?" he said briskly. "You're supposed to know all the best ways of putting something across, aren't you?"

Malcolm left her standing in the office while he strode off towards the cold store. As Caroline hadn't yet finalised the details of their meals, she returned to the kitchen and Florence Dacre. She didn't see Malcolm hurrying back to the office as soon as she reached the house.

He needed to be alone, to be unobserved while he digested this news. A part of him was thankful that Anne wasn't keeping him out of her life by excluding him from their protest group, the other half was perplexed by the prospect of having Caroline present whenever he and Anne were together.

He might have known Anne would hedge herself around with some means of protection. Couldn't she understand, though, that what he needed was to have her company, undiluted? Had she never seen how he relaxed while able to confide in her, while sharing their philosophy about life?

Despite all misgivings, Malcolm was determined to be agreeable when he and Caroline set out for that meeting. They were using the Jaguar, and even the fact that she was driving must not be allowed to irk him. He would concentrate on the fact that he was still to see Anne, no matter how many other people would be present.

The gathering was small compared with many that he'd attended – designed as a preliminary sorting of priorities. The Mayor of Ashford was proposing to launch a Rail Charter for the County of Kent. The aim was to attract a thousand influential local people as signatories.

Sitting beside him, Caroline could hardly fail to notice Malcolm scanning those present for a glimpse of Anne Newbold. She herself had already observed that their doctor was not among the familiar faces who had greeted them with a nod or a smile. Wryly, she noted that her husband was not alone in eagerly awaiting Anne's arrival: their village postmaster, who was in the chair, repeatedly glanced at his watch before eventually announcing that they should give Dr Newbold a few more minutes.

While everyone waited for the meeting proper to begin, a good deal of amusement arose out of the misfortunes surrounding the Channel Tunnel and its proposed rail link. No one had forgotten how the first train through the tunnel had actually arrived late. Another fairly recent crisis was the resignation of Dr John Prideaux, Chairman of Union Railways – the company planning the railway link. Someone remarked that perhaps these problems augured well for the success of their own intentions!

Anne hastened in minutes afterwards, apologising for being late and explaining that her evening surgery had been particularly heavy. Caroline sensed immediately that, along with Anne, a certain dynamism entered the hall. As discussion progressed on the major points to be put forward, it was Anne who offered the strongest arguments and she, rather than the chairman, who seemed to encourage others to speak up for their particular concerns.

Several times, Malcolm expressed anxieties peculiar to those who farmed the area in addition to possessing homes whose quality of living would be affected. Caroline noticed he spoke strongly, making all points succinctly.

She was already feeling that her own presence wasn't required. These people, who had managed well enough without her during the preceding months, would more than adequately convey their viewpoint until some agreement was reached over every aspect of the rail link construction.

Towards the end of the meeting the highly organised minutes secretary gave her résumé of matters scheduled to be tackled. Yet again Caroline, who hadn't been invited to express a single thought, reflected that she couldn't feel more superfluous. I shall tell Anne what I think, and that I shan't come along with Malcolm again unless or until they give me a specific task.

She did not say anything of the kind. Anne made that impossible, appearing with their chairman, to say how pleased they all were that Caroline was offering her expertise. To remind anyone that no one had called on her to contribute would have been churlish.

When they arrived home the answerphone had recorded Lucy's message, pressing Caroline to give another talk about low-cholesterol eating. Several members of their residents' association regularly went along to a nearby senior citizens group, and were sure that any information she might offer would be welcomed there.

"It would be more important for them perhaps," Lucy persisted when Caroline called her. "Some of the people in our flats are, as you saw, quite active. These poor dears, on the other hand, are at an age when reminders of how sensible eating can help may actually prove life-saving."

Caroline again protested that someone qualified would be more suitable, but Lucy was insisting that this was another group which would be more inclined to listen to an ordinary woman speaking from experience.

"They don't want a lot of technical know-how, do they, nor the sort of jargon that comes from years of training."

Caroline did need to feel that she was doing a bit of good somewhere, especially following her wasted attendance at the rail link meeting. And now that she had coped with one talk of this nature, a second would seem far easier, and good cause for re-using the information she had collated.

She would also use the visit to check that Lucy was quite well – not that Lucy seemed other than very fit, especially with organising another gathering in prospect. Caroline was noticing that her mother flourished when given something fresh to tackle.

Discussing dates, Caroline unashamedly chose an evening when she knew that Malcolm had a meeting.

She was surprised when Anne telephoned to say she was sorry that Caroline couldn't attend with Malcolm. What sounded like

Anne's disappointment left her itching to say that she'd chosen somewhere where she would be useful instead.

But saying that would be childish, Caroline thought. Content to let matters ride so long as she *was* going elsewhere, she merely said, "Some other time perhaps."

Lucy's friend Vinnie was one of the members of the club which Caroline was addressing. The three of them arrived early in the Jaguar and Lucy was steering Vinnie's chair into the hall as the audience began trickling through the doors.

Caroline saw the Admiral among them and wondered if he might be in charge here too, but an indomitable Scottish lady was quickly introduced as "Chairperson". She proved herself assertive once the last members of the audience had settled into their seats, and soon had Caroline marvelling at her unhesitating manner. She tackled announcements and, eventually, introduction of their speaker without recourse to even one note.

That puts me on my mettle to deliver this lot with equal assurance, thought Caroline, rising to begin.

The people present today seemed less attentive than those at the flats, causing her to harness all her old PR skills to allay any restlessness and hold their concentration. Altering the order slightly, she quickly referred to Malcolm's attack, inviting them to consider how good it would be if people were able to reduce the risk of similar threats to life simply through paying attention to what they ate.

She had sensed correctly that more than one of those present had suffered the scare of a heart attack or stroke, a glance towards the rows of seats revealed heads nodding their understanding. Murmured agreement rose towards her.

Encouraged, Caroline launched in with how she had begun reorganising the family's diet, telling frankly of feeling resentful of implications that she had not known how to keep her husband healthy. This made everyone laugh, and she recognised that she was winning their approval.

From there, the talk went much as the earlier one had done, leaving her feeling that perhaps she'd accomplished something, despite the short attention span of some of those present. The numbers who came up afterwards to ask for more detail, or to compliment her seemed to confirm that she could feel satisfied.

Caroline drove Lucy and her friend away from the meeting and was unfolding Vinnie's wheelchair on the pavement when she saw Paul approaching.

"Where's Captain tonight?" she asked with a smile after he greeted them.

Paul sighed, his eyes darkening. "You've not heard then? I had to leave him with friends. Our luck ran out, we were spotted one day going back into the flats."

"Oh, no." Caroline immediately felt saddened. How Paul must be missing Captain's company.

"Suppose it was my own fault for ever attempting to conceal his existence there, but . . ."

"But you'd always have been alone without him."

"It certainly isn't much fun."

Vinnie hadn't met Paul previously and was introduced, then immediately invited him in for supper. "I'm not letting Caroline drive off without something, and it sounds as though you have no one waiting at home for you."

As soon as the door was unlocked, Scamp appeared, bouncing around his mistress's wheelchair until Lucy scolded him for impeding them.

"If you don't calm down, Scamp, none of us will get into the house ever!"

It was then that the Yorkie recognised Paul and flung himself at him. Laughing as he picked up the dog, Paul accepted an energetic licking of his face. He carried Scamp indoors.

"Maybe I should have had a little dog like you," Paul said ruefully to him. "You'd be easier to hide."

"That he wouldn't!" Vinnie exclaimed, gesturing to them all to sit. "Have you never heard a Yorkie yapping?"

Vinnie had already prepared supper and asked Lucy to wheel in the laden trolley while she filled the kettle.

"Anything I can do?" Caroline enquired.

"Indeed not," came the response. "You've done your share for the evening, delivering that talk."

Paul was smiling towards her as he fondled the dog who had settled on his shoes.

"Another one on that diet of yours?"

"Yes. Only it isn't really *my* diet, is it?"

"From what I heard before, you have made it yours – adapting the restrictions to a whole range of menus."

Caroline smiled back. "You make it sound much more agreeable than my husband seems to find it!"

"I just wish I was the lucky person to have you catering for me."

His words were light enough, but from what she knew of his background Caroline was aware that Paul must long to have someone at home when he returned each day. She met his glance, and found her own gaze held by the intensity of his blue eyes. Unbidden, pulses were awakening deep inside her and even along the surface of her skin, a restless urgency difficult to withstand.

I can't sit still, she thought wildly. *Cannot endure this surge that feels like new life beginning.* And yet how could she do other than sit? She would never explain to Vinnie or her mother, if this inner ferment obliged her to spring up from her chair.

Supper provided a diversion and – Caroline hoped – at least directed some attention away from herself. Paul tackled the food with relish, making her wonder if he could be neglecting himself, until she reflected silently that his well-being was hardly her concern.

When supper was finished Caroline didn't know how to leave, did not wish to. Anchored by Scamp's adoration, Paul appeared content to linger. She thought of home, of Malcolm returned by now from the meeting, of Christopher. She saw so little of her stepson now that he was working for Julian.

Thinking of Chris resurrected an awkward memory – his annoyance on that one occasion when she'd been home later than he expected after a visit to Folkestone. Tonight she would be later still. And this time Malcolm was at home.

"Does Scamp need exercise, Vinnie?" Her own voice surprised her, contradicting as it did the conscience bidding her leave. "If I take him now, you and Mother can have a nice chat."

Paul rose with her, took the leash from Vinnie while Caroline was thanking her for supper.

She missed Captain as they strode towards The Leas, but was glad that Paul seemed enchanted with Scamp, now trotting busily along. The autumnal night had darkened overhead and out to sea, conjuring a breeze that chilled her body still fevered with excitement. He saw her shiver and she felt his arm, tentative at first about her shoulders, then drawing her against his side.

Paul was warm and smelled of shower soap, his shirt seemed garden-fresh like newly dried laundry. He told her of the pub where he had lingered in solitude, surrounded by tables occupied by couples, laughing and chattering while they relished drinking outdoors. His mouth tasted of beer when he paused to kiss her.

"I contrived seeing you tonight," Paul admitted. "Lucy mentioned you'd be over here."

It was the worst thing he could have said. Caroline drew away from him. Trying to be firm without being unkind, she turned and began walking back towards Vinnie's home. Beyond that another home was waiting. Her own.

"Take the dog in for me, will you," Paul said tersely. "I'd hate to embarrass anyone else tonight."

Ten

T heir local action group had been cheered that night by news that some mid-Kent MPs were joining them to protest about the continuing uncertainty regarding the route of the rail link. The Ashford Mayor's Rail Charter appeared to be publicising all the dissatisfaction felt throughout the county. Malcolm and Anne both seemed quite elated as they went out to her car.

"Pity Caroline couldn't make it," she remarked.

Malcolm thought she was implying that she'd hoped to see Caroline there.

"Over in Folkestone, something her mother arranged." He felt sure Anne had known not to expect her, but perhaps he should play along.

"Sorry it clashed. We ought to use her, you know."

"As a chaperone?" His tone was sharp. This game wasn't really amusing.

"As someone skilled in PR."

"Was that why you asked her in the first place, though?"

"To help present our campaign, yes."

"I'm not a child, Anne."

"Then you'll understand," she said steadily, starting up the engine.

They had almost reached the village when she asked how he was. "Really, I mean."

"OK. Still losing a bit of weight, keeping to your wretched diet."

"That wasn't what I meant."

Malcolm sighed. How swiftly that elation had subsided. "Perhaps I should make an appointment at your surgery, maybe you'll listen there . . ."

"I'll listen now. It isn't talking that's wrong, it never was."

"But the mood has gone, the mood where we *could* talk."

"I don't believe it has. It's taken a bit of a shaking, that's all."

"I'll not easily forget that."

"Nor will I," Anne admitted ruefully. "Don't know how I could have been so – so lacking in sense."

"Oh, I do," Malcolm asserted. "It's because we're good together, two halves . . ."

"No, Malcolm."

The house was in darkness. He had known Christopher would be late, but had expected Caroline home before him. He couldn't help being glad that she was not.

"Come in for a drink . . ."

"No, thanks."

"Only for a drink. It won't matter if—"

"If the others walk in on us. *I* know that, because I mean to ensure it. Even so, I'm tired, love, and I've a letter to write when I get home. A difficult letter, concerning a complaint someone's made."

"About you?"

Anne laughed, he sounded so incredulous. "No one's infallible."

"And you're not just making excuses?"

"Not just that, no." *But we do need time now*, she thought: *to recover our wits and adjust our outlook.*

"I only need to talk."

"Come to surgery then. Your suggestion. You know I never tell patients I'm pressed for time."

Crossing the empty hall it seemed larger than ever, cold. Malcolm strode through and along to the kitchen. He would make himself a sandwich, their evening meal had been hours ago. No one should be expected to sleep when they felt so ravenous.

In the refrigerator he found a chunk of cheese, the Red Leicester of which he'd been particularly fond until forbidden dairy produce. These days he was obliged to watch Christopher relish cheeses. Well, they hadn't deprived him of initiative along with everything else! Before beginning to slice into the cheese, he broke off one corner, popped it into his mouth.

Slowly, Malcolm chewed, savouring its taste as a chocoholic

might savour chocolate. The fridge door still was open, he began looking for the low calorie spread that masqueraded as butter. Through its semi-transparent box he saw the piece of leftover beef. Just thinking about its succulent flavour, he salivated, reached for the container.

Malcolm began humming to himself as he carved from the beef. The first slice was smaller than the rest, he rolled it neatly, placed it in his mouth, and licked his fingers. He was by now accustomed to the fatless roasting advocated by his wife, relished the flavour of garlic and a lingering hint of the wine in which the meat was cooked.

He could hardly wait to tackle his sandwich. First, though, he must cut some bread. The granary loaf seemed to be resisting the knife when he started sawing away. The first two pieces were quite thin, not quite the substantial slices he had visualised. He hacked off two more, gave all four a coating of the spread.

He didn't rate those first two pieces good enough for his beef, stuffed them with cheese instead. He would eat those now, leave that superb meat as his final treat.

Caroline came in while Malcolm's mouth was full. On her way through she'd called "You all right, darling?" She wasn't accustomed to finding him in the kitchen. When she was near enough to see, she couldn't restrain an exasperated groan. Before him on the table was the remaining half of the cheese sandwiches, together with the beef.

"Cheese? *And* you're into that beef! You heard me say we were having that tomorrow with salad."

"There's plenty left . . ."

"No, there isn't. But that's not the point, is it? Well, is it? I don't go to all this trouble planning all our meals around the things you're supposed to avoid just for the fun of it."

Malcolm swallowed down a mouthful. "Thought that's what you did enjoy – you seem to be in your element telling all and sundry what you're doing."

"No, I'm not. Anyway, if I was glad to talk to other people that was only because they have enough sense to realise that filling yourself to the brim with high-cholesterol foods will do you no good."

"God, but you do sound self-righteous! Don't know how they can stand your lecturing."

"I don't lecture, all I do is—" Her voice trailed off, she swung around and strode away from him. If she remained there they would only continue until they became inextricably enmeshed in a thorough slanging-match.

Left to himself again, Malcolm found his appetite had waned. But he didn't mean to have Caroline deprive him of that beef. Although it took him several minutes he ate every last sliver of juicy meat.

It seemed almost like the need to make confession, yet Malcolm – who years ago had abandoned his solid C of E upbringing – would never have used that simile aloud. Ridiculously, that overindulgence was weighing on his mind. He felt compelled to explain how goaded he'd been.

He went over to Anne's in good time for evening surgery the following day. When his turn came he couldn't avoid noticing the swift raising of brown eyebrows which accompanied her gesture towards a chair.

"Something wrong?" she enquired. *A little tersely*, he thought, as if not quite trusting him to keep to permissible matters.

"I know, I know," he said hastily. "It was only last night we met. It's just – suddenly, I seem incapable of doing any one thing right."

Her expression showed concern, but did he detect beyond that a considerable effort to be patient?

"Look – Malcolm, I didn't really mean that we should settle here to discuss – well, certain difficulties."

"I know that. It's not the reason I'm here. At least – well, I suppose if I wasn't making such a mess of all that, I might have been less inclined to go off the rails."

"Go off the rails? What's this? You'd better tell me, hadn't you?"

At last, Malcolm grinned. "It isn't really so terrible. Or only to Caro because she sees herself as custodian of my alimentary system. Had a bit of a binge when I got in last night, couple of sandwiches. Beef, and you know how that's rationed where I'm concerned. And cheese."

Anne's hazel eyes lit, she laughed. "Is this the first time that you've slipped so wickedly?"

Malcolm nodded. "I'm rarely granted the opportunity!"

"I'm sure that even if Caroline hasn't quite forgiven you, you might begin to forgive yourself. Restrictions are tough, and their being for your health's sake doesn't render them any less irksome."

"So you don't really think it matters?"

"Only if you don't have the sense to keep such indulgences to a minimum. Perhaps you ought to remember, though, that digestion does take more physical effort than we're ever conscious of. We don't want you putting too much of a strain on that heart."

Suspecting that she believed he'd wasted her time, Malcolm thanked Anne and left Birch Tree House. He must make his peace with Caroline, then try and dismiss the entire, rather silly, business.

Later that night Anne was trying to dismiss what Malcolm had told her. Initial amusement had turned to concern as soon as surgery was ended and she was free to reflect on the implications of what Malcolm had done. She was well aware of the clinical reasons for overindulging in food; among them – all too frequently – was the aching for comfort when other physical satisfaction was denied.

So long as this is a one-off and Malcolm doesn't keep gorging, no harm should be done, she assured herself. Yet she continued to dwell on what was, after all, a quite minor event. Why did she suppose that she was the person to blame?

I shouldn't have let this situation develop, she admitted to herself again, daunted by feeling doomed because of creating these forbidden yearnings. And not only in Malcolm.

Anne felt weighed down by the whole wretched business. It was becoming a disproportionately large preoccupation. She needed time to herself in order to think, restore some balance, resurrect her sense of humour.

She hadn't taken a holiday all year, realised suddenly how much she wanted to get away.

Next morning Anne telephoned through to book accommodation in Harrogate. Finding a locum to stand in during the week she would be absent hadn't proved difficult, and she believed she had everything well organised.

The problem arose on the day she was setting out. Her car wouldn't start, and when she rang the garage they reminded her that the car was due for its MOT. She realised then that a major service was also long overdue.

"I'd leave it with you if I could only start the thing," she told them. "It won't hurt to go by train."

In fact, not having to drive would suit her, leave her free for all that thinking.

The garage valued her custom and spared a mechanic to get the car started and deliver her to the station in Ashford. He left her with assurances that the car would be ready on her return.

Thrusting her case aboard the London train, Anne realised how thankful she would be to just let go and unwind. Any country doctor relied so heavily on their vehicle that its failing to start always aroused tension. Only now was her ready acceptance of this alternative method of transport removing today's initial anxiety.

Stowing her luggage and removing her coat, she willed herself to begin that holiday here and now. She might need to do some serious thinking, but must first clear her mind by forgetting everything beyond the present moment.

A man seated opposite to her looked vaguely familiar. Anne didn't believe he lived locally, she hadn't noticed him on the station at Ashford. He seemed settled in his seat, she could believe he'd been in the carriage all the way from the coast. Mentally, she shrugged, glad to dismiss the possibility that she could know him.

At Charing Cross the man helped with her suitcase, Anne thanked him, naturally, before hurrying out to find a taxi. When he was the person beside her in the queue, it would have been churlish to reject his suggestion that it might be useful if they could share a cab.

"Are you aiming for another station too?" he enquired.

"King's Cross, actually."

"So am I."

Refusing to share with him now would have been against her native Yorkshire thrift. More sure than ever that he looked familiar,

Anne concluded that he must be from another local action group. When they were seated in the cab, she decided to satisfy her curiosity.

"Forgive me if I'm wrong, but I feel as though I know you from somewhere." It might sound like a line, but she trusted that there was enough about her appearance to assure anyone that she wasn't attempting to pick him up!

The man laughed, amiably. "I get around quite a bit, putting the case for my work, I guess."

"You're not in medicine as well?" She began to wonder if they had met professionally.

He laughed again. "Hardly."

"So you're not one of the many people from all that time in medical school, or during more years than I care to admit as a GP."

Instead of enlightening her, he posed a couple of questions. "In Kent somewhere? Or is it that *your* holiday here is all but over?"

"Your first guess was right. It is Kent where I settled after I'd done some of my training in the south. And you . . .?"

"I'm living in Folkestone at present, just off home for a break."

"Same here, or to my home county at least. All at once I'd had enough."

"You're on your own then, not married?"

He sounded surprised that she was single. Strangely, Anne felt pleased.

"No, I – it's a demanding life. Few men who aren't doctors themselves really understand the hours. It'd have had to have been someone with an enormous tolerance factor. What about you?"

She had noticed he wore a ring, but how significant was that?

"No, I'm not married now. There is someone – *special*, though . . ."

He hadn't known how much he wanted to tell somebody. Every time that he saw Caroline he recognised how important she'd become to him. Yet he could hardly forgive his own impulsiveness which had trapped him in a situation that seemed so hopeless.

When they discovered they were catching the same train north, he helped Anne with her case again, and seemed to take it for granted that they should travel together.

Anne concealed her private amusement; perhaps here was the distraction that she needed.

He noticed that she appeared willing to listen, was glad to continue to confide.

"My wife died tragically, making me feel that there'd never be anyone else. That I didn't want there to be. Then I met this amazing woman who is just about my ideal . . ."

"That's nice," said Anne.

"It would be, if she weren't married," the man added swiftly. "She's not the kind to contemplate an affair either, any more than I am really."

Anne smiled. "These days, it's always good to hear that some people still draw the line somewhere, so many don't."

"To make the situation even more impossible, her husband needs her more than ever now. Had a heart attack a short while after Caroline and I met in May. Poor chap was having a rough time of it, anyway. He's a fruit farmer, no longer doing so well as he was, I gather he was even obliged to stop employing his son."

Anne swallowed down a gasp. Already thinking it was a coincidence to be learning of another Caroline whose husband suffered a recent heart attack, she was really shaken now. What were the odds against hearing this about the couple she knew so well? One of whom she'd come close to loving.

"I couldn't do anything that might break them up," Paul went on. "Even if she would contemplate it."

"It wouldn't be right, would it?" said Anne quickly.

But her eager imagination was working on a whole new series of possibilities. She already liked this man who introduced himself as Paul Saunders. She could believe he might be good for Caroline. Malcolm was no longer entirely happy about his marriage. If he should ever be on his own again, he'd need a good friend, someone to rely on. Anne knew where he would turn.

"I keep telling myself to forget her. That is proving anything but easy. *Knowing* that Caroline feels better for our meetings makes it so difficult to deny us both."

Then why do so? Anne yearned to suggest. *Take her, leave Malcolm free to . . .* Ruefully, she shook her head. It wouldn't do, would it? She withdrew swiftly, beyond the professional façade that she'd believed was left behind in her surgery.

Paul had been watching the guardedness in her eyes. "Sorry – I must be boring you to sobs. Didn't mean to. I should never have expected you to understand."

"Oh, I understand," she assured him. "Just don't ask me to advise."

He grinned. "Not sure I want advice. I'm on my own too much, that's all. Even my dog had to move out. On my way to see him now."

Paul went on to relate how the secret of Captain's presence in the flats had come out, resulting in the dog's lodging with friends. "My own fault in the first place for trying to keep him there. But after my wife died he wouldn't settle, poor thing."

Anne frowned. Hadn't he mentioned that his wife's death had been tragic? She didn't mean to question him, concentrated instead on talking about the dog. "And what breed is Captain?"

"German Shepherd. His sheer size means I can't fail to miss him about the place."

"But you'd miss him anyway, even if he were a tiny terrier."

Like the Yorkie Caroline was walking that first day. Why did everything lead back to her? Was he simply obsessed? Or was such a firm bond developing that he was meant to think of her everlastingly – to make her a part of his future?

"How long have you lived in Kent, did you say?" Anne enquired, determined to keep him off the subject of Caroline Parker. For her own peace of mind more than his!

Paul told her about his work and the possibility of remaining in Kent after the lines under the Channel were completed. "I'm a bit of a specialist on tunnelling, and may be required – if only to keep tunnels for the rail link to a minimum."

Anne's eyebrows soared. "Oh, dear! I'm afraid I'm busy opposing the route of that rail line – or at least, in any of the forms offered to date."

He grinned. "You're not alone in that, I'm sure. And my interest is only in giving a civil engineer's assessment of the various options. I do understand the need to minimise local disturbance, just as much as comprehend the urge to keep down costings."

He paused for a while then smiled. "You didn't say exactly where you live – is it in Ashford?"

"Not far from there." She'd no intention of revealing details. This chance meeting was providing more than enough to stimulate the imagination. And *emotions*, most of all her emotions.

That's if the meeting was pure chance, a part of her insisted – in her more fanciful days she might have believed the encounter was meant to happen. As a trigger for reflections on Caroline Parker's loyalty to Malcolm. Or lack of loyalty?

By the time she eventually left the train Anne was feeling more stressed than when she was first setting out for Yorkshire. Paul had departed at the previous station, with the suggestion that they might travel back together in a week's time.

She had evaded that idea. "Not certain I'll manage a full week. Depends how my locum copes." She made a mental note to leave a day early, just in case.

Her feelings in turmoil, Anne took herself off for a walk as soon as she had booked into her Harrogate hotel. The hotel a little way out of the town, she took a lengthy stroll before she reached the Valley Gardens, her intended destination. By the time she was wandering along paths and pausing to admire the final blooms of a very late flush of roses, she was quite exhausted. And despite the November sun, this northern air felt bitingly cold.

I'm a bit of a fool, she admitted silently to herself, and hoped that the conclusion *had* been silent! Tired like this, and still agitated, she wasn't at all certain that she was fully in control. And despite her emotions, she was extremely hungry.

At least she wasn't obliged to return to her hotel for a meal. When arranging somewhere to stay she'd believed she would have the car, and had decided not to tie herself down to dining in every evening.

Thankful for the freedom to eat at the nearest likely looking place, Anne crossed towards a smart, if unpretentious hotel.

The dining room was busy, three-quarters full and many of the people present seemed, like herself, to be taking a late holiday. A table for one in a corner near the window suited her admirably, providing a view of passers-by to distract her from feeling awkward about sitting on her own.

The conversation with Paul Saunders had generated too much fuel for that wretched imagination, which was refusing to be suppressed. No matter how well accustomed Anne was to being out on her own, today she seemed unable to cease picturing how it might feel to have a companion, one certain companion. By the time she had eaten and decided to hail a cab for the hotel where she was staying, Anne resolved that she must take a firmer grip on herself. She would use these few days to will herself to accept that she could not entertain such fantasies.

The walking helped, long and hard over once-familiar moors and dales which she reached by bus or train, journeys where she revelled in reacquainting herself with her native dialect. Using public transport reminded her of the friendliness of Yorkshire folk – a factor which she hadn't consciously missed, though only perhaps because her work always brought contact with so many people.

Gradually, Anne noticed that, striding over rough moorland or lingering in picturesque hamlets, she was feeling less perturbed. As exhaustion drifted away on stiff breezes or began to evaporate while she absorbed the splendour of some half-forgotten landscape, she felt renewed, recognised that she was being strengthened to face the real world to which she would soon return. The world where she would never endanger either her own career or anyone else's marriage for the sake of indulging dreams.

Anne spent her last day in Yorkshire in the gardens at Harlow Carr. Although she never had sufficient time for much serious gardening, she was interested in improving the plot surrounding Birch Tree House, and had heard a great deal about this place.

Fortified by the coffee which she bought before going round the gardens, she paused on the terrace to gaze out over the pleasing contours. She had expected the experimental beds filled with trials of this plant or the other, but hadn't anticipated that the grounds as a whole would have been designed quite so elegantly. Even today, while autumn hovered towards winter, there was plenty to take the eye. And perhaps more scope for noticing plants which could provide brightness after summer's colours had waned.

I'm going to enjoy this, Anne resolved and, as the day progressed, was surprised how total her enjoyment became. When she returned to her hotel late that afternoon it was with a notebook crammed with ideas for improving her own half-acre. And a mind quiet at last in the knowledge that her life could still hold fresh interests.

Keith Goodrich, the doctor who had stood in for Anne, was surprised to see her a day early, but quite happy to accommodate her suggestion that he stay around for the period arranged.

"That way I should have a chance to go through your notes with you," she told him. "Be sure that I'm *au fait* with what's happened." And that would be a luxury. Normally there was little enough time for catching up on events before a locum was obliged to depart.

"There hasn't been much in the way of crises," he assured her. "But there has been one sad event, I'm afraid. I have the details here somewhere, kept the records out to show you. Parker, the name was—"

Anne shuddered. "Not – not Malcolm Parker?" she demanded, her head already reeling dizzily while blood pumped in her ears. *God, don't let it be Malcolm . . .*

"That might have been the name. The family are farmers, fruit."

She gasped, swallowed, tried to speak and had to clear her throat. "Or was it Isabel Parker?" she asked, desperate that it should be someone other than Malcolm. Where was the sense in anything when she had gone away to think things through, to resolve to sacrifice whatever she herself felt. For *his* sake.

And then Anne remembered. Neither Isabel nor Graham Parker were patients of hers. It couldn't be that part of the family.

"Ah – here it is." Dr Goodrich drew the record card, with his own notes, out of the buff envelope. "Oh, yes. I remember. It was the infant who was to be called Malcolm. The son's fiancée was staying there. Such a lovely house, The Sylvan Barn. Her own parents were away from home when she went into premature labour."

"You mean – you mean it wasn't Malcolm himself at all? It was just – whatever they call Nick's fiancée who—"

"Went into premature labour. Didn't I say? The baby isn't likely to be viable – although we judged him to be something like thirty-four weeks, he's pitifully small. But that's not the only problem."

"Go on . . ." Anne prompted him.

"Don't know up-to-date details, I'm afraid. Mother and child were rushed to hospital, of course. The paediatrician confirmed that I was right to suspect there was some kind of internal trouble with the child. I've not heard whether they've carried out the intended exploratory operation yet."

"But we can do so much more these days," Anne began.

"Where the infant is otherwise strong, yes. I'm not at all happy that that would be the case in this instance."

"You're afraid there could be even more complications?"

"I certainly don't hold out much hope."

"I've got to go over and see them," Anne decided, and was thankful she now had the car back from the garage.

Caroline opened the door of The Sylvan Barn to Anne, shadowed eyes and a wan complexion evidence of the family stress.

"I've just got back from that short break," Anne told her. "Had to come over as soon as I heard."

"Come in, I'm glad you have. It's all been so dreadful – most of all, because of the feeling of helplessness."

"Is – is the baby still alive?"

"Being kept alive. Did your locum explain the consultant decided to operate?"

Anne nodded.

"It was worse even than they'd feared. Poor mite had a massive obstruction of the large intestine. I understand they did what they could to correct that. Then they discovered various other internal irregularities. You'd know what the implications are, I'm afraid all we took in was that he is unlikely to survive."

"How dreadful. How's Bianca coping, and Nicholas?"

"Trying hard to be brave, but she was in no condition for a shock like this. The birth took her totally by surprise – not unnaturally, the poor girl went into a bit of a panic." Caroline paused, glanced at her watch. "Look – I'm sorry, can I offer you tea or coffee or something? I'm not thinking straight, was just rushing back to the hospital. Along with Bianca's parents we're trying to ensure that she and Nick aren't left on their own there. Her mother and father run a business, so I'm doing a lot of covering . . ."

"I'll come with you," said Anne. "Got to see them today. Easiest for organising things, as well, my locum's still at the surgery."

They went in Anne's car and as soon as they were on the road Caroline began describing the dreadful day when it had all begun.

"We were so happy. For a long time now Malcolm has seemed very much better, and he's been getting on so well with the boys again. Even with Chris, and as you can imagine that hasn't always been easy of late. We'd had a nice meal, and Nick and Bianca insisted on clearing away afterwards. Suddenly, there was this sort of wail from the kitchen. Bianca dashed out of there, and headed straight for the cloakroom.

"I ran to see what was wrong. I'll never forget how the poor child looked. Doubled-over with pain, and blood everywhere already. Dr Goodrich arrived almost immediately, but the baby was there before him. I was upset because we hadn't been able to get Bianca to a bed. She gave birth in all that mess on the cloakroom floor.

"At first, I blamed that, blamed *us* for not looking after the poor girl better. Afterwards, the hospital said that'd made no difference, but you still wonder . . ."

"I'm sure you needn't," Anne consoled her. "From what Keith Goodrich told me, nothing during the actual birth could have affected his condition."

"I hope you're right. There's enough to cope with, without feeling we're to blame."

"I gather that the hospital people are giving a gloomy prognosis."

"Couldn't be worse. They had a talk with Bianca and Nick this morning, to prepare them. There isn't a scrap of hope. Rightly or wrongly, the paediatrician is requesting that they consider giving their consent to organ donation."

"Oh dear, as bad as that."

Caroline sighed. "Dreadful, isn't it? I can see that the two of them can barely bring themselves to contemplate losing him."

"And it is only the machinery that's keeping him going?"

"Oh, yes. That was explained after he was brought back from theatre."

"Seems cruel, I know, when parents have to be told that so soon. But it's often far worse for them in the long run if they're allowed to build up false hopes."

"A blow like this makes you believe all your hopes have been false, that you were wrong to begin making plans again. This has hit Malcolm hard, you know. He'd just started really looking forward to having a grandchild. It seemed to me that he needed that feeling of continuity, something to cling to."

I want to hold him, though Anne miserably. *I need to talk this through with him. I need to be the one who helps him through this trauma.*

"We'll all have to be gentle with him for a while," she told Caroline. "Distress is harder for men, isn't it, they can't have a good bawl."

Anne recognised then that sobbing her heart out was what she most felt like doing. Weeping for all the Parker family. For her own inability to help them. To help *him*.

Driving the car between the bollards near the hospital entrance required a great effort of concentration. She recognised how debilitated she felt, not at all the doctor who was trained to help patients endure this kind of tragedy.

Her colleagues in the hospital would expect her to urge the young couple to make sure that their infant's organs should be used to help other babies. But he was Malcolm Parker, named for his grandfather, she could not leave her own emotions out of this. God, but how in this world were any of them going to feel up to making a decision?

Eleven

Caroline led the way to the ward where Bianca was seated beside her son's cot. The woman at its other side looked around forty, but a forty worn down by recent anxiety.

"This is our doctor Anne Newbold, Frances," Caroline began. "Anne – I'd like you to meet Bianca's mother Frances Lomax. You've met Bianca, haven't you?"

"Actually, I haven't. Hello, Bianca, Mrs Lomax . . ." said Anne. "No, please don't either of you get up."

Both Frances Lomax and the girl had half-risen, murmured hello, and flopped back on to the hard hospital chairs. As introductions went, these felt graceless and muddled. The doctor wished with all her heart that the situation didn't render such things immaterial.

"I am so sorry," she continued. "I just wish there was something I could suggest." She would never grow accustomed to bearing the insoluble with other people. Painful treatments, she could explain, and serious operations. In those circumstances she could try to make them appear not only necessary but acceptable. Today, she could see nothing acceptable in the reality surrounding them.

Caroline seemed equally at a loss and, understandably, drained already of compassionate words. Eventually, it was Frances who broke the oppressive silence.

"I suppose I'll get off home now you're back, Caroline. Adrian will come in this evening."

"So will Malcolm," Caroline assured them.

"Nick's somewhere around," Frances told them as she gathered together her belongings ready for leaving.

"Think you'll find him in the chapel," Bianca murmured. "Not that it'll do any good."

"I'll see if I can find him, have a word," said Anne, turning from the cot-side as Frances Lomax bent to kiss Bianca.

Anne was surprised when the woman caught her up in the corridor.

"It can't be pleasant for doctors when they know there's no hope," Frances said, surprising her again. "And I do understand there's no hope for Baby Malcolm. I just wish one of us could get through to either Bianca or Nick. They're not facing the truth, you know, not really."

"No. Well, maybe they've got to have more time. Though I'm sure you don't need me to tell you that no amount of time will make them find this anything but diabolically hard."

"Did – did Caroline mention the hospital people are asking for their consent to organ donation?"

Anne nodded gravely. "She said it had become that serious, yes."

"It's almost as though neither of them is listening. Yet Bianca's always been clever. And Nick is brighter still."

"They're both very young."

"Too young to bear this, that is for certain."

"I'll do all I can. Even though I'm afraid that might not amount to more than talking."

Nicholas was in the chapel, the only person in its quiet interior, looking all the more dejected for being alone. The building was modern, light, so many of its windows were plain, with only the one of stained glass, above the altar.

Red, gold and purple were beaming down in rays, transforming the drab grey of his knitted sweater. His head was bowed low over clenched hands, the long ponytail had slid sideways, revealing a nape of neck perturbingly vulnerable.

I'm no use here, thought Anne despairingly. And then – *he is Malcolm's son. I must not fail him.*

"Nick," she said quietly, sliding into the pew beside him, placing a hand on his shoulder. "I've left your moth – Caroline with Bianca. Do *you* need to talk?"

"Yes," he said at last, raising his head and sitting back on to the edge of the pew beside her. "And I can't say this to any of them. They're all too *involved*. They might think I'm not, that I'm being too – dispassionate. I'm not, anything but. Only you see, I've thought and thought, and the hospital people *are* right. There is no other way. If we don't consent to transplants, his whole little life will be wasted." He sighed. "Shall I ever be able to make Bianca understand how I feel?"

"You can only try. We could work on it here perhaps."

He is depending on me, Anne realised. And knew there could be no going back. If she were ever to dream of having Malcolm she would destroy more than his marriage, more than the relationship his sons have with him. With Caroline. They all belong together.

"I can't avoid considering how *I* would have felt, if someone could have come forward with something that might save our baby," Nick went on. "I'd have been so thankful, for the rest of my life."

Anne smiled slightly although her heart could not lift. This young man, whose anxious eyes reminded her of those of a child in trouble at school, had worked out far more than she had dared to imagine.

"We'll put that across to Bianca, somehow. We'll manage it," she assured him.

After returning to the ward with Nicholas, Anne looked into the cot, and realised that earlier she had been unable to bring herself to do so. Heaven knew, she'd had enough of a grounding in seeing people – even infants like this – connected up to the machinery that was the only means of keeping them alive. Today, was different. Until a few moments ago, she had been afraid of what she might see.

An early resemblance to Malcolm perhaps, some familiar feature that would tug at her already-aching soul? That likeness was there, in a miniature Parker chin, and surely that downy-soft hair was the exact brown of his . . .

"Nick thinks you should talk," she began tenderly, moving to stand behind Bianca and place gentle hands on her shoulders. "I think that's a good idea. There's a room along here, isn't there?"

"I'll fetch you immediately if there's any change," Caroline assured them when the girl shook her head, reluctant to leave.

The young couple wanted Anne with them. She wouldn't have refused, although she felt they needed to be alone to thrash out the horror of this situation.

All they wanted was a bridge, though, someone less daunting than the consultants, but who still could confirm their own interpretation of what they'd been told. Anne took a few moments to manage a quick word with one of the doctors, then went to the young couple.

Seated beside Bianca, her hand firmly clasped in his, Nicholas began, his voice a moving blend of sadness and the resolution of having decided.

"We can't keep him like this forever, darling. We both know that really, don't we? It wouldn't be right to condemn him to just lying there, attached to all those wires and tubes. Besides, we can't know for sure that he isn't hurting."

Any certainty he'd felt was waning already. Nick paused and looked to Anne.

She nodded. "Just – tell Bianca what you said to me minutes ago."

Nicholas inhaled slowly. "I've thought and thought, and I'm afraid the hospital people *are* right. There is no other way. If we don't consent to transplants, our – our baby's whole little life will be wasted."

"Nick! Don't you feel *anything*? How terribly hard this is?" Bianca's haunted eyes gleamed with tears.

Bianca had never felt more alone. For the first time in her life, she couldn't hope that even one other person understood. Nick wasn't with her any longer, he'd not be sounding so *rational* if he was experiencing this massive, massive pain.

"It's the worst thing that could've happened. But it's made me consider how *I* would feel, if someone were offering him even a faint hope of surviving. If they hadn't let their own distress make them – well, selfish, I guess."

Bianca choked on a sob, screeched at him: "It isn't selfish to need our only child to live." She wanted to shake Nick until he noticed, and shared, this anguish.

"I'm not saying it is. We're both yearning for a baby we can take home, Baby Malcolm but—" Nicholas was unable to say another word. He glanced despairingly towards the doctor.

Anne swallowed down the lump in her taut throat. "It must be the most difficult thing in the world right now for you both to even contemplate *not* having him there. For you to see, to hold, to care for. Sadly, everyone here seems terribly certain that he could never exist out of that ward. What's even worse, he might be kept alive for months, maybe even longer, without knowing who you are, without knowing anything."

"But *is* he in pain?" Bianca demanded. Still sore and exhausted from the birth, she couldn't let their infant's life slip away. Where was the point of it all? Where the point of anything now?

Anne experienced a fierce empathy for this need to be assured that keeping the baby alive wouldn't harm him. But she was obliged to be truthful. "I doubt if anyone can be sure. He has no means of letting us know, has he, love?"

"Because he can't get through to us. And we can't get through to him. That's what's so bloody frustrating." After all those months, their child was no longer a part of her.

"Not much of a life for him, is it? Darling?" Nick was asking.

"But I can't tell them to – just switch off, to flick his life off as if . . . as if . . ." Bianca gulped. Bearing this child didn't bestow the right to erase his existence. But inside her head Nick's words were forming a refrain: "Not much of a life for him. Not much of life for him. Not much of a life . . ."

"If we had to – if, I couldn't end it for him."

"You know you're the only ones who can decide. But you needn't have to make the next move," said Anne softly. "If – if you were, at some time, ready – I could tell them for you. There'd be forms – forms which only you could sign, but you needn't talk about it at length unless you wanted to."

Bianca was quieter now, worn down by distress, beginning to wonder why she was fighting Nick on this. No one had spared them the facts. None of these doctors could be blamed for her refusal to believe what was happening.

"You're saying we don't really have much of an alternative, aren't you? Had we – had we better get it over today?"

"Perhaps when your parents are all here, to be with you?" Anne suggested, still moved by how young this poor girl seemed.

"Actually, no." Bianca shook her head. "I'll only go all soft if they're here. Nick's right, and we've got to be – be grown-up about it. They will let us hold him, won't they? Before they – before—"

"Of course, my dear, of course. For as long as you both need."

"But it's got to be soon, today. Or I'll never agree."

Anne turned as Nick hugged Bianca. Tears were running down his face.

Caroline and Anne left them alone with the infant just for a while. They had stayed close by during the gruelling formalities which would abstract what little life remained in Baby Malcolm, and provide a more complete life for some other child.

"Poor kids," said Anne as they walked away to find the cup of tea that neither of them really wanted. "They've experienced so little of life themselves before they're faced with one of its most harrowing disasters."

"They're standing up to it well, though," Caroline remarked. "I wouldn't have thought either Nick or Bianca had it in them. Just shows how readily we underestimate those we love."

Anne nodded. "At least their youth allows plenty of time in which to conceive a whole string of babies. Did you hear anyone say they were telephoning Bianca's parents to tell them the decision?"

"Nick offered, but Bianca said not to. I suspect she's afraid they might fuss rather. Think she'd go to pieces if anyone were to overdo the concern, however loving."

The two women were drinking tea when Caroline stood up.

"I think I'll give the Lomaxes a call. Frances will be home by now, should have told him this morning's news. They ought to know what's happened since, if only to give them time to prepare themselves. Accepting the situation is bloody difficult for all of us."

Frances Lomax sounded relieved. Evidently she had half-expected that Nick and Bianca would reach this conclusion. She would have preferred to have said her own goodbyes to her infant grandson, but understood Bianca's need to avoid prolonging the whole wretched situation.

Somewhat easier in her mind after speaking with her, Caroline rang the farm.

"He's died, hasn't he?" said Malcolm, anticipating the worst as soon as he heard her strained voice.

171

"Not exactly, no. At least, I'm not really sure. Anne and I left them on their own with him. It was what they wanted. But they've had to decide about making his organs available for donation."

"Which amounts to the same thing," he said grimly. "Poor little blighter. And poor Bianca and Nick. What in the world can we do for them, Caro?"

"Don't know, love. Once it's – *over*, we'll just have to see. She'll most likely need to be with her own parents, I would have thought."

"Bring them home – bring them home to us, Caro. We'll look after them."

Rejoining Anne, Caroline asked how soon she believed the equipment sustaining the baby might be switched off. She was also wondering how long he would last after that.

"I've no idea, I'm afraid. Depends if they already have potential recipients in mind for the donor organs. If there are children somewhere waiting now, the surgeons could need to speed things up."

Ultimately, this proved to be the case. The young couple's farewell to their baby was not prolonged. Caroline suspected this could have been for the best. There was no way that any of them would ever feel the same after losing him, but they would all need to think about picking up some kind of normal life again.

Bianca surprised Caroline by wishing to come to The Sylvan Barn for a few days instead of going to her own mother. She gave no reason, but Caroline and Malcolm alike were pleased, and really felt rather better.

"It's your doing, of course," Malcolm told her one night in bed. "You're proving all over again what a compassionate woman you are."

One person who felt quite awkward about having his brother and Bianca there was Christopher. He had been to the hospital only the once, and had been appalled to see such a tiny person attached to so much equipment. When told that the baby would never get better he had sympathised with Nick as soon as he saw him. But finding the right words to commiserate exhausted itself there.

"I feel so dreadful about the whole wretched business," he

confided to Amanda, thankful to escape to the vineyard the following day. "There's so much I ought to be saying, so much that I feel,
but the words just won't come out."

"I'd have thought you always knew how to behave correctly,"
Amanda exclaimed. "You're so assured, not all horribly gauche like
me."

Chris grinned. "Well, now you know." And he *wanted* her to
know. These weeks since coming to work for her father had
generated an extraordinary kinship with Amanda. It did him no
harm to have her recognise that he experienced uncertainties. He
hoped that some sort of fellow-feeling could help her to accept some
of the many misgivings about herself.

"I want to do something to help," Amanda announced on the day
he explained that the baby's short life was over. "Send flowers, that
sort of thing. When's the funeral?"

Chris told her. "Only they just want flowers from closest family.
They're asking anyone else to donate to a fund for hospital equipment – paediatric stuff."

Amanda said nothing more. Chris was giving her a look, but she
still could not speak. She hated feeling like this, *excluded*. She
wanted to shout that she *was* family. Wasn't Caroline her mother,
her real mother! She knew how it would be, could picture it quite
plainly. This girl who was loved by Nick, was loved by Caroline as
well, would be hugged when she ached with grief. Would be kissed
each night before bed, as she herself had been kissed. In the time
long ago, which seemed now to have happened to some quite
different person.

Her mother always was kind, loving. No one needed to be
domesticated in order to *care*, to show that caring.

Amanda knew she hadn't responded well to being hugged, to
similar demonstrations of affection. And now she admitted the
reasons. Neither her mother nor her father had understood, no one
else had known that she'd recognised quite early on how imperma-
nent their home life felt. The temperament which inclined her
towards a creative career generated its own intense sensitivity. A
glance, a word spoken in haste, other words withheld – had so often
at that time demonstrated to her their family's fragility. When the

split came there had been no comfort whatsoever in being right. Only this emotionally freezing acceptance had enabled her to survive.

No one had ever been permitted to see how she *grieved* for the mother whom she so often had thought dead to her. Certainly, no one today would learn how she yearned for the arms which might ease this everlasting sense of loss.

"You could contribute something," Chris told her. "They'd be pleased, Amanda."

She shrugged. Even to Chris, she would not confide her idea. Scarcely ready for it yet, she was beginning to understand what she must do. Just in case she failed to muster her will to carry out this intention, she would keep it to herself.

The coffin was white, the smallest any of them had ever seen. On that blustery day with chilly rain darts stabbing their faces as they solemnly crossed the churchyard, Malcolm was dreadfully afraid he would blub.

Ahead of himself and Caroline now, flanked by Frances and Adrian Lomax, walked Bianca and his son. His heart surged with pride in them both. Nicholas was proving more sensible than Malcolm ever had hoped. Practical in making arrangements for this infinitely sad event, gentle yet firm in preventing Bianca from giving in completely.

He marvelled that the pair were already making plans, looking beyond this abysmal day – perhaps to avoid examining too closely all that it meant, certainly to witness that they did have a future.

Nick had told him last night: they were returning to Cambridge. Sooner than either family wished or thought wise, but Bianca's GP had given the OK. And the girl's tutor had insisted over the phone that she still had her university place.

This could be the solution for the pair, Malcolm supposed. Back in Cambridge, both would work, would fill their minds with matters other than the baby they had lost. Being compelled to think might spare them some degree of having to *feel*.

"All right, love?" Caroline's whisper at his side made him smile a little, nod. And reminded him how her presence throughout these blighted days had kept everyone going. Seeing today Frances Lomax's tendency to fuss (however well intentioned) had refreshed in him awareness of his own wife's fine judgement. Somehow, he knew not how, Caro encouraged people to renew their own purpose.

She has always done that, he acknowledged silently, minutes later when they slowly turned to leave his namesake, his first grandchild. Years ago the death of Sue, which once had felt like the end of Malcolm himself, had proved to him Caroline's worth. A strength which her slender person belied, and one which he surely must cease taking for granted.

In some ways, he supposed, her qualities were inherited. Lucy was with them, naturally, as so often when his family encountered trouble. Word of the decisions made regarding Baby Malcolm had brought Lucy homing in, arriving in a bit of a state after a difficult journey in fog-bound trains, but arriving nevertheless. An hour after her appearance at the house, she was her normal reassuring self, finding words for the bereaved couple when the rest of them were drained, torn apart by struggling to express or suppress emotions.

Throughout the trauma preceding the funeral, and on this day, Lucy remained a constant; empathising in full, yet sufficiently composed to become a prop for them all. She had taken Nick in hand, Malcolm had noticed, walking with him in the cold garden, letting him talk, leaving Bianca free to talk (or not) while she spent hours in the kitchen with Caroline.

Afterwards at The Sylvan Barn another grandmother caused Caroline several moments' anxiety. More subdued than normal and severely pale, Isabel looked ramrod straight as ever while she walked across the entrance hall to speak with the young couple.

"Do you think we ought to intervene?" Caroline asked Lucy who was beginning to help her take around refreshments.

Lucy shook her head. "You mustn't, Caro darling. Isabel's the senior member of the family, she has a right to say – well, her piece. And I don't suppose, today, that they *could* be made to feel much worse."

In fact, Caroline need not have worried. Isabel Parker might be opinionated, but those opinions were garnered through a long life's experiences. Grief was something all-too-frequently familiar to her.

"I've already told you how sorry I am, my dears," she began, her old eyes glistening with tears. "For once in my life, I wish I knew a few words of sure comfort. There are none really. That much I have learned."

"That's OK, Grandmother," said Nick.

"We – we're glad that you are with us today," Bianca added.

"But *I* need to be a bit of use, don't you see?" Isabel persisted. "To help, to be able to – to do something. To share. We're all hurting today, you know – not with the same intensity of you yourselves, I understand that. But all hurting. Once – sometimes it feels like a hundred years ago – but once I'd have tried to infect you with a little of my own faith. But that faith too, has grown shaky with the years, almost as shaky as I've grown myself."

"Gran, you're not," Nick protested.

A faint smile warmed her eyes. "You see only as much as you are meant to see, don't forget. Life deals cruel blows, as you already know, it toughens you up. Unless you're the kind to go under." Isabel sniffed, her old self briefly visible. "Never could quite bring myself to give in, you know. I reckon that faith – barely though I acknowledge its existence – is what's sustained me. If we were all that certain that there was someone, somewhere, sort of *holding* us, it wouldn't be called faith. Or belief. There aren't too many certainties around, are there?"

Isabel paused, reflecting, and then nodded as though deciding to say something further.

"When I was a girl, a committed church-goer, I was perturbed by our old vicar declaring that we're never given more blows than we're able to endure. Many's the time that I've disputed that claim from the depths of anguish. But I am still here, and freely admit surviving hasn't entirely been my own doing."

Isabel was turning away when she swung around and went back to them.

"Need I say, that was for your ears alone? Doesn't do to let my image slip too severely!"

*   *   *

Only when the bereaved couple had gone to their bed that night and the Lomaxes and the rest of the Parker family departed, had Lucy admitted how tired she was, and followed her daughter upstairs.

And now, much later, sitting with Chris, Malcolm was tempted to remind his son how fortunate they were, that they must do more to make Caroline feel appreciated. But before he said one word Chris had thoughts of his own, needed an ear while he expressed them.

"It's made me think, Dad, today. About – well, losing people. All those years ago when Mum died, I didn't understand."

"You were too young. And then there was Caroline, making everything easier."

Christopher interrupted. "I know, but listen *please* – this time's so unfair. The baby being so little, and that. Not knowing anything. Makes you wonder why. Unless – I couldn't say this to Nick, of course, but unless it was to provide whatever – whatever organs they needed to keep those other little ones alive. Only that's no real answer because you wonder why Nick and Bianca? They never deserved this. What did they do wrong?"

"Nothing. Not one thing. Christopher. You're learning life isn't fair. We get on with it. Best we can. And we're provided with help. I did learn that."

"Caroline? I said – I do know. She's always been a super mum. I'm sorry I don't really remember what life was like with my real mother, but—" He had said enough. He wouldn't tell his father that if he'd been able to choose he'd have chosen a mother like Caro. If he ever married, he hoped it'd be to someone as good.

"You'll always be all right, Christopher. I mean – well, should that scare I had earlier this year flare up again in earnest, the family will remain in good hands."

"Dad? You're not feeling off again, are you?"

The concern in his son's tone warmed Malcolm. Smiling, he shook his head. "Not in the least. Just – like you, made aware of the realities."

The reality of the following morning was hard to endure. Caroline could hardly bear to let Bianca and Nicholas leave. There seemed so much unsaid, so many ways of helping which had not even come to mind, so little that she had *done*. And both of them, bless them, appeared so valiant.

Thanking Malcolm and herself, Lucy as well, for being so supportive, they had rushed about loading up the little car, preparing to take up their independent lives once again.

And they're hardly more than children themselves, thought Caroline, hugging them in turn, aching with inexpressible love. If she might only hold them for ever more, not turn them away to get on with the healing process.

Through heavy rain that afternoon a car drove up, one which Caroline didn't recognise at all. For a moment she didn't recognise the driver either – a young woman in an expensive-looking trouser suit. Its shade was pale turquoise, the tailoring skilful; when the woman leaned into the back of the car the trousers still appeared faultless.

Carrying a huge bouquet of flowers, the woman looked towards the house. From the office window, Caroline finally recognised the face, ran through the deluge to greet her.

"Amanda! Darling, you look stunning!"

Her daughter blushed. "Thanks. Brought these for Bianca. Had to do something, didn't know what on earth to say, so – well . . ." Amanda sighed awkwardly, shrugged.

"Come into the house."

"How – how are they? Nicholas and Bianca?"

"Sit down." Caroline had led the way across the hall and into the drawing-room. "Actually, they're not here now."

"You mean they've gone to her parents? Not far away, is it?" She had come this far, wouldn't give up for the sake of another mile or two.

Caroline shook her head. "No, but it's Cambridge they've gone to, I'm afraid. They needed to get back to work again."

"Oh." Disappointment made Amanda wilt inside her elegant suit. Caroline thought she suddenly looked nearer fourteen than twenty.

"You mustn't be upset. Bringing those gorgeous flowers was a lovely gesture, nothing changes that. I shall tell Bianca tonight, she said she would ring me."

Amanda stood up, rushed forward, and pushed the flowers

towards her mother. "You take these then. Might make you feel better. Can't have been easy for any of you."

"Thank you, Amanda, thank you very much. They are lovely." Burying her face in the scented blooms, Caroline smiled across them at her daughter.

Amanda smiled back, gave her an awkward shrug. "Glad they're all right. First time I've ever chosen any flowers."

Her words made Caroline think. Had numerous facets of maturing been omitted from Amanda's life? In how many ways had she suffered as a result of that broken marriage?

"Do you want a coffee?" she suggested. "And I'd like you to see the house . . ."

"Coffee first, please. I need to calm down a bit. I've only just got that car, rather a worry – it's so very shiny!"

Caroline smiled again as she headed towards the kitchen. "I wondered who was arriving in such a gleaming car. Didn't even know you'd learned."

She was pleased when Amanda walked with her, continued speaking.

"Didn't Chris tell you? I didn't talk about it much, except to Dad, never thought I'd pass first time."

"What else have you been doing since I saw you last? How's the music . . .?"

"Actually, I've decided not to take it up, not professionally, that is. I know really that I'd never be brilliant. I'm doing a correspondence course – journalism. Dad thinks there might be an opening on the magazine. If not, on someone else's."

Lucy arrived back from Maidstone while Caroline was giving Amanda a tour of the house.

"Great heavens, this is a marvellous surprise!" she exclaimed, and turned to Caroline. "Did you arrange it specially, because I haven't seen this young lady for such an age?"

"No. Amanda was hoping to see Bianca and Nick. She brought them these beautiful flowers."

"What a thoughtful gesture. Well, I'm delighted to see you again, Amanda. And looking so glamorous! I hope that doesn't mean you're afraid a hug might mess you up . . .?"

179

"Of course not, Gran." Amanda proved that by launching herself on Lucy.

When the pair drew apart, Caroline looked across at her daughter. "Do you want to sit and talk, or would you like to see the rest of the house?"

"Both! I've got heaps of time, told Dad to expect me when he sees me. I'm trying to cure him of worrying when I'm out in the car."

"From a parent's viewpoint, I'd say that's a vain task," Lucy told her. "Your mother would never believe how anxious I become when she's driving back and forth between here and Folkestone."

"I've never seen your flat, have I?" said Amanda, sounding quite plaintive. "Can I visit one day? Or drive you home perhaps?"

"We could take her back together," Caroline suggested. "You intend leaving tomorrow, don't you, Mother?"

When Lucy nodded, Amanda smiled. "I can make tomorrow, but only if we use my car. Just tell me what time to pick you both up."

Malcolm came across from the office as soon as he had a spare moment. He'd been busy today, catching up on matters neglected during the family crisis. Seeing Amanda arrive, he had been glad for Caroline's sake, thankful that this totally unexpected visit would give her something fresh to think about.

He was less surprised than his wife by Amanda's smart appearance – on the rare occasions when he had met the girl she had been dressed for some special event. Today, though, he noticed for the first time ever that she was developing a likeness to her mother: given a few more years, Amanda could be really attractive.

"Doesn't she look smart?" Caroline exclaimed as the three of them waved her daughter off.

Later that day she realised that no matter how Amanda had looked she wouldn't have been more thrilled to see her. She only hoped that this might be the beginning of a fresh relationship between them.

If, yesterday, she had looked ahead trying to recognise any potential means of improving the family situation she would never have dared to dream that Amanda would come here. Now that her daughter had taken this step Caroline could only pray that she herself might begin to handle communications between them more skilfully.

It was another chance, one that she didn't really deserve, but it was a challenge – one that frightened her totally. God, but she mustn't ruin everything between them this time!

Twelve

W ith that day, when Amanda drove Caroline and Lucy over to Folkestone, everything seemed to improve. From the second that her daughter greeted them excitedly as she came rushing into the house to help load Lucy's belongings into the car, Caroline began to feel happier.

The day was cold, but bright, with none of the dreadful fog over which Caroline had spent a few sleepless hours. She was relieved, nevertheless, that Amanda took the A20 rather than the motorway. Even without the summer holiday traffic the M20 always seemed to carry enough commercial vehicles to render it quite busy.

Smiling ruefully, Caroline reflected that she was proving just as anxious a parent as her ex-husband. And wasn't this (though she'd not have admitted as much to Amanda) because her ideas were regrettably sexist? From the instant that her stepsons had qualified to drive she had accepted that they were capable of handling a car on any road!

"Bianca rang us last night, as she'd promised," she told Amanda. "When I explained about the flowers she was quite touched, and asked me to be sure to thank you for such a kind thought."

"How did she sound?"

"Not as bad as I feared. I expected that she would hate going back to Cambridge to face explaining about the baby. In the event, she didn't have to. Nick had telephoned one of their friends, as well as Bianca's college. He's very thoughtful."

"They both are," her daughter asserted. "Chris is just the same. You don't need to explain, he somehow senses what you're about, what you're feeling."

"You get on well with him then?" said Lucy.

"We're great friends, have been since just after he started at the vineyard."

Caroline was surprised Chris had never mentioned that. In fact, he rarely spoke of Amanda at all.

"But for him, I'd probably still be grinding away at the violin instead of studying journalism. He persuaded me that I ought to have a bit of fun, tackle something which will lead to my meeting people."

"Like your mother," Lucy reminded her. "I've been meaning to ask, Caroline, are you willing to do any more talks about diet?"

"Only if absolutely pressed, I never favour repetition. What I really want is to get back to PR work. Though it won't be for a while yet. Malcolm has to have some assistance in the office."

"He could employ someone, surely," suggested Lucy. "Free you to follow your own career."

"Why not?" said Amanda. "Go for it, Mother."

That's all very well, thought Caroline, but I can't, not yet. Today was simply a brief respite amid the distress of losing Baby Malcolm. For the present she needed to be around in the farm office, and suspected Malcolm needed to have her there.

Lucy was in the front of the car ready to direct Amanda once they arrived in Folkestone. Caroline had enjoyed watching the pair of them *en route*, noticing how Lucy smiled while she observed how competently the girl changed gear and coped with traffic.

Lucy seemed to be relish her own efficiency which ensured that she directed Amanda towards the seafront flats very easily, and to just the right spot for convenient parking.

"So this is it then, Gran? I'm going to see your lovely home at last."

Lucy chuckled. "Better wait until you've seen the interior before you call it lovely! I'll be surprised if you approve of my style, Amanda."

Caroline and Lucy were the ones to be surprised, as Amanda exclaimed over pieces remembered from visits to Lucy's previous home when she was a child.

"I always loved this comfy sofa, and the chairs. And isn't that the table you used to have near the window?"

Lucy nodded. "As it stands by the window in my sun room now. Normally, I move it away from there as winter approaches. This year, I haven't had the heart, I love the sea too much."

"So do I!" Amanda enthused. "Can I come and stay? I wouldn't be a nuisance. I could bring my books. And I'd walk for miles here."

For one moment Caroline felt the pain of envy. Never once had Amanda hinted that she would wish to stay at The Sylvan Barn. She suppressed the feeling, firmly. Until yesterday she hadn't believed that she might ever see her daughter there. This was much too soon for becoming dissatisfied with the present situation.

As Amanda drove back to The Sylvan Barn she mentioned something she'd read in the *Kent Messenger*. "Malcolm must be delighted that Kent County Council are backing local protests about the delays to that rail link scheme, and are also making a fuss about the potential level of noise it will produce."

"Was this in last week? We'll have to look at that. There's a lot of catching up to do."

"Don't suppose you'll even have thought of opening the papers while you were all upset about the baby."

"Quite. Thanks for mentioning it, glad you happened to notice."

"Oh, I've always loved to read what's happening around you. I make Dad buy the *KM* every week."

Caroline swallowed on the lump rising in her throat. She would never have imagined that Amanda was at all interested in their situation. But the subject of journalism had prompted her daughter to explain that her own ambitions had arisen after meeting Sarah Dwight from Julian's magazine.

"She is rather glamorous, isn't she?" said Caroline.

Amanda grinned. "I don't kid myself that I'll ever look like that, but I mean to enjoy trying! I'm lucky Father can afford to provide a few decent outfits."

As soon as the sentence was out, though, Amanda apologised. "Sorry – not tactful, was it? Not when you've been having a bit of a lean time."

"Don't worry, we're over the worst again, 'til the next crisis. Did your father mention we'd been through a sticky patch?"

Amanda shook her head. "Chris, of course. We talk a lot."

Only after Amanda had driven away did Caroline experience the real sadness. Looking out the relevant copy of the *Kent Messenger* to discuss with Malcolm, the truth of the situation hit home. Her own daughter had been obliged to purchase this wretched paper to learn what was happening around them. They'd never had the kind of relationship where she'd simply call at the house, or even phone.

Heartened by reading about this support they were receiving from people in authority, Malcolm tried to reassure Caroline that night.

"I'm certain you needn't worry about the way you behaved towards Amanda in the past. That's all over now that you've restructured the relationship. You couldn't really fail her entirely. No one on this earth could have been more supportive towards Nick and Bianca throughout their diabolical tragedy."

Malcolm took her in his arms in the wide bed, holding her to his firm body until Caroline felt every pulse awakening to him.

Love me then, she thought, *make me feel really better.*

They lay like that, close, quiet. Minutes later, her husband's even breathing told Caroline that he was asleep. She ought to feel glad that this proximity gave him peace. Was she utterly selfish to long for some quite different feeling?

Anne seemed surprised to find Caroline waiting at Birch Tree House. They chatted for a while seated at either side of the desk. It was ten days after the report of the Kent County Council calling for major alterations to the rail link route. The latest news was of the tunnel itself where commissioning tests evidently had run into trouble.

"But I don't suppose you've come here to discuss all this, have you? How may I help, Caroline? Is it to do with your concern for Nicholas and Bianca?"

"No. From all accounts, they're surviving pretty well now they're back at university. Work seems to be providing a solution, however temporary." Caroline paused, sighed. "It's me, actually, or us. I've never been clear since Malcolm's attack whether or not having sex could be – well, dangerous."

"Shouldn't be, not after all these months. Any tests we've done since he came out of hospital have only reinforced our belief that he's made a good recovery."

Caroline nodded. "He seems fit in every other way. Well – if you're sure. I just – well, it feels as if there's something missing all the time."

"As there is, assuming you enjoyed a good physical relationship before." Anne was trying hard to concentrate on the difficulty from Caroline's point of view, struggling to ignore what she knew from Malcolm's. "I – I *could* recommend that you both see a specialist, if you wish."

"No, not yet," said Caroline hastily. "I'd hate him to get the impression that he was somehow – well, failing me."

Anne willed herself not to shirk a task which she would rather avoid. "I could approach this in such a way that he need never suspect you've consulted me. Call him in for a routine check-up, that sort of thing, bring up the question that way."

"Only if you really needn't mention this chat."

"Meanwhile, it doesn't hurt for the woman to take the initiative, you know."

Caroline's smile was rueful. "Not sure how that chauvinistic man of mine would react!"

Anne steeled herself to sound encouraging. "Worth a try, though, perhaps? Doesn't sound to me as if you have a great deal to lose. Maybe the necessary closeness will work, especially if you manage to create an undemanding atmosphere."

"It's certainly high time that this was sorted."

"Could be that Malcolm is feeling that way too. And you mustn't dwell too much on the possible effect upon his heart. My guess is he would benefit greatly from – from the release."

Anne provided her with a list of reading which would explain more about heart function, and reminded her that counselling would be made available, should they find no other solution.

Long after her last patient had departed Anne remained at her desk, thinking. If it wasn't exactly guilt that she felt, it was something closely akin. She'd never set out to make Malcolm want her, but a small part of her *had* been warmed by being needed.

And that must end. She had acknowledged as much already. Any alternative was impossible.

Malcolm was due that other check-up. Anne forced herself to bring up the matter, and was confronted with the attitude she'd expected.

"Think of Caroline, think of your marriage," she persisted. "What it means to her, what it should mean to you. Especially after everything she's done to see you all through these past weeks. And months."

Malcolm was silent, frowning.

Anne felt obliged to keep on at him, regardless of her own feelings. "It's not some massive sacrifice anyone's expecting from you, after all. But you could give it your best. You might even enjoy it."

"Not sure that's as responsible as you try to make it sound. What if we have children? We're not fully in the clear financially yet, and supposing I snuff it? What'd become of a young kiddy then?"

"I can provide contraceptive advice."

"No, thank you." She was the last person from whom he'd accept such a thing!

Malcolm reacted by shelving the matter. He'd never be any good if he tackled the issue with Anne's words ringing through his head. He needed some spontaneity, after all – would wait until the moment was right.

Malcolm's waiting continued well into the following year. Caroline was driven to insist that they must work something out. He immediately mentioned his dread of their having children. That particular prospect appealed to her, rather than alarmed. It always had done, which was why they'd never used contraception before. But Malcolm was afraid of more responsibility. Her not conceiving in the past proved nothing now. Sufficiently perturbed to consult their doctor again, Caroline came away disturbed as much as relieved. Anne had prescribed the pill.

Although that ended Malcolm's stalling, it didn't fully solve the difficulties. Even when they made love Caroline couldn't help wondering miserably if he really seemed to be going through a ritual purely to please her.

If the rest of her life were less rewarding, Caroline might have decided to thrash the matter out with Malcolm again, reluctant though she was to risk jeopardising their marriage which in all other ways seemed fine. As things were, anyway, she was becoming more satisfied with her professional life. Over Christmas they had found the time to talk about the future.

Malcolm hadn't forgotten her ambition to re-establish her career. He promised she should tackle PR work alongside time in the farm office, for a trial period. If her career took off again, he would employ someone new to work with him.

Elated, Caroline began contacting former clients, and used all her old skills to publicise her own business. Delighted, she soon found that she was earning once more – modestly, at first, but earning from work which she loved.

By the time that she felt justified in ceasing to put in an appearance in Malcolm's office, he appeared quite content to find someone to replace her. When he found Hugh Edmonds, a man with experience of fruit-farming plus an accountancy qualification, it seemed no one could have been more suitable.

Throughout that summer Caroline relished her work, greatly relieved to see Malcolm happily accepting that he wasn't the only man with some understanding of farming fruit.

Having someone else around to share problems within the trade was preventing him from becoming too pessimistic. In early spring when foreign imports further threatened local growers the two men had followed closely the National Farmers' Union delegation putting their difficulties to the House of Commons. Much later that year, as the EC scheme offering to pay apple growers to quit was announced, Malcolm was tempted by the compensation being made available. Eventually, talking the matter through with Hugh convinced him that there was no way they should agree to the scheme. After all, it stipulated that accepting such a payment would prevent their replanting apples within fifteen years.

Caroline was delighted when Malcolm admitted that the money which her business now brought in was creating a difference. He no longer felt compelled to seek the most financially viable option.

With frequent visits from Amanda to enhance what little spare time she had, Caroline's contentment was growing.

The one depressing factor that year was further disappointment for Nick and Bianca. They had survived that first dreadful, empty Christmas only through talking and thinking about starting another baby. Unfortunately, after conceiving their first infant so readily they now seemed unable to do so again.

Although Bianca's parents and all the Parker family were offering a lot of support, no one could fail to see how depressed the poor girl was becoming. By Christmas 1994 she had abandoned her university course, and was working in a Cambridge bookshop. Her originally slight figure had grown thinner still while she drove Nick to despair with her refusal to eat anything substantial.

Fully occupied with her PR business, Caroline hadn't repeated the occasion when she'd attended a meeting about the rail link, but Malcolm's reports of alternating progress and frustration indicated that nothing altered vastly. The innumerable incidents and delays within the Channel Tunnel itself did little more than amuse them – even when a special gathering of VIPs suffered a new Eurostar train's failure. Less amusing and a source of consternation was the car fire aboard one of the trains which caused passengers to flee.

That fire occurred in December 1994, during the following month another tunnel blaze had one hundred travellers obliged to escape.

"If you took on their PR work, you'd make the proverbial fortune," Malcolm remarked with a smile. "There's no project ever that's been more in need of good publicity."

Caroline smiled back, but she wasn't looking for that kind of business. Among her original clients who had been glad to return was a professional novelist now living in Bruges. A prolific writer, he needed good promotion over here for each book as it came out. Although prepared to return to the UK for the occasional personal appearance, he was happier to rely on Caroline for keeping his work before the media and potential readers.

The year that he won a Crime Writers' Association Silver Dagger Caroline was introduced to several of his fellow writers. As soon as they began approaching her for assistance in publicising their work (and themselves) she discovered that this was something which she enjoyed thoroughly. To her, writing had a certain mystique, rendering it more exciting than the products or manufacturing companies which she might be expected to promote.

Amanda, now an assistant art editor with a national weekly was happy to share her mother's enthusiasms, always eager to push her into being more adventurous. Privately, Caroline was rather amused. Who could have anticipated that Amanda, who once had seemed so unprepossessing, might now be persuading others that ambition should entertain no limits.

It was Amanda who, a couple of years later, encouraged Caroline to open her own website on the Internet. "You've got to keep up with trends, Mother, or no one'll take you seriously, will they?"

Experience in a large office fitted with every facility so far invented prepared Amanda for inducting her mother in the intricacies of the Internet, an experience which they both found fascinating.

Malcolm tended to find this adoption of modern technology amusing. "I'm only thankful that you had your own telephone lines installed now that you're spending so much time with your new toy."

Caroline could have been annoyed by his attitude, but the mass of new clients eager to employ her skills left her too preoccupied to be offended. If she were to take on much more work she would soon be needing an assistant.

"You could always ask me," Amanda suggested one evening when she had arrived for a meal at The Sylvan Barn only to discover her mother still seated at the computer.

Caroline gave her a look. "You mean that, don't you? Before we took such a drastic step, you'd have to consider very carefully. You could have much better prospects remaining in journalism."

"But would you like us to work together?"

Would she! Caroline couldn't imagine anything which seemed more clearly guaranteed to erase all the old misgivings and misunderstandings. She must be fair, though, and that would mean not attempting to persuade Amanda to join her.

She was happy enough now with the way that things were turning out. Whenever Nick and Bianca came to Kent, Amanda got on well with them both, and seemed one of the few people capable of hauling Bianca out of her dejection. The months of fearing that they would never again look forward to having a baby had finally ended when Bianca conceived again. Their sadness was all the more intense when at almost three months she suffered a miscarriage.

"She's my friend, I've got to see her," Amanda exclaimed on hearing the news, and prepared to set out for Cambridge.

"Do you want me to come along?" Christopher offered.

It was January and although the weather wasn't too dreadful, he was wondering how Amanda would cope with the journey if snow should set in.

Amanda was happy to have Christopher's company, although she insisted that they must travel in her car.

"Fine with me," Chris agreed. Fond though he still was of his MG, it tended to be mighty cold for long journeys in winter.

Talking animatedly as they so often were, the pair set out, watched by Caroline who waved them off feeling extremely thankful that Chris had so readily become the older brother that Amanda had been lacking.

For Chris, having Amanda to himself for a few hours was a rare experience. All too often they met only while her father or other people were present. He liked Amanda a great deal, yet without fancying her at all, and had always resisted suggesting they spend a bit of time together. She might have misunderstood his intentions. They were not related, of course, but the complexities of her father having once been married to his stepmother always felt to him to create a kind of barrier.

Chris was no fool, and noticed that his own father appeared watchful, alert to possible signals that Amanda's fondness was becoming dangerous. They had talked more than once, he and his dad, and Chris was in no doubt that Malcolm would be more comfortable if he learned his younger son had met some other girl he wished to marry. In fact, Chris was hoping for someone with his stepmother's qualities.

He felt no urgency to settle down. He and his friends went to clubs, occasionally got slightly drunk, more often enjoyed an evening at the cinema. Work occupied much of his time, and of his thoughts, especially since Julian had set up the bottling plant justified by vastly increased production. Christopher remained delighted as well as a little surprised that the job which had started as simply an experiment had escalated into such an absorbing interest.

The visit to Cambridge was less traumatic for him than it became for Amanda. Calling at the hospital where Bianca had been taken they learned that the girl was already discharged, recovering at home.

Whey-faced, Nick met them at the door and was embraced by them both. His expressive eyes were so desperately sad that Chris found no other means of consoling his brother. Amanda sought out Bianca in the bedroom upstairs, and that was where the two spent most of the weekend.

Bianca had been tearful in the past when she'd confided to Amanda the desperation of being unable to conceive a second time. With this pregnancy ended in such dejection, she was too distressed to weep, too disgusted with her misfortune even to rage against it. Mainly in silence, she stared dismally through the window, seemingly oblivious to Amanda's attempts at offering comfort.

"I wish I knew what to do, or what to say, Bianca," Amanda admitted when it was finally time for her and Christopher to leave. "I've not been a bit of use, I know. And I did so want to help you."

Bianca surprised her with a hug. "You have – you came here. One day – if that day ever comes – when I begin to feel better, I'll tell you how much that mattered."

"Perhaps next time will be all right," Amanda suggested in what she hoped was an optimistic voice.

Going out to her car to travel back to Kent she told Chris he'd better drive. She could hardly see for her tears, tears that continued during most of the journey.

They were still depressed about Bianca's loss when Caroline's Internet link brought her a surprise. Not by e-mail or fax, but in a familiar voice over the phone.

"I'm delighted to learn that your business is thriving. Love the website! Did you design it yourself?"

"Paul! I—" Caroline was so astonished that she had to pause, catch her breath. "Well, the ideas were mine, but someone from Amanda's office helped set it up."

"Good, good."

He sounded rather hesitant, the opening words might have been rehearsed. Caroline thought he sounded far less certain of how to proceed.

"How are you, Paul?"

"OK, thanks. And you – the family . . .?"

"Surviving. Nick and Bianca are having a rotten time of it. Did Mother tell you?"

"The bit about losing the baby, yes. Never see Lucy now, I left Folkestone ages ago."

"I see." She had resigned herself to not seeing Paul again. Why then should she feel this perturbed because of not having known where he was?

"Are the young couple still having no luck then?" he enquired.

"Afraid that's so. It's really getting them down."

"Sorry to hear that." Again there was a pause. "Actually, Caroline, lovely though it is to chat, this call is really about business. As soon as I discovered you were in harness again I was sure you're just the person we need."

"Oh, in what way?"

"Could you meet me for lunch one day? So I can explain."

She couldn't fail to agree. Whatever Paul might have in mind, she wouldn't forgive herself if she passed up this opportunity to see him.

They met in an intimate restaurant not far from Ashford. Noting the Les Routiers sign beside its name, Caroline smiled to herself. Paul was out to impress.

He was waiting near the bar and smiled widely the moment she walked in. She hadn't forgotten how compelling his eyes were, yet their force almost made her gasp while his gaze held her own.

He ordered their drinks and they studied the menu. Caroline found herself glancing to his face repeatedly. She might have been seeking reassurance that they really were together. At last.

"Where are you living now?" she asked while their meal was being prepared.

"Not far from here, in fact. I rented a cottage, means I can have Captain with me again."

"That's great."

Paul nodded. "Infinitely better, for us both. Captain became quite obstreperous during our separation."

"And are you working locally as well?"

"Didn't I say?"

The words came out readily, yet Caroline sensed that he'd purposely delayed telling her.

"No. Go on . . ."

"Still similar work, and allied to the same scheme. I'm one of the civil engineers initially producing information on the viability (or otherwise) of tunnelling being used along part of this rail link."

Caroline's eyebrows soared. "Does that mean we can expect that disturbance *will* be minimised for people living nearby?"

"Not necessarily, I'm afraid. All anyone can be certain of is the matter receiving fair assessment."

"If anyone else said that, I'd make a rude comment! Oh, Paul – why did you have to be involved in this wretched thing?"

"It's the job I do. Like it or not, this kind of project is my bread and butter."

"And when it passes the planning stage?"

"We're the people who work out the structural practicalities."

"So you'll be around in Kent for some long while." After such an age of not even knowing where he was, she needed this reassurance.

"In contact with you, if you agree to assist what we're doing. The entire scheme has suffered a bad press from day one. It's high time we made folk appreciate the scale of it all. What it will do for them."

Caroline was shaking her head.

Paul was reaching over to grasp her hand when the waitress came to take them to their table. He waited until Caroline was seated then took his own chair, smiled across, reassuringly.

"There's no one I'd rather work with, and I know I could convince my colleagues as to your suitability. Just think, Caroline – we could use every kind of media publicity. Presentation which you would create, to show everyone that this project is right, that no one need fear any part of it."

She snorted in disbelief, began toying with the exquisitely presented food which she suddenly did not want.

"Do you always need to be attuned to everything you promote?" he asked. "I'd have said you're professional enough to put all you've got behind anything you take on."

"I hope I am, but—"

"There'd be time enough for us to work out ways of putting it across. As soon as it's decided who'll be responsible for the actual construction of the line, we need to start up a campaign. Initially, to counteract that mass of negative publicity."

Caroline was trying not to listen. She was here with Paul, at long last just across this table from him. Her own eyes were exercising the well-learned routine of seeking his, of seeking his approval. If only she could overlook all that his present work entailed, she might feel free to enjoy his company. His company now, however briefly, for a couple of hours.

"Please, Caroline. It would give your business an enormous boost. Think about it. There is no one I'd rather have."

She read in those candid eyes how greatly he longed to have this reason to see each other repeatedly.

"I – I need to think, would have to consider what might be entailed."

"Just let me know. And please – let your decision be the right one."

Caroline began to wonder – was this a chance which she couldn't ignore, the opportunity which would supply those never quite forgotten hopes? A totally innocuous means of meeting Paul again?

Thirteen

E ven three or four years afterwards Caroline wondered occasionally what her life would have been like if she had agreed to do all the PR work required for improving the poor image of the Channel Tunnel rail link.

She had refused, of course, as she'd suspected all along that she would. No matter how tempted by the prospect of continual attention for her work, to say nothing of cooperation with Paul Saunders, she couldn't dismiss Malcolm's strong objections to the route of that railway line.

Telling Paul her decision was meant to have been easy. She had rung his mobile number, prepared to explain quite coolly why she could not agree.

The warmth of his voice when he recognised hers had thrown Caroline, especially when it was followed by his eager, optimistic, "Well, then . . .?"

She'd loathed telling him, and was soon feeling quite distressed. It was so evident that he hadn't anticipated that she would refuse the work.

"Caroline, no! I was so looking forward to seeing you, to meeting to—"

Interrupting to remind Paul that she'd given him no cause to believe she might take on the job sounded cruel in her own ears.

He sighed. "True, I suppose, only I couldn't help hoping. I thought we were friends. Don't you know how much you've come to mean to me?"

There was nothing she might say.

"Caroline, Caroline – I need to continue seeing you."

"I'm sorry." And so it ended.

The rail link was now being constructed. With or without assistance from someone in her profession, the consortium responsible for management of the project was issuing occasional information. At the end of August in 1999 their local press had covered progress to date. One article mentioned that the civil engineering of Section One was likely to take around two years. Caroline could assume that Paul had remained somewhere in her area.

She thought of him still, but no longer with any sense of yearning. He had influenced her life; at one time, to the point where she might have had him dominate her whole existence. But now she could let him go. *Almost*, she wished that she might learn he'd moved right away from Kent.

As for the rail link itself, the developers had set up a special initiative with a workshop, inviting conservation groups, local councils and voluntary organisations to discuss environmental projects. It seemed that they were finally learning to consult the people most affected by the scheme, increasing the hope that the rolling countryside of Kent might not suffer too catastrophically as a result of that railway line.

Although interested, Caroline was too busy to give the matter a great deal of time. Her PR company was flourishing, and she was happier than ever. Most of all, because Amanda had joined her, and was proving a committed assistant whose journalistic experience seemed to give her an understanding of good promotional work.

From time to time, she stayed overnight at The Sylvan Barn when perhaps she and Caroline had been out on a job together, or less frequently for a family gathering. Amanda was enjoying being included, especially whenever Chris was present. Her mother was thankful that they could provide a second home now that Amanda was dealing with a major change in her life.

During the previous year Julian had re-married – not (as Caroline might have supposed) some glamorous female like Sarah Dwight. He had settled contentedly with a widow of similar age to himself, a smart woman with wide interests and a love of travelling. They were abroad now, on a November trip to South Africa.

As Julian delegated much of his own work, Christopher's position at the vineyard naturally included further responsibility. He relished the opportunity to demonstrate how capable he was, and seemed not to mind the long hours which prevented a very active social life.

To his father's concern, Chris was still a bachelor, and if he had marriage in prospect he hadn't confided in any of them. He visited The Sylvan Barn quite often, although he now lived in Sussex close to the vineyard.

Caroline was pleased that Nick and Bianca were back in Kent, and that they had married two years ago when Nick first started teaching at one of the best schools in the area. Bianca had studied further and obtained the degree fitting her for a career as a librarian. Those who knew her well were only too aware that this was no more than a distraction. Something to turn her mind from the absence of children, before that absence turned her mind completely.

Caroline and the rest of the family had witnessed Bianca's brave survival of four miscarriages. While feeling the distress with her, the hardest part seemed being able to do nothing. Isabel Parker surprised Caroline by continuing to offer Bianca and Nick a great deal of understanding.

Only last weekend Caroline had cringed instinctively when she noticed her mother-in-law taking the two young people aside during Kate's birthday party.

"I can't tell you how delighted I am that you decided to marry and settle in Kent, you know. And that you're so evidently working at your good relationship. I've been looking through some of the things that have been passed down to me through the family, and I'd like you to see if you wish to have them for your new home. Mostly, they are books – and I know you both love reading."

Nick hesitated, wondering what Bianca would wish. "That's very kind of you, Grandmother, but—"

Bianca interrupted him. "We'd love them all, I'm sure. How thoughtful of you, just when we need something to make our house more of a home."

Isabel nodded approvingly. "I know you two will take care of them, especially anything that looks valuable. You'll keep them from tiny hands when your turn finally comes and you do have a family."

Bianca was blinking hard, and Nick was looking concertedly at her, but Isabel placed a hand on the girl's shoulder and spoke earnestly.

"I know life seems unfair, my dear, and I wish fervently that I could help. I can only try and encourage you to be determined that this won't make you lose hope completely. I've always suspected, you know, that negative thinking breeds its own trail of misfortune."

"That may be true," Nick argued quietly. "But there are limits to how long you can endure disappointments."

"Then use us," Isabel insisted. "Use *me*. Talking's one of the few things I can still do. And listening, of course, though most of you here would say I'm not the best person for doing that!"

Caroline had missed a great deal of what was being said but she caught the final few words and contained a smile. She need not have worried. The old girl was beginning to recognise her failings. And she was being kind to Bianca and Nick, no one could fault her treatment of them.

Hugh had worked alongside Malcolm for so long and so successfully that, these days, whenever Caroline suggested that they might take a holiday Malcolm's only concern was whether they could afford a break.

Mainly due to her workload they hadn't managed to get away during 1999, and Malcolm was the one who was urging her to take time off. Originally, they had discussed the possibility of going away for Christmas, or even to celebrate the Millennium. But, although the farm was on a better financial footing, Malcolm refused to contemplate paying out some of the amounts being expected for accommodation in good hotels.

"If we wait until we're into the New Year, we'll avoid these extortionately high charges."

On impulse, she and Malcolm had attended the local church service at noon on the first of January, and Caroline had thought particularly of Bianca and Nick during the prayer: "In a world of despair give us hope, in a world of sadness and tears show us your joy . . ."

The words seemed to reassure Caroline about the pair. She was feeling elated as she set out with Malcolm for Madeira, glad to be getting away from the cold and damp of England. She was justified in taking a break from responsibilities. Amanda had progressed so well over the years that she had no qualms about leaving her in charge of the business.

Caroline saw him first while she and Malcolm were queuing to check in for their flight. Paul was hurrying past, with a tremendous amount of baggage on his trolley, so much that Caroline wondered where he could be holidaying, and for how long.

Distracted by trying to watch where Paul was heading and utterly shaken by seeing him again, she scarcely took in what the woman behind the check-in desk was saying. Malcolm was beside her and gave her a prod in the back.

"Wake up, darling, this isn't like you. She wants your bag on the conveyor."

Caroline complied and moved to one side as Malcolm began discussing their seat allocations with the girl. Scanning the distance and middle-distance, Caroline tried to spot Paul's distinctive white hair among the crowds. That's it, she thought despairing, just that brief tantalising glance, and then – nothing.

They did meet again, forty minutes later while she was choosing a paperback book. Seeing her first, Paul glanced across from the maps he was examining and called to her.

"Caroline! How wonderful – I am so pleased to see you."

Replacing a book on the shelf, she pushed her way through the crowd to greet him.

"I saw you earlier, while we were checking in," she exclaimed. "Was afraid that was all I'd see of you."

Paul's expression was wry. "All but, as it is. Only got minutes before I must be on my way. Just wanted a decent map, might not be able to get a good one I can understand over there."

"Sounds like you're off on quite an expedition . . ."

"More than that, Caroline. Today's flight is only the start. I mean to settle out in Japan – making my way out there, gradually, seeing something of the world *en route.*"

"Japan? Why Japan?"

His keen gaze sought hers, held on in that way once so familiar. "Why do you think? Nothing in the UK for me, is there?"

At that moment Malcolm shouted, impatiently, from beside the cash desk. "Caroline, what's keeping you? Don't you know our flight's been called?"

Paul grasped her hand. His fingers cool yet firm on hers, he caressed the inner side of her wrist.

They said goodbye, his voice husky, her own almost non-existent.

"Someone you know?" Malcolm asked casually as he hustled her towards the gate where their aircraft was loading. "A client?"

"He might have been," said Caroline, so shaken that she felt almost incoherent.

"Might have? Do you mean he turned down your services?"

"No. Actually, Paul used to be a friend of my mother."

"Oh, is that all." Satisfied, Malcolm forgot Paul Saunders. He was forgetting everyone but Caroline now. He had relinquished every last regret about Anne. She had made that easier by ensuring that his relationship with his wife was fully restored. And by showing that she was pleased for them.

Caroline was afraid that she would never forget Paul. She cursed the fate that had provided this one, chance, final encounter. She even cursed the fact that it had prevented her from buying that book. With its pages open before her she could have pretended to read throughout this flight. Would have been free to adjust.

Paul had wanted her to understand that he was going right across the world. To get away from thoughts of her? Perhaps their friendship hadn't been dismissed so readily as she'd believed. By either of them.

The hotel on Madeira was beautiful, from its position quite close to Reid's it provided splendid views, and Caroline was too agitated to care. Malcolm had unwound rapidly, was eager to explore all the facilities of the place before they ate that evening. He talked more than usual, enthused about the wine and the food, and made plans for all that they would do on the following day. Caroline tried to focus on what he was saying, to add appreciative comments – and suspected that she was beginning to bewilder him.

Their hire car took them up into the mountains next morning, and they walked for a while gazing all around at the lush green of steep-sided valleys. They stopped to eat lunch in a small place which appeared to be frequented mainly by local people. Normally, she would have revelled in the atmosphere as much as the dishes they were offered. Today, nothing about her felt at all normal.

In their hotel room that evening Malcolm pointed out just how disorganised she was. Caroline was searching for her perfume when he chanced to look across.

"You haven't unpacked everything yet, have you? This isn't like you, Caro – you always used to fill all the bathroom shelves with neatly arranged possessions. To say nothing of every drawer a hotel provided! What's wrong, darling? You are pleased to be here, aren't you?"

"Of course, of course. It's just – oh, I don't know, seems to be taking me a long time to feel reorientated."

Malcolm laughed. "Hope you're not losing your ability to unwind, just when I'm rediscovering the art of relaxing."

He appeared deeply concerned for her, and most attentive during dinner. Afterwards he insisted that they should stroll towards one of the local bars.

The wine they'd had with their meal combined with the vodka she drank as they sat gazing out towards the harbour. And it did help, Caroline decided as they walked arm-in-arm back to their hotel. She could almost forget Paul for tonight, and was thankful that Malcolm had discovered the best means of helping her overcome that dreadful uneasiness. She only hoped now that while learning to subdue all that wretchedness she hadn't forgotten anything important.

All anxieties seemed finally driven from her weary brain. The moment they reached their room Malcolm took her into his arms, kissed her fervently, and pressed her close against his firm body.

"You're where you belong, Caro my love. You're not to feel

unsure about anything. We've weathered so much together, we both work too hard. Well – this is *our* time. I'm going to make up to you for all past disappointments."

They might have been the lovers from those early days of their marriage. Certainly, Caroline could recall no occasion during the past few years when they had made love so fiercely. Lying breathless afterwards and completely sated, she understood how desperately she had needed Malcolm to drive away all wayward thinking so forcefully.

This new attunement spread into the rest of their days on Madeira. They explored the island with an eagerness which left them both feeling renewed, younger.

As soon as they arrived home, their appearance of well-being was confirmed. Amanda and Chris had laid on a surprise supper, and each in turn exclaimed that the holiday seemed to have rejuvenated them.

Malcolm readily agreed. These days, he was well aware of being fortunate, he'd found a brilliant assistant in Hugh, which freed him to appreciate living with Caroline. This holiday had convinced him to enjoy each day of being together.

She herself was greatly relieved. That encounter with Paul at the airport had threatened to ruin everything for her. She wouldn't have believed how shocked she would be to learn that he was getting away as far as possible from England. From her? But she had been hauled out of all those negative thoughts by her husband. And now their marriage felt strengthened.

Amanda had worked well in her absence. She had organised a book-signing for one of their authors, and with a local poet on their list she was planning a combined luncheon and reading.

"She wasn't keen at first to read the poems herself in public, but I persuaded her that a reading will have more impact. Now I'm hoping to get Meridian television interested."

"Be good if we can manage that," Caroline approved. "Poets get too little publicity."

"They certainly aren't easy to promote, are they. But provided we pull this off we could try something similar for others."

Much as she had eventually loved that visit to Madeira, Caroline was happy to be back at work. So often now Amanda made Caroline feel proud. Maybe, she herself wasn't such a poor mother after all. This daughter of hers had somehow found her right niche, and was proving that no one could have responded more satisfactorily to guidance.

They went together to their poet's lunchtime reading, and shared the joy of hearing compliments from the writer herself, as well as from people attending.

"You've done a thoroughly good job, Amanda," said Caroline as they drove home afterwards.

Her daughter grinned. "You're glad I'm not still scraping away at my violin then, and moping around Father's bungalow?"

"It would have been rather a waste, wouldn't it?" But what pleased Caroline greatly was the way that Amanda frequently treated The Sylvan Barn as her home, and shared her time between The Barn and her father's place.

Life seemed especially good whenever Lucy's visits coincided with having Amanda to stay. The pair so evidently relished being together, and Caroline loved arranging outings for the three of them, making up for the past.

The only slight flaw on such occasions was that she herself suddenly had begun to tire more easily, and sometimes felt unwell in her daughter's car. Perhaps that was due to Amanda's exhilaration which did create the need to drive as fast as traffic conditions permitted.

After a run down to the south coast which had otherwise been delightful, Caroline felt so unwell that she rushed into the downstairs cloakroom and vomited. For days afterwards the sick feeling continued, until Caroline became convinced that something peculiar was affecting her digestion.

Anne Newbold greeted her at the surgery with a raised eyebrow. "It's a long time since I had you in here. What's troubling you? I rather gathered from Malcolm that your holiday had done you both the world of good."

"As it had, but that's weeks ago now." Caroline began describing her symptoms. "Maybe I'm making a fuss unnecessarily, but I need to be sure. So much has gone wrong for our family, hasn't it? I've stopped thinking 'that can't happen to us'!"

Anne told her to undress and lie on the examination couch where she gently felt around Caroline's abdomen. Finding nothing untoward, she straightened her back, and smiled reassuringly.

"Periods all right? Everything quite normal?" There could be a problem in that region, she supposed, in which case prompt investigation was advisable.

"Oh." Caroline paled, began breathing agitatedly. "God, I never thought! I haven't seen one since – since before our holiday."

"But – you're on the pill. Although it's not always one hundred per cent. You are still taking it?"

"Yes – yes. At least – oh, Anne, what have I done?" Caroline sat upright. "I did forget, overlooked it completely first couple of nights away. I seemed to be so – disorientated, I guess, I just didn't think."

"We'll do the usual tests, have the result very quickly."

"But what if I am pregnant – will having taken the pill since then have harmed the baby?"

"Caroline, calm down – you'd not be the first to have this occur after forgetting on a couple of occasions." She paused, thinking, wondering how to phrase the next question. "You would go through with it then? You were originally uneasy enough about a possible baby to seek contraception."

"Of course I want the baby, how can you ask? Let's see to those tests, I need to know, one way or the other."

The truth was still a surprise, but one which delighted Caroline more than dismayed her. She did wonder how Malcolm would react, she could only hope that his consistently improved health would allow him to be optimistic about their future. For the present, just for a little while, she needed to consider the prospect of another baby, without being affected by anyone else's opinions.

This was all so strange, such a peculiar succession of events had combined to create this new life within her. She alone knew how that final meeting with Paul had disturbed her – disturbed sufficiently to fail to even think about the supply of pills at the bottom of her suitcase.

It was several days before Caroline decided she must tell Malcolm her news. For once, she was glad that Amanda wasn't spending the weekend with them, and when Nick and Bianca turned down her invitation for Sunday lunch it seemed to provide the ideal opportunity for talking.

Malcolm was in good spirits already, Hugh had asked to be considered as a partner in the farm. After discussing the idea, Malcolm had agreed, and they were finding that Hugh's investment would enable them to expand.

Although initially against the idea, Malcolm had eventually acceded to the suggestion from Chris that they might devote some acreage to growing vines. This promised further security against times when imported produce threatened the home market for their other fruits. More than that, it provided opportunities for cooperating with his son again.

They had finished their meal early that Sunday afternoon and were sitting over coffee when Caroline began to tell Malcolm what was happening.

"You know I've not been feeling too brilliant recently, darling. Well – I went to see Anne the other day."

"You're not ill? Don't tell me it's something serious?" Malcolm looked so apprehensive that she smiled reassuringly.

"Not ill, no. But this has come as quite a shock. The thing is, I'm pregnant, darling."

"You can't be, you're on the pill. You are, aren't you?"

"I was, yes. Guess I slipped up. Came off it soon as I knew, naturally."

He looked pensive. "Yes, well – this *is* a shock, as you say. Don't suppose you're very happy to – to let things take their natural course. Interfere with your career, and all that."

His rather gruff manner was making Caroline suspect that Malcolm was appalled. She swallowed down a sigh, shook her head.

"No, the career's not the worry. It's more wondering what you really feel. You've said for so long that we don't need further responsibilities."

"Oh, things aren't so bad as they were, are they? Actually, once I

206

get used to the idea, I believe I'll be thrilled by the prospect of having a youngster. Yes, Caro my love, thrilled."

If she'd needed further convincing, the hug he gave her would have provided that, but she was assured anyway by the light in his grey eyes. Thankful to have the house to themselves, they talked and talked about the differences a baby would make to their lives. By nightfall Caroline was blissfully happy.

Malcolm's reaction was soon overshadowed by the response elsewhere. Amanda was less than enthusiastic about the news, and this perturbed Caroline for days. Eventually, it was Chris who relayed her daughter's fears.

"She's still ridiculously insecure, Mum – we've got to allow for that. She's terrified that the new baby will supplant her."

Caroline sighed. "Guess I should have anticipated that. Somehow, I'll have to ensure she understands no one could ever do that. And you – what do you think?"

Christopher laughed. "Apart from the fact that it's hard to imagine the old man still doing it, I suppose it's OK! So long as you're going to be all right."

"Despite my age?" said Caroline, and laughed with him.

The persons she really dreaded telling were, of course, Nick and Bianca. And rightly so, as it turned out. No matter that she had chosen her words carefully, leading up to the news with a reminder of how ill she had been feeling. Caroline was distressed by the incredulous horror in Bianca's eyes.

"*You?*" her daughter-in-law demanded. "But you're too—"

"Bianca love," Nick interrupted with a warning frown.

"Ancient?" Caroline tried to make a joke of her age, but none of this was in any way amusing, least of all for Bianca.

"Sorry, sorry," the girl said, while the pain in her eyes hurt Caroline far more than any words she might have flung at her.

If she hadn't caught the end of something Bianca was saying to Nick as they were going out to the car, Caroline might have begun to hope that now that the truth had emerged Bianca would begin to accept it.

"I know, Nick, I do know that I can't spoil everything for

every woman who becomes pregnant. I'll keep my emotions to myself now. But I do wonder why it's always us that can't manage it."

Caroline wept that night, came close to suggesting to Malcolm that terminating the pregnancy could be better for everyone. By the following morning, however, she was sure that she would do nothing to harm this infant of theirs. The only child which they were likely to have together.

Despite her certainty on that day, the disturbance caused within their family did make her continue to wonder if having the baby was creating too much distress for too many people.

Strangely, even when her sister Kate declared she was shaken by the news, their mother-in-law's reaction was the one that reassured Caroline.

"Surprised though I am, I'm not at all displeased. I shall be happy to welcome another grandchild. And it will do Malcolm a power of good. Needs something to demonstrate he's not been aged too completely by heart problems."

Although Bianca tried to appear unmoved by Caroline's condition, her carefully guarded expression whenever they met began to prove just as disturbing as overt distress. Caroline wished she knew what she could do, but was obliged to accept Malcolm's assertion that there was nothing.

To some degree Caroline's misgivings eased with the waning of her sickness, and gradually Amanda appeared to overcome whatever fears she entertained regarding the inevitable changes at The Sylvan Barn. By the time that Caroline was emphasising that Amanda would be expected to take on more responsibility for their clients, their good relationship seemed to be recovering.

Malcolm was the person whose attitude surprised Caroline most of all, the prospect of becoming a father again regenerated him. He was filled with a fresh enthusiasm for life, energised with plans for the future.

Caroline wasn't in the least sorry to visit the ante-natal clinic along with everyone else. Even her early embarrassment, because of being pregnant again in her forties, had evaporated. She had Anne

Newbold to thank for that, she supposed, just as she owed Anne a great deal for many of the improvements in her life.

She could smile now recalling the early days when Anne had insisted that she should attend surgery along with all those ridiculously young mothers-to-be on Tuesday afternoons. But she had been embarrassed, especially when she'd been taken for a prospective grandmother on one occasion before her condition became evident to anyone who really looked at her.

"Here with your daughter, are you? Which one is she?" the girl she later knew as Meg had enquired.

"Actually, no. I'm the one who's pregnant."

Caroline hadn't missed the covert amusement between several of the women who to her looked little more than children themselves.

Some of those young women were here today. Caroline appreciated having familiar faces in the hospital corridor, friendly greetings from women trying to arrange their enlarging persons on tiny chairs to endure the inevitable waiting.

Sitting beside a girl in black leggings and an expanding T-shirt, Caroline was surprised by the cheery, "Hello, Caro – I know you from Birch Tree House, don't I?" A squarish face which she now recognised as Meg's turned towards her.

Before she had got out more than a swift confirmation, the girl was continuing: "You having your scan as well today? It'll be all right, you don't have to worry." Meg paused with a giggle producing a wobble that rocked them both. "Listen to me – telling you what it's like. You're the expert on all this, aren't you, with a family already."

Caroline nodded, smiled, refrained from saying she suspected nobody had even thought up these scans when Amanda was born. Twenty-plus years ago.

"This is my second, though," Meg confided, pulling down over her hair the droopy purple velvet hat that was the reason Caroline hadn't realised earlier who she was. "I'm just praying it's a lad this time. Can't afford more than two, and Cherie's a girl, of course. My chap's going to have the 'snip'. Good, isn't it – the way you don't have to keep on having kids just 'cos you want your fun!"

Smiling even more widely, Caroline agreed. "We live in very enlightened times. There are some clever people."

"I bet your husband's clever. I'm right, aren't I? You've got that look about you. Said to myself first time I saw you 'There's a woman that's got a chap who's made something of himself.' It always shows, you know – success. Rubs off on them that's lucky enough to live with them."

Meg was beckoned by the nurse, halting Caroline's rapidly forming response. Which seemed just as well. For all her currently fashionable gear, Meg's notions were positively Edwardian! Caro hadn't believed any female still existed who subscribed to the idea of the man being the only one entitled to success. Or capable of achievement. One half of her regretted there being no time for explaining about her years spent running a PR company, but then her other half shrugged. Misconceptions concerning her life could not affect her. The facts were as she knew them to be, facts that she had learned to accept.

Still surprised by Meg's outlook, Caroline continued to ponder during the intervals between her various tests and examinations. And then she forgot the girl while she grew perturbed. Emerging from routine, she must prepare for the actual scan.

Visualising the experience, Caroline always was afraid that she wouldn't be able to make sense of anything she saw on the screen. When the time came, she discovered to her chagrin how right that supposition had been. The image looked sort of wavery to her, or was that because her eyes had misted at the prospect of what she considered her first introduction to their offspring?

The professional voice *sounded* patient the second time that various areas of that on-screen pulsing mass were indicated to her, but surely she was being labelled idiotic? A fool. Too stupid to appreciate the wonder of it all. Or was it the wonder of the experience which came between herself and total comprehension?

"And as you can see, Mrs Parker, your baby is a girl."

Still feeling foolish, she hadn't been certain enough of what was present (or absent, she supposed) on the screen, Caroline grinned. "Just what we both hoped for."

The task was completed and she left with a photograph that

seemed no more recognisable as human than the moving original. Swiftly, she inserted the photo in her diary. Only in private, with Malcolm, would she study it again.

Meg and another of the prospective mothers from their village were comparing pictures, turning them this way and that, exclaiming as they might over holiday snaps. Meg's voice drifted towards her: "Good thing he hasn't had the 'snip' yet – I'm not going to go through life without that lad I want!"

Caroline was simply very thankful that, so far, their baby was reported to be doing well. She would be happy to have another daughter, but Malcolm was the one who would be ecstatic. He'd had enough of boys, he professed, while remaining proud of both sons, now that Nicholas had such an excellent job, and Christopher so responsible a position in a flourishing vineyard.

Malcolm would enjoy having a little girl about the place. She would compel him to relax. Caroline could picture them: the tall man, quite elegant now that he was so much fitter, and the tiny daughter. A child who would enchant him. He was ready for a bit of enchantment, a diversion along with the responsibility.

For herself, a new daughter would be good. A further chance, a second opportunity to prove that she was no longer a failed mother. Some of the mistakes she had made with Amanda had been retrieved. Those tentative strands of a new relationship had held for six years or so now. The bond between them strengthened. Amanda was proving forgiving. Only Caroline herself knew how bitterly she regretted all the years that had gone before, the years so achingly short of perfect.

Deep in reflection as she headed along towards the outer door of the hospital, she was jolted into the present by the beaming face, the "Hello, Caroline!" So sudden the greeting that she first believed the girl to be yet another of Anne Newbold's patients, she was startled when she really looked at her.

"Bianca! Are you here as well for the—?"

The girl nodded. "Ante-natal clinic, yes. Promise you won't breathe a word. Nick doesn't know yet. We've both been so gutted, so many times when – well, you know . . . I've not told my mother either. You mustn't say, if you happen to see her."

"Anything you wish, anything at all. I am just so pleased . . . so very pleased." Caroline hugged her then, felt how slender Bianca seemed, felt her own bump between them, was glad for them both. So very glad.

"Is it very early yet?"

Bianca nodded, looking serious beyond her smile. "My GP's only just confirmed it, but I'm taking no chances. That's why I'm here today. Don't tell anyone, but I sold a piece of jewellery. Dad wouldn't like that, it was a pendant he gave me. But I've got to get it right this time. Paying to see a top consultant."

Caroline gave her another hug. "Bless you, love. Hope it goes well for you. Come and see us soon, don't forget."

Her step felt light, hurrying to the car. If only Bianca could keep this baby to full term, they would all feel so much better. She herself could enjoy her own infant, in anticipation and when it – *she* – arrived. There'd be no more awkwardness, no watching Bianca for tell-tale signs of understandable envy barely concealed. Nick would lose that unnatural brusqueness behind which his grief had gnawed. Even Chris wouldn't be unaffected. He would be freed again to exhibit his normal exuberance towards his brother, for so long he'd treated him quite cautiously.

The roadside grass looked parched as Caroline drove home towards The Sylvan Barn, but the nearby hedge swayed beneath wild roses. On the hill rising to her right, fields stood sandy-gold with ripening grain, rippling gently before the breeze. *I could paint that*, she thought, and was reminded of Paul. Only very briefly, she felt the old dismal ache. Dismissing it was becoming easier.

Approaching the farm up the narrow lane, she smelled the last of the strawberry crop, saw to either side of her apples, pears, plums, trees soon to be mature with fruit. The yearly renewal, a perpetuation just as eloquent as the family succession she once had supposed would be represented by Bianca. And now her own astonishing fruitfulness would precede the girl's.

You never quite knew, never could tell, even the earthly cycle came up with surprises: the late frost, bumper crops, the blight no one could anticipate. Yet somehow it all survived. As did they themselves.

Malcolm was at the office window, looking out for her. As she left the car his gaze met hers, held on, and Caroline felt a surging pulse of attraction. All the way to the door of The Sylvan Barn, she sensed that he was watching her. And yet she was thankful he was speaking to someone on the phone and wouldn't come across to the house immediately.

Her own footsteps echoing through the quiet hall emphasised her solitude, and Caroline was relieved. She needed this time on her own, needed to control her feelings.

Even though the tears creating this lump in her throat were joyful, Malcolm must not see them. Their life together had seemed so fragile, there must be no risk of misinterpreted emotions. They had endured so much. *And they had survived.* Gradually now, she was coming to terms with the news that had affected the whole family so profoundly. Today, with confirmation of further details, she was beginning to look forward.

By this time next year their lives would have changed again, drastically, but in a way which would confirm how right she had been to make the decisions that she had, to make those choices.

There would be regrets: no one could live and avoid contemplating the "might-have-beens", the "what-ifs", the "just supposings". But she had surrendered the past on that day when the truth shattered her.

Malcolm's key scratched in the lock, the door opened and he strode across towards her.

"You all right?" he asked. "How did it go?"

"Fine. Fine, darling." And, she thought, remembering meeting Bianca there, everything (please God) might be coming right for them again too.

Malcolm hugged her close. They kissed.

"Sure the hospital people are happy with you, Caro? You really are OK?"

She smiled, nodded. Slowly at first, she had accepted the situation, and was now beginning to see it as part of a pattern, the design that was their lives. This first summer of the new millennium suddenly seemed glorious, the fruit ripening in their orchards a reminder of continuity, of her personal harvest.

Beyond their own acres a great deal had changed. They themselves were fortunate that so small a section of their land was sacrificed to this massive scar of the rail route under construction.

Looking forward today she could smile, and feel certain that *together* they would tackle everything ahead of them with this fresh sense of purpose.

CENTRAL 5.8.00